**St. Martin's Paperbacks Titles
by Julianne MacLean**

Captured by the Highlander

Claimed by the Highlander

Seduced by the Highlander

Be My Prince

Claimed
by the
Highlander

JULIANNE MACLEAN

St. Martin's Paperbacks

CLAIMED BY THE HIGHLANDER

Copyright © 2011 by Julianne MacLean.
Excerpt from *Princess in Love* copyright © 2012 by Julianne MacLean.

For information address St. Martin's Press, 175 Fifth Avenue, New York, NY 10010.

ISBN: 978-1-250-01627-0

Printed in the United States of America

St. Martin's Paperbacks edition / April 2011

St. Martin's Paperbacks are published by St. Martin's Press, 175 Fifth Avenue, New York, NY 10010.

10 9 8 7 6 5 4 3

He was banished, and in his absence all was lost. But soon, his time will come. The sleeping lion will wake, and when he does, the MacEwens will hear his roar.

—*The Oracle, March 3, 1718*
The Western Isles of Scotland

Claimed
by the
Highlander

Chapter One

Kinloch Castle
Scottish Highlands, July 1718

The dream startled her awake mere minutes before the siege began.

Gwendolen MacEwen sat up with a gasp and turned her eyes to the window. *It was only a dream,* she told herself as she struggled to calm her breathing. Later she would call it a premonition, but for now, she was certain it was just the trickeries of sleep causing this terror in her heart.

Giving up any notion of slumber, she tossed the covers aside, sat up on the edge of the bed, and reached for her robe. She slipped it on for warmth against the pre-dawn chill as she rose to her feet and padded to the window, lured to the leaded glass by a faint glow of light on the horizon.

A new day had begun. At last. She closed her eyes and said a silent prayer that it would bring her brother, Murdoch, home from his travels. The MacEwens needed their chief, and if he did not soon return and claim his birthright, she feared someone else would—for there had been some talk of discontent in the village. She'd heard it from her maid, whose sister was married to the alehouse keeper. And after the dream she'd just had . . .

The horn blew suddenly in the bailey.

Unaccustomed to hearing such a clamor while the castle still slept, Gwendolen turned from the window. *What in God's name . . . ?*

It blew again, a second time. Then a third.

A spark of alarm fired her blood, for she knew the meaning of that signal. It was coming from the rooftop, and it spoke of danger.

Gwendolen rushed to the door, flung it open, and hurried up the tower stairs.

"What's happening?" she asked the guard, who was pacing back and forth through the early morning chill. She could see his ragged breath upon the air.

He pointed. "Look there, Miss MacEwen!"

She rose up on her toes and leaned out over the battlements, squinting through the dim morning light at the moving shadows in the field. It was an advancing army, approaching quickly from the edge of the forest. Some were on foot, others mounted.

"How many men?" she asked.

"Two hundred, at least," he replied. "Maybe more."

She stepped away from the wall and regarded him soberly. "How much time do we have?"

"Five minutes at best."

She turned and locked eyes with another clansman, who exploded out of the tower staircase with a musket in his hands. He halted, panic-stricken, when he spotted her.

"They came out of nowhere," he explained. "We're doomed for sure. Ye should escape, Miss MacEwen, before it's too late."

Immediately incensed, Gwendolen strode forward, grabbed two fistfuls of his shirt, and shook him roughly. *"Repeat those words again, sir, and I will have your head!"* She swung around to face the other clansman. "Go and alert the steward."

"But—"

"Just do it!"

They had no leader. Her father was dead, and their current laird of war was a drunkard who was not even within the castle walls, for he'd been spending his nights in the village since her father's passing. Her brother had not yet returned from the Continent. They had only their steward, Gordon MacEwen—who was a brilliant manager of books and numbers, but no warrior.

"Is your weapon loaded?" she asked the flustered clansman. "Do you have enough powder?"

"Aye."

"Then take aim and defend the gate!"

He hurried into position, while she looked out over the bailey below, where her clansmen were finally assembling in answer to the call. Torches had been lit, but everyone was shouting in confusion, asking too many questions.

"MacEwens, hear me now!" she shouted. "An army is approaching from the east! We will soon be under attack! Arm yourselves and man the battlements!"

Only in the hush of that moment, as all eyes turned toward her, did she realize that she was still wearing her dressing gown.

"You there!" She pointed at a boy. "Arm yourself with a sword! Assemble all the women and children. Take them to the chapel, bar the doors, and stay with them until the battle is ended."

The boy nodded bravely and dashed off to the armory.

"They are MacDonalds!" a guard shouted from the opposite corner tower. It was Douglas MacEwen, a good friend and able swordsman.

Gwendolen gathered her shift in her hands and ran to meet him. "Are you certain?"

"Aye, look there." He pointed across the field, now shimmering with mist and morning dew. "They carry the banner of Angus the Lion."

Gwendolen had heard tales of Angus MacDonald, forsaken son of the fallen MacDonald chief, who had once been Laird of Kinloch. He had been a Jacobite traitor, however, which was why the King granted her father Letters of Fire and Sword, which had awarded him the right to take the castle in service to the Crown.

There were whispers that Angus was the infamous Butcher of the Highlands—a renegade Jacobite who hacked entire English armies to pieces with his legendary death axe.

Others said he was nothing but a treacherous villain, who was banished to the north by his own father for some secret, unspeakable crime.

Either way, he was reputed to be a fierce and ruthless warrior, faster and more ferocious than a phantom beast on the battlefield. Some even said he was invincible.

This much was true at least: he was an expert swordsman, who showed no mercy to warriors and women alike.

"What in God's name is that?" She leaned forward and squinted, as a terrible sense of foreboding poured through her.

Douglas strained to see clearly through the mist,

then his face went pale. "It's a catapult, and their horses are pulling a battering ram."

She could hear the heavy, muted thunder of their approach, and her heart turned over in her chest.

"You are in charge here until I return," she told him. "You must defend the gate, Douglas. At all costs."

He nodded silently. She patted him on the arm with encouragement, then hurried back to the tower stairs. Seconds later, she was pushing through the door to her bedchamber. Her maid was waiting uneasily by the bed.

Gwendolen spoke without flinching. "We are under attack," she said. "There isn't much time. You must help gather the women and children, go straight to the chapel, and stay there until it is over."

"Aye, Miss McEwen!" The maid hastened from the room.

Closing the door behind her, Gwendolen quickly tore off her robe and dropped it, without a care, onto the braided rug. She hurried to the wardrobe to find clothes.

Just then, a sudden, violent pounding began at her door, as if an animal were bucking up against it.

"Gwendolen! Gwendolen! Are you awake?"

She halted in her tracks. Oh, if only she were asleep, and this was still the dream, playing tricks on her mind. But the sound of alarm in her mother's voice quashed that possibility. She hurried to answer the door.

"Come inside, Mother. We are under attack."

"Are you certain?" Onora looked as if she had already taken the time to dress for the event. Her long curly hair was combed into a hasty but elegant twist, and she was wearing a crisp new gown of blue and white silk. "I heard the horn, but thought surely it must be a false alarm."

"It isn't." Gwendolen returned to the wardrobe and pulled a skirt on over her shift. "The MacDonalds are storming the gates as we speak. There isn't much time. They have brought a catapult and battering ram."

Onora swept into the room and shut the door behind her. "How utterly medieval!"

"Indeed. They are led by Angus the Lion." Glancing briefly at her mother with concern, Gwendolen hunted around for her shoes.

"Angus the Lion? Forsaken son of the MacDonald chief? Oh, God help us all. If he is triumphant, you and I will be doomed."

"Do not speak those words in my presence, Mother," Gwendolen replied. "They are not yet inside the castle walls. We can still keep them at bay."

This was, after all, the mighty and formidable Kinloch Castle. Its walls were six feet thick and sixty feet high. Only a bird could reach the towers and battlements. They were surrounded by water, protected by a drawbridge and an iron portcullis. How could the MacDonalds possibly overtake such a stronghold?

She longed suddenly for her brother Murdoch. Why wasn't he here? He should have come home the moment he learned of their father's death. Why had he stayed away so long, and left them here without a leader?

Her mother began to pace. "I always told your father he should have banished each and every member of that Jacobite clan when he claimed this castle for the MacEwens, but would he listen? No. He insisted on mercy and compassion, and look where it got us."

Gwendolen pulled on her stays and her mother tied the laces. "I disagree. The MacDonalds who chose to remain here under Father's protection have been peaceful and loyal to us for two years. They adored Father. This cannot be their doing."

"But have you not heard the ugly rumors in the village? The complaints about the rents, and that silly debacle over the beehive?"

"Aye," Gwendolen replied, tying her hair back off her shoulders with a simple leather cord. "But it is only a small number who feel that way, and only because we have no chief to settle disputes. I am certain that when Murdoch returns, all will be well. Besides, those who chose to remain never supported the Jacobite cause to begin with. They do not want to participate in another rebellion. Kinloch is a Hanoverian house now."

She got down on her knees and reached under the bed for the trunk. It scraped across the floor as she pulled it out.

"No, I suppose it is not their doing," Onora said. "They are farmers and peasants. This is the vengeance of the warriors who would not take an oath of allegiance to your father when he proclaimed himself laird two years ago. That is what we are facing now. We should have known they would return to take back what was theirs."

Gwendolen opened the trunk and withdrew a small saber, then rose to her feet and belted it around her waist. "Kinloch is not theirs *now*," she reminded her mother. "It belongs to the MacEwens by order of the King. Anyone who claims otherwise is a traitor to England and in breach of the law. And surely the King will not allow this powerful Scottish bastion to fall into the hands of enemy Jacobites. We will soon have assistance, I am sure of it."

Her mother shook her head. "You are very naïve,

Gwendolen. No one will be coming to our aid, at least not in time to save us from having our throats slit by that savage rebel, Angus MacDonald."

"Kinloch will not fall to them," Gwendolen insisted. "We will fight, and by God's grace, we will win."

Her mother scoffed bitterly as she followed her to the door. "Don't be a fool! We are outnumbered and leaderless! We will have to surrender and plead for mercy. Although what good it will do, I cannot imagine. I am the wife and you are the daughter of the clansman who conquered this castle and slayed their chief. Mark my words, the first thing the Lion will do is take his vengeance out on *us*!"

Gwendolen would not listen to any more of this. She moved quickly out of the chamber and into the corridor, where she paused to adjust her sword belt. "I am going to the armory to fetch a musket and powder," she explained. "And then I am going up to the battlements to fight for what is ours, in the name of the King. I will not let Father's greatest achievement die with him."

"Are you mad?" Onora followed her to the stairs. "You are a woman! You cannot fight them! You must stay here, where it is safe. We will pray for our lives and think of a way to contend with those dirty MacDonalds when they break down your bedchamber door."

Gwendolen paused. "*You* can stay here and pray, Mother, but I cannot simply sit here and wait for them to slit my throat. If I am going to die today, so be it, but I will not depart this life without a fight." She started down the curved staircase. "And with any luck, I will live long enough to shoot a musket ball straight through the black heart of Angus MacDonald himself. *That* you can pray for!"

By the time Gwendolen reached the battlements and took aim at the invaders on the drawbridge below, the iron-tipped battering ram was smashing the thick oak door to pieces. The castle walls shuddered beneath her feet, and she was forced to stop and take a moment to absorb what was happening.

The frightful reality of battle struck her, and all at once, she felt dazed, as if she were staring into a churning abyss of noise and confusion. She couldn't move. Her fellow clansmen were shouting gruffly at each other. Smoke and the smell of gunpowder burned in her lungs and stung her eyes. One kilted warrior had dropped all his weapons beside her and was crouching by the wall, overcome by a fit of weeping.

She stared down at him for a hazy moment, feeling nauseous and light-headed, as cracks of musketfire exploded all around her.

"Get up!" she shouted, reaching down and hooking her arm under his. She hauled him to his feet. "Reload your weapon, and use it to fight!"

The young clansman stared at her blankly for a moment, then fumbled for his powder.

Gwendolen leaned out over the battlements to see below. The MacDonalds were swarming through the broken gate, crawling like insects over the wooden ram. She quickly took aim and fired at one of them, but missed.

"To the bailey!" she shouted, and the sound of dozens of swords scraping out of scabbards fueled her

resolve. With steady hands and an unwavering spirit, she reloaded her musket. There was shouting and screaming, men running everywhere, flocking to the stairs . . .

"Gwendolen!" Douglas called out, stopping beside her. "You should not be here! You must go below to your chamber and lock yourself in! Leave the fighting to the men!"

"Nay, Douglas, I will fight and die for Kinloch if I must."

He regarded her with both admiration and regret, and spoke in a gentler voice. "At least do your fighting from the rooftop, lassie. The clan will not survive the loss of you."

His meaning was clear, and she knew he was right. She was the daughter of the MacEwen chief. She must remain alive to negotiate terms of surrender, if it came to that.

Gwendolen nodded. "Be gone, Douglas. Leave me here to reload my weapon. This is a good spot. I will do what I can from here."

He kissed her on the cheek, wished her luck, and bolted for the stairs.

Hand-to-hand combat began immediately in the bailey below. There was a dreadful roar—close to four hundred men all shouting at once—and the deafening clang of steel against steel rang in her ears as she fired and reloaded her musket, over and over. Before long, she had to stop, for the two clans had merged into one screaming cataclysm of carnage, and she could not risk shooting any of her own men.

The chapel bell tolled, calling the villagers to come quickly and assist in the fight, but even if every able-bodied man arrived at that moment, it would not be enough. These MacDonald warriors were rough and battle seasoned, armed with spears, muskets, axes, bows and arrows. They were quickly seizing control, and she could do nothing from where she stood, for if she went below, it would be suicide, and she had to live for her clan.

Then she spotted him. Their leader. Angus the Lion, fighting in the center of it all.

She quickly loaded her musket and aimed, but he moved too quickly. She could not get a clear shot.

A scorching ball of terror shot into her belly as she lowered her weapon. No wonder they called him the Lion. His hair was a thick, tawny mane that reached past his broad shoulders, and he roared with every deadly swing of his claymore, which sliced effortlessly through the air before cutting down foe after foe after foe.

Gwendolen stood transfixed, unable to tear her eyes away from the sheer muscled brawn of his arms, chest, and legs—legs thick as tree trunks, just like the battering ram on the bridge. There was a perfect, lethal symmetry and balance to his movements as he lunged and killed, then flicked the sweat-drenched hair from his eyes, spun around and killed again.

Her heart pounded with fascination and awe. He was a powerful beast of a man, a superb warrior, magnificent in every way, and the mere sight of him in battle, in all his legendary glory, nearly brought her to her knees. He deflected every blow with his sturdy black shield, and swung the claymore with exquisite grace. She had never encountered such a man before, nor imagined such strength was possible in the human form.

She realized suddenly that her mother had been correct in her predictions. There was no possibility of defeating this man. They were all doomed. Without a doubt, the castle would fall to these invaders and there would be no mercy. It was pointless to hope otherwise.

She moved across the rooftop to the corner tower where her bedchamber was housed, and looked down at the hopeless struggle.

This had been far too easy a charge for the Mac-Donalds. To watch it any longer was pure agony, and she was ashamed when she had to close her eyes and turn her face away. She had wanted so desperately to triumph over these attackers, but she had never witnessed a battle such as this in all her twenty-one years. She'd heard tales, of course, and imagined the evils of war, but she'd had no idea how truly violent and grisly it would be.

Soon the battle cries grew sparse, and only a handful of willful warriors continued to fight to the death. Other MacEwen clansmen, with swords pointed at their throats, accepted their fate. They laid down their weapons and dropped to their knees. Those who surrendered were being assembled into a line at the far wall.

Gwendolen, who had been watching the great Lion throughout the battle, noticed suddenly that he was gone, vanished like a phantom into the gunsmoke. Panic shot to her core, and she gazed frantically from one corner of the bailey to the other, searching all the faces for those gleaming, devilish eyes. Where was he? Had someone killed him? Or had he penetrated the chapel to ravage the women and children, too?

She spotted him, at last, on the rooftop, clear across the distance, standing on the opposite corner tower. His broadsword was sheathed at his side, and his shield was strapped to his back. He raised his arms out to his sides and shouted to the clansmen below.

"I am Angus Bradach MacDonald! Son of the fallen Laird MacDonald, true master of Kinloch Castle!" His voice was deep and thunderous. It rumbled mightily inside her chest. "Kinloch belongs to me by right of birth! I hereby declare myself laird and chief!"

"Kinloch belongs to the MacEwens now!" someone shouted from below. "By Letters of Fire and Sword, issued by King George of Great Britain!"

"If you want it back," Angus growled, stepping forward to the edge of the rooftop, "then raise your sword and fight me!"

His challenge was met with silence, until Gwendolen was overcome by a blast of anger so hot, she could not control or contain it.

"Angus Bradach MacDonald!" she shouted from the dark, outraged depths of her soul. "Hear me now! I am Gwendolen MacEwen, daughter of the MacEwen chief who won this castle by fair and lawful means! I am leader here, and *I* will fight you!"

It was not until that moment that she realized she had marched to the edge of the rooftop and drawn her saber, which she was now pointing at him from across the distance.

Her heart pummeled her chest. She had never felt more exhilarated. It was intoxicating. She wished there was not this expanse of separation between them. If there were a bridge from one tower to the other, she would dash across it and fight him to the death.

"Gwendolen MacEwen!" he shouted in reply. "Daughter of my enemy! You have been defeated!"

And just like that, he dismissed her challenge and addressed the clansmen in the bailey below.

"All who have taken part in usurping this castle, and

are in possession of lands that did not belong to them—you must forfeit them now to the clansmen from whom you took them!"

Gwendolen's anger rose up again, more fiercely than before. *"The MacEwens refuse!"* she answered.

He immediately pointed his sword at her in a forceful show of warning, then lowered it and continued, as if she had not spoken.

"If that clansman is dead or absent today," he declared, "you may remain, but I will have your loyalty, and you will swear allegiance to me as Laird of Kinloch!"

There was another long, drawn-out silence, until some brave soul spoke up.

"Why should we pledge loyalty to you? You are a MacDonald, and we are MacEwens!"

The Lion was quiet for a moment. He seemed to be looking deep into the eyes of every man in the bailey below. "Be it known that our two clans will unite!" He pointed his sword at Gwendolen again, and she felt the intense heat of his gaze like a fire across her body. "For I will claim this woman, who is your brave and noble leader, as my wife, and our son, one day, will be laird."

Cheers erupted from the crowd of MacDonald warriors below, while Gwendolen digested his words with shock and disbelief. He intended to claim her as his wife?

No, it was not possible.

"There will be a feast on this night in the Great Hall," the Lion roared, "and I will accept the pledges of all men willing to remain here and live in peace under my protection!"

Murmurs of surrender floated upward through the air

and reached Gwendolen's burning ears. She clenched her jaw and dug her fingernails into the cold rough stones of the tower. This was not happening. It could not be. Pray God, this was still the dream, and she would soon wake. But the hot morning sun on her cheeks reminded her that the dreams of a restless night had already given way to reality, and her father's castle had been sacked and conquered by an unassailable warrior. Moreover, he intended to make her his bride and force her to bear children for him. What in God's name was she to do?

"I do not agree to this!" she shouted, and the Lion tilted his head to the side, beholding her strangely, as if she were some sort of otherworldly creature he had never encountered before. "I wish to negotiate our terms of surrender!"

Her body began to tremble as she waited for his response. Perhaps he would simply send a man to slit her throat in front of everyone—as an example for those who were bold enough, or foolish enough, to resist. He looked ready to do it. She could feel the hot flames of his anger from where she stood, at the opposite corner of the castle.

Then the oddest thing happened. One by one, each MacEwen warrior in the bailey below turned toward her, and dropped to one knee. They all bowed their heads in silence, while the MacDonalds stood among them, observing the demonstration with some uneasiness.

For a long time Angus stood upon the North Tower saying nothing, as he watched the men deliver this unexpected defiance. A raw and brutal tension stretched ever tighter within the castle, and Gwendolen feared they would all be slaughtered.

Then, at last, the Lion turned his eyes toward her.

She lifted her chin, but his murderous contempt seemed to squeeze around her throat, and she found it difficult to breathe.

He spoke with quiet, grave authority. "Gwendolen MacEwen, I will hear your terms in the Great Hall."

Not trusting herself to speak, she nodded and resheathed her saber, then walked with pride toward the tower stairs, while her legs, hidden beneath her skirts, shook uncontrollably and threatened to give out beneath her.

When at last she reached the top of the stairs, she paused a moment to take a breath and compose herself.

God, oh God . . .

She felt nauseous and light-headed.

Leaning forward and laying the flat of her hand upon the cool stones, she closed her eyes and wondered how she was ever going to negotiate with this warrior, who had already defeated her clan in a brutal and bloody campaign, and claimed her as his property. She had nothing, *nothing,* with which to bargain. But perhaps she and her mother could think of something— some other way to manage the situation, at least until her brother returned.

If only Murdoch were here now . . .

But no, there was no point wishing for such things. He was not here, and she had only herself to rely on. She must stand strong for her people.

She took one last look at them. Angus the Lion had quitted the rooftop and returned to his men. He was giving orders and wandering among the dead and wounded, assessing the magnitude of his triumph, no doubt.

A light breeze lifted his thick golden hair, which shimmered in the morning light. His kilt wafted lightly around his muscular legs, while he adjusted the leather strap that held the shield at his back.

Just then he glanced up and saw that she was watching him. He faced her squarely and did not look away.

Gwendolen's breath caught in her throat. Her knees went weak, and something fluttered in her belly. Whether it was fear or fascination, she did not know. Either way, it did not bode well for her future dealings with him.

Shaken and agitated, she pushed away from the wall and quickly descended the tower stairs.

Chapter Two

Standing on blood-soaked ground, Angus watched as his enemy's daughter disappeared into the East Tower. The instant she was gone, he cupped his shoulder with one hand and tried to roll out the pain, but realized it was worse than he thought. He grimaced, then shoved hard and fast with the heel of his palm to jostle the joint back into place. Slowly, he walked to the other side of the bailey, where he took a moment to recover.

It had been a hard battle. His clothes were stained with dirt, sweat, and blood—some of it his own—but it had all been worth it, for this was *his* home. *His* castle. The MacEwens had no right to it.

And his father was dead.

He turned and faced the carnage, and felt the renewed arousal of his fighting spirit as he recalled the courageous lass who had raised her voice and interrupted his moment of triumph. She was a dark and radiant beauty, which somehow added fuel to the fires of his antagonism. He did not want a beautiful wife, and he hadn't even given a single passing thought to what the daughter of his enemy might look like. Her comeliness—or lack of it—was of no concern to him. She was an instrument, nothing more, which was precisely why her beauty and bold conduct had lifted the hairs on the back of his neck.

Angus rolled his shoulder again to work out the pain, and resolved to forget her, for now. He would not let her spoil this moment. He had come too far not to savor this victory.

With a passionate cry of triumph that echoed off the castle walls and roused the attention of his men, he unsheathed his sword and thrust it into the ground. Then he lowered himself to one knee and bowed his head on the shiny basket hilt.

Relief flooded through him, though it was tainted with grief. His father had been dead for two years, and Angus had not known until these past months. In the meantime, Kinloch had fallen into enemy hands, and his clan had been absorbed into another.

He had waited too long to return.

His cousin Lachlan came to stand beside him. "It doesn't seem right," he said, thrusting his sword into the dirt as well.

Angus looked up. "Which part?"

"The part where a man must raise an army to invade his own home."

Angus rose to his full height and regarded the cousin and friend who had spent the better part of two years searching for him, found him on the outer fringes of the Western Isles, and helped him to raise an army and fight for what was theirs.

"Perhaps it's destiny," he replied, "for surely I can have no greater purpose than this. I have drawn my sword on behalf of my home, my clan, and my beloved Kinloch. Perhaps this is to be my redemption, a chance to make up for past sins."

He turned his eyes toward the shattered castle gate, then to all the casualties that littered the ground. There had been terrible losses on both sides.

"And what of the dead?" Lachlan asked, taking in the wretched sight of the fallen warriors.

"We will honor them. The MacEwens fought bravely." He inclined his head at Lachlan. "A testament to their leader, perhaps?"

"Aye, she was something of a fireball—and a bonnie vision, besides." Lachlan's dark eyes narrowed questioningly. "Think you'll be able to manage her?"

"Do you doubt me, Lachlan?"

"You just took her home and destroyed half her clan. I doubt she'll be overjoyed to share a bed with you."

Angus wrenched his sword out of the dirt and slid it into his scabbard. "I don't care how she feels." He had no patience for emotional women, and this was certainly no love story. She knew that as well as he did. "Her father stole Kinloch from us. She will settle that debt." He started toward the Great Hall.

Lachlan pulled a flask out of his sporran and took a drink. "I shouldn't have to tell you to watch your back," he said. "Her saber may have been small, but it had a sharp point."

Angus heard the warning, but gave no reply.

Gwendolen entered her bedchamber and found her mother waiting anxiously at the window.

"Oh, my darling," Onora said, "thank heavens you're alive. I expected the worst. What has happened?"

Gwendolen shut the door behind her and spoke plainly. "The MacDonalds have broken through the main gate. There was a battle, and they have taken the castle.

Angus the Lion has declared himself chief, and he means to claim me as his wife in order to produce an heir, and unite our two clans." She was surprised by how calmly she could explain everything, when her insides were careening with dread.

Her mother stared blankly at her for a moment, then laughed aloud. "He means to *claim* you? Good God, does he not realize what century this is?"

"Clearly not." Gwendolen paused. "You should see him, Mother. All the stories about him are true. He is exactly what they say—mighty, violent, and fearsome. I was frozen with astonishment as I watched him exchange blows with our strongest, most skilled warriors, and I could not breathe when he spoke."

Her mother strode forward, fascinated. "So it's true then. He is fierce, and unconquerable?"

"Very much so."

"And he intends to take *you* as his wife?"

"Aye. I am not sure what to do."

Onora threw her hands up. "Are you daft, Gwendolen? You will accept him, of course. What other choice is there?" She turned toward the looking glass, pinched her cheeks for color, and ran her fingers through her long, curly locks of auburn hair. For a woman of her age, she was remarkably beautiful. Her lips were full, her cheekbones finely sculpted, her figure slender and trim. "This is very good news," she said. "I must say, I am greatly relieved."

"Relieved? How can you possibly be relieved?"

Onora turned. "Don't be such an idealist. There is no way out of this. The Lion has taken the castle, and we are at his mercy. He could kill us both, but he is willing to spare *you* at least, and not only that, he wants to wed you. What more could you ask? Your position here will not change. In fact, it will improve. Mine, however . . ." She paused and returned her attention to the looking glass. "That is yet to be determined." She wet her lips and puckered them. "But do not worry for me. I will negotiate for my own life and position."

Gwendolen laughed bitterly. "*Negotiate*. That is exactly what I must do a few short minutes from now. But with what, I ask you? As you said, we are at his mercy. We have no power. He has declared himself chief and has terrorized every warrior who still breathes. Those who would not surrender are dead."

Onora faced Gwendolen with fire in her eyes. "Which is why you are going to submit to him. In every way."

"Submit . . ."

"Aye." Her mother took hold of her wrist. "You are going to do exactly what he tells you to do, Gwendolen, and if you have any sense in that pretty little head of yours, you'll act like you enjoy it."

Gwendolen ripped her arm away. "Why don't *you* submit to him, Mother? If anyone knows how to please a man in bed, it's you, not me."

"I assure you, I would submit in an instant if I was the one he wanted. But he wants *you*, which is exactly what he shall have, or we'll both be dead. Now listen to what I say. You must be docile and agreeable. And for heaven's sake, make yourself more presentable. Put on a prettier gown." She reached out to untie the laces of Gwendolen's stays. "He has offered you a gift—a chance to preserve our status here. You must thank him, and lure him to your bed."

"Lure him to my bed?" Gwendolen shoved her mother's hands away. "He has laid siege to our home. I will not simply lie back and wait for him to lay siege to my body, as well. I will go to the hall and meet him there, with dignity, as Father would have done."

"And say what?"

"I will negotiate the terms of our surrender."

Onora scoffed. "You are forgetting that we have already been defeated. Surrender is no longer an option. He will laugh at you."

Gwendolen backed away, then realized that she did, in fact, have some power. "That is where you are wrong, Mother. He wants something from me—a child—and I shall inform him that *I* will not be conquered quite so easily as this castle. More importantly, if I can buy us time, there is a chance that Murdoch will return and restore our freedom."

"Gwendolen!"

Heart beating erratically in her chest, she walked out and shut the door behind her, then quickly made her way down the curved staircase, ignoring her mother's outraged calls, which echoed through the vaulted stone passageways.

As she approached the hall, her stomach turned somersaults. She was about to confront and challenge a ruthless, battle-seasoned warrior, who thought nothing of ramming through castle gates and slaughtering entire armies before breakfast.

Physically, she was no match for him. That was certain. He was mighty and strapping, and he could slaughter her too in a single heartbeat, if he was so inclined. But no matter what happened, she would not show her fear. She was the daughter of a Highland chief, and she had the allegiance of her people. She would face him on equal ground.

Thankfully, the hall was empty when she arrived, which awarded her a few minutes to collect her thoughts and decide how, exactly, she was going to address Angus Bradach MacDonald. She paused just inside the arched entry, behind the dais, and turned her eyes to the impressive display of MacEwen heraldry. Heavy silk tapestries draped the walls, flags and banners hung from the rafters, and their family crest had recently been carved into the stonework.

She glanced toward the heavy chair that her father had occupied until recently. When he had presided over this hall, feasts and celebrations were the order of the day. Laughter, music, and poetry filled the nights with culture and amusement. There was no threat of war or tyranny. He was a good man, a strong and fair leader, but all of that would soon change if she did not stand up to this new conqueror. Tonight, there would be subjugation, forced oaths, and peril for those who refused to submit.

Unless, of course, she could exert some influence, however small . . .

She stepped up onto the dais and approached the empty chair. *Help me to be brave, Father, for I wish to do my duty for the MacEwens.*

Her prayer was interrupted, unfortunately, by the sound of footsteps entering from the bailey. Gwendolen glanced up. Her pulse quickened as she beheld her enemy, Angus the Lion, at the far end of the hall.

Not yet aware of her presence, he paused just inside.

He looked up at the highest peaks of the ceiling, then his cool gaze moved along the string of MacEwen banners, hung from the wide wooden beams.

Gwendolen observed the finer details of his appearance—the dark kilt and tartan draped over his shoulder and pinned with a heavy silver brooch that had been polished to a brilliant sheen. He was an enormous man. That much she already knew. But up close, she could see that his hands were large, as well, which was especially distressing, to say nothing of the weapons he carried. In addition to the shield on his back and the heavy claymore belted at his waist, two pistols were tucked into the belt, and a powder horn was slung across his chest. A dirk was sheathed in his boot.

She looked more closely at his face, and felt rather anxious.

It was a face both rugged and beautiful—flawlessly proportioned, with a full sensuous mouth and a fine, patrician nose. His eyes were pale blue, as clear as ice on a winter lake, and yet they smoldered with fire. A curious commotion began inside her—an unusual trepidation, a shiver of heat that spread to her toes. She had to work hard to control it.

The great Lion studied the tapestries, the walls, and even the stones in the hearth, then his big hand went to the hilt of his broadsword, and his eyes narrowed in on her.

Before today, Gwendolen had not known what it felt like to be held in the gaze of a man so breathtaking. She had to focus on her sense of balance in order to remain upright on her feet.

Angus, on the other hand, appeared wholly relaxed,

though there was something intense and frightening about the way he looked at her. A lingering bloodlust from battle still coursed through his body, no doubt.

If she was going to get through this, she would have to remember that he wanted something from her. She was not entirely without power.

His hand still resting on the hilt of his sword, he crossed the length of the hall with menacing determination. Her heart galloped inside her chest. By the time he reached the dais, she was feeling the same wild and reckless exhilaration she had felt on the rooftop when she challenged him with her small sword, and declared herself brave enough to fight him.

"Get down off there," he said.

"Why? So you can look down on me?"

"Aye. Your family stole my home. You are thieves. The whole lot of you."

Her body raged, and she worried suddenly that she might faint from all the mayhem.

"You look pale, lassie. Are you ill?"

"No. I am fine," she told him, until she thought better of it. "I beg your pardon. I wish to retract that. I am not fine. I am disgusted."

He took a step forward and scoffed. "Disgusted? By *me*?"

"Aye. Did you expect otherwise?"

He stared at her with threatening resolve. "It's not the response I was anticipating, but it matters not. This castle is mine now. I've claimed you as my wife. Those are the facts."

She inhaled slowly in order to gather her wits about her. He was disturbingly succinct and to the point, with no consideration for politeness.

"And what am I supposed to do with those facts?" she asked. "Call everyone in and prance about the hall with delight?"

"Nay, there won't be any public prancing, lassie. Whether you like it or not, I'll be having you in my bed tonight—and *that* we'll do in private."

She took a deep breath, working hard to calm her rising hostility. "So soon?"

"Not soon enough, if you must know. I didn't expect to be wedding such a beauty."

Gwendolen laughed. "You think to get what you want by flattering me?"

The corner of his mouth curled up into a sinister grin. "I already got what I wanted, lass. Don't need to flatter anyone."

"And what was it, exactly, that you wanted?"

"Was it not obvious when I broke down the castle gate? I wanted Kinloch, and now I have it."

She swallowed hard. "Of course you do."

Neither of them said anything for a moment or two. Gwendolen was fighting to maintain a semblance of composure and dignity, while he seemed quite unabashedly distracted by the curve of her breasts and hips.

"Did I not ask you to get down off there?" he repeated, while tilting his head to the side. "Or do I need to come up and haul you down like a sack of turnips? I'll oblige you, if that's what you wish, but I'm weary from battle and in no mood for hauling vegetables. So get down off there, woman. Don't make me tell you again."

Gwendolen took careful note of the threatening message of command in his voice, and approached the edge of the dais. She stepped down, squared her shoulders, and stared up at him. He looked her over from head to foot, then leaped up onto the dais and strolled from one side to the other, as if he were taking measurements.

Gwendolen remained silent while he seated himself in her father's chair and lounged back comfortably, his long muscular legs stretched out in front of him. "Home at last," he said.

Again, he looked up at the MacEwen heraldry. He sat without speaking, and she knew he was pondering the future. Or perhaps recalling the past.

She watched his face for some insight into his mood and intentions. Sitting there like a sprawling lion, he appeared in absolute control, with no doubt whatsoever in his mind that he was now Laird of Kinloch, and she was to be his obedient wife and servant.

He was in for a rude awakening.

"Where is your brother, Murdoch?" he asked. "Why is he not here to defend Kinloch and protect his people?"

"He traveled abroad to visit Rome and educate himself. He believed a strong leader should be enlightened and knowledgeable about the world—an aspiration which I doubt *you* would understand. He left before my father died."

"But with your father's death, why has he not returned?"

She regarded Angus with steady eyes. "I am not certain he knows of it. We have dispatched a letter to him, of course, but have no way of knowing if he has received it. I am hopeful, however, that he will return any day. Perhaps unexpectedly."

It was an intentional strike at the Lion's arrogance. She wished him to know that his victory this morning may have seemed effortless, but the MacEwens would not continue to be easy prey. He should be on his guard.

Angus rested an elbow on the arm of the chair. "Will he be difficult?"

"I hope so."

He studied her with careful scrutiny. "I suppose the real question is whether or not *you* will be difficult."

"Oh, definitely."

His brow furrowed with displeasure, and she regretted the brash reply, when she had come here to negotiate in a civilized manner. She half expected him to rise up out of the chair and show her the back of his hand. He continued, however, to sit calmly, relaxed, but with a focused expression that made her feel as if she were standing before him naked. Her cheeks flushed with heat.

"Do you understand, lass, that I have already claimed you as my wife?"

"I heard as much when you shouted my marriage proposal from the rooftops, instead of asking me directly."

He cocked his head to the side. "Do you wish me to get down on bended knee?"

"Not particularly."

He nodded, as if he were reaching a number of conclusions about her character and temperament in these moments, based on her replies.

He sat back. "Good, because I'm not the romantic sort."

"You don't say. I am astonished."

There was a fluttering in the rafters above, and his eyes lifted. He caught sight of the tiny bird that had been nesting in the hall for as long as she could remember. It flew out the open arched doorway to the bailey.

"No one has been able to get rid of that bird," she told him. "Maybe you'll have better luck. Or maybe the poor defenseless creature has just realized what calamity has befallen her home, and has finally flown the coop."

"We'll see," he replied, rising to his feet, as if he had grown bored of the conversation and had much more important matters to attend to.

She hastened to step forward before he could dismiss her. "All that aside," she blurted out, "I would like to negotiate the terms of my surrender."

His eyes settled upon her again and he spoke in a patronizing tone. "Your surrender . . ."

"Aye. I told you I would resist you, and I will, in every sense of the word, unless this situation can be resolved to my liking."

For a long moment he stared at her, as if he could barely comprehend what he'd just heard. A dark scowl passed across his features, and yet there was something else . . . Was it possible that he was enjoying her insolence?

"To *your* liking," he repeated.

"Aye."

A muscle clenched in his jaw, and any hint of interest vanished, as she realized she had struck a very bad note. It was obvious from the rising tide of fury in his eyes that he was not accustomed to hearing such demands from people, much less a woman he had just claimed as his possession. He was used to being feared.

He stepped down from the dais and approached her. She took a step back. It was one thing to speak to a conquering warlord seated in a chair, ten feet away. It was quite another to be standing at eye level with his chest—so close, she could see the bloodstains in the individual fibers of his shirt, and smell the fresh aroma of his sweat.

Slowly, carefully, she lifted her eyes.

He was glaring down at her with blistering antagonism. "I'll hear your terms now," he said.

Thankful that his sword was still sheathed in the scabbard and she was still in possession of her head, Gwendolen cleared her throat. "I want you to honor the conditions you offered just now to the people of my clan, but I have something else to add."

"Speak, then."

She wet her dry lips. "Those who must forfeit their homes, but choose to stay and pledge allegiance to you, will be given compensation from the Kinloch treasury. I understand that there will be no compensation given to those who leave, but I must be assured that if that is what they choose, they will be permitted to leave freely, without fear of death or retaliation by your warriors."

"Agreed," he replied.

Surprised by the swiftness and ease with which he accepted her first request, she nevertheless proceeded with caution. "I petition also that my mother will be treated with the appropriate respect due to her, as the widow of a past Laird of Kinloch. She will keep her apartments and jewels, and she will sit at our table."

"Agreed," he said. "Anything else?"

She swallowed thickly. "All members of the Mac-Ewen clan will have rights equal to the MacDonalds in all matters."

He thought about that one for a moment. "If they

pledge their allegiance to me tonight, I give you my word that they will have equal rights."

She realized suddenly that she was perspiring, and wiped the back of her hand across her damp forehead.

"Lastly, in regard to our marital union . . ." All at once, her belly swarmed with butterflies, and she had to swallow hard to keep her voice steady. "I request that you do not claim your husbandly rights until our wedding night."

That one, oddly enough, was the only application that gave him pause—and soon after, his eyes smoldered with rising sexuality. "Are you a virgin, lass?"

"Of course," she replied incredulously.

He studied her expression, then his gaze dipped lower. Time seemed to stand still as he lifted a hand and traced a slow finger along the line of her jaw, down the center of her throat to the valley of her cleavage, then along the breadth of her neckline from shoulder to shoulder, as if he were drawing a smile with his rough, callused fingertip.

Gwendolen shivered, for no man had ever touched her like that before, and this man was far more intimidating than most. He slanted a seductive glance at her, and all her bravado from moments ago poured out of her like water. Her skin seemed to burn with fever under his fingertip, and it made her head swim in churning circles.

She felt suddenly inept when it came to negotiating for anything. Perhaps her mother was right. Perhaps she should simply be thanking him.

"That's a considerable demand, lass. I'd venture to call it impudent, and I've no interest in wedding a woman who doesn't know her place."

"And what is my place, exactly?"

"Your place will be in my bed. Pleasing me."

She was having a devil of a time getting air in and out of her lungs. "I understand," she said shakily, "that if I am to be your wife, it will be my duty to provide you with an heir. I only ask that I have time to prepare myself for that . . . *obligation.*"

His eyes narrowed with dark, sensual resolve. "What's the point in putting off the inevitable? One way or another, you'll be on your back, and I'll be having my way with you. You might even find you enjoy it."

"Enjoy it?" she scoffed. "I think not."

His gaze lingered on her lips, and her insides seemed to melt into a big warm puddle of sensation as he cupped the side of her face in his hand and let his fingers play in the wisps of hair over her ear. "Since we're negotiating the terms for your total and complete surrender to me," he said, "I'll agree to your blushing request on two conditions."

"I am listening." She struggled to banish the color from her cheeks.

"I'll leave your sweet, luscious maidenhead intact, as long as you agree to be amiable toward me between now and then. Never again will you defy me in front of the clans like you did this morning, nor will you resist or dispute my authority over Kinloch. You will support my rule, both publicly and privately."

Could she agree to that? she wondered uneasily.

Yes. She would agree to anything, if it meant he would not touch her like this, or attempt to take her this very night. And perhaps, before that moment arrived, if she was blessed with good fortune or mercy from above, her brother would arrive and save her from that fate.

"Fine. What is the second condition?" She worked hard to ignore the fact that his thumb was now gently brushing back and forth across her chin.

"When your brother returns like a hero on his white steed"—he said, as if he had read her mind—"which I am certain he will, your allegiance will be with me, your husband, and you will not betray that vow."

"But what will become of my brother? This castle is his birthright, too. You cannot simply expect him to—"

A flash of anger burned in the Lion's eyes. "It is not his birthright. It is mine. But your brother will have a choice. He can pledge an oath to me, and with that oath, he will be given land and a position of rank and stature. If he refuses, he will be free to leave."

She paused, for she did not believe it. "Would you promise me—would you give me your word of honor as a Scotsman—that you will not kill him?"

Angus stepped back. "Nay. For if he raises his sword against me, or any other MacDonald, I will slice him in half without hesitation."

Gwendolen looked down at the floor. She did not doubt his word in that regard, and for the first time, a true feeling of defeat swept through her. He was a powerful foe, and she was out of her depth.

"I will agree to those terms," she said, consoling herself with the fact that she had at least attained some compensation for her people. And the Lion would not attempt to bed her that night. Perhaps, with any luck, her brother would arrive soon with an army of redcoats, and drag this Jacobite rebel off to the gallows for treason. She would try to get word to Murdoch about the urgency of their predicament, and cling to the hope that even after the forfeiture of her innocence, the castle could still be reclaimed. All hope was not lost.

It would be her sacrifice, she supposed. Her virtue in exchange for the eventual freedom of her clan.

Gwendolen looked up and found herself gazing into the unyielding blue depths of his eyes.

"Are we done now?" he asked. "Did you get what you wanted?"

"Aye." But she felt completely unraveled.

"Then seal the agreement. Prove to me that your word is true."

"How?"

The tone of his voice changed in that moment. He spoke in a low, husky whisper. "Pledge it with a kiss."

Before she had a chance to object, he pressed his mouth to hers, and the floor seemed to shift under her feet. She had never been kissed before, not once in her life. She had lived a virtuous existence, determined to evolve into a woman very different from her mother, who used sex as an instrument of power over men.

But this was not the same as that. Not at all. Gwendolen had no power here. She was completely beguiled and could do nothing but bend and soften to the strength of his will.

He slipped his hands around her waist and pulled her close, and her head tilted back under the pressure of the kiss—so urgent and probing, it sent her body reeling. All at once, this artless, naïve pledge of hers felt like a promise of profound physicality and commitment. He was demanding her complete surrender and capitulation, here in this room, by the joining of their mouths and bodies, and she had no idea what to do, but to respond.

He tipped his head to the side and cupped the back of her neck with his hand, parting her lips and sliding his tongue inside to mingle damply with hers. The kiss drew out an involuntary whimper of submission.

Then—just as she was becoming acquainted with the sensation of their lips and tongues colliding gently—he drew back from the kiss and ran a finger across her flushed cheek.

"I believe you *will* enjoy it, lass," he said in a gruff voice, "when the time comes."

Gwendolen's legs nearly buckled beneath her. "I most certainly will not."

He turned away and started toward the bailey.

"Wait!" she said.

He stopped, but did not turn.

"There is one more thing." Gwendolen strode forward tensely.

He turned his head to the side.

"I want my family's heraldry to remain here in the hall, beside yours."

For the longest time, he stood with his back to her, refusing to speak. A knot of uncertainty tangled up inside her stomach.

At last, he turned. "You were doing so well, lass. Why did you have to spoil it?"

"Spoil what? I am only asking for what is rightfully ours. My father was granted possession of this castle by the King of Great Britain, and our name cannot simply be erased from its walls."

Another warrior entered the hall. He, too, was imposing like Angus, but his hair was black as night, his eyes dark as sin. He stood just inside the door.

Angus spoke over his shoulder. "Lachlan, come here

and escort my future bride to my bedchamber. She needs to be taught a lesson or two about the rules of war and the meaning of surrender. Lock her in and put a guard at the door."

"What?" Gwendolen's heart began to pitch and roll. "I thought we had an agreement."

"We did, and I confess, I enjoyed the negotiations. But you shouldn't have stepped over the line, lass. I told you, I have no interest in wedding a woman who does not know her place. It's time you learned yours and understood the limits of my tolerance." He frowned at her. "I am not a kind man."

"I didn't step over any line. I only asked for one more thing."

"The negotiations were finished," he said. "That's the end of it. Now go with Lachlan, and wait for me in my bed."

The other warrior strode across the hall and took hold of her arm. "Don't fight it, lass," he said. "You'll only make things worse for yourself."

"How can it possibly get any worse than this?" she asked.

He chuckled softly. "You don't know Angus."

Chapter Three

The instant the door slammed shut behind Gwendolen and the key turned in the lock, she squeezed her eyes shut. She had to fight against the overwhelming urge to scream her lungs out and pound her fists up against the door. She felt desperate enough to do it, but alas, she had never been the type of woman who succumbed to temper tantrums. They accomplished nothing.

Besides, Angus the Lion hardly struck her as the sort of man who would be moved by such childish displays. In fact, she doubted he would be moved by much of anything, for his heart seemed forged of steel. There was nothing gentle about him, nothing whatsoever. She had not recognized a single breath of tenderness or compassion in his character. He had treated her like an object. He expected her to fear and obey him, and he made it clear that if she did not, he would use her body to teach her lessons about insubordination. He also intended to use her to breed a child for political purposes—and perhaps to satisfy his savage lust.

Lifting her eyes, she looked around her father's private chamber. No one had made use of the room since his passing, but Gwendolen had nevertheless instructed the servants to come in and dust once a week, and change the bed linens, for she'd wanted the room prepared at all times for her brother's return. Now it seemed she'd had it prepared instead for her enemy. And for her own deflowering.

She crossed to the bed, where sunshine beamed in through the leaded windows and cast bright squares of light on the crimson coverings. The book her father had been reading lay open on the table beside the lamp. No one had touched the book, nor had anyone moved his shoes, which remained exactly where he'd left them, beside the bed, on the night he died.

Gwendolen looked down at them. They were well worn and formed to the shape of his feet.

What was it about a man's shoes that made it seem as if he were still alive in the world, and would eventually come home? They were concrete evidence of his existence, she supposed—a part of his physical being. They reminded her of his courage and strength.

She knelt down and ran a finger over one of the leather toes and resolved that she, too, would continue to be brave. No matter what happened, no matter what her conqueror did to her, she would not fall apart. She would not succumb to the power he'd wielded over her in the hall just now, when he'd sealed their bargain with a kiss. She had been caught off guard, that was all, and it would not happen again. Next time she would be prepared for his touch, and the sensations it aroused, and would not become spellbound. Let him come now, and she would fulfill her part of the bargain with courage, dignity, and decorum.

Footsteps sounded in the corridor, and a key turned

in the lock. Her conqueror entered the room, and she suddenly found herself wishing that destiny was not paying such close attention to her lofty aspirations.

She rose to her feet.

"I told you to wait for me in bed." He gestured toward her with a hand. "Yet, here you stand before me doing the opposite. Are you simpleminded, lass? Or just inept when it comes to following orders?"

"I am the daughter of a great laird, not one of your minions."

"But you are soon to be my wife."

"Soon, perhaps," she replied. "But we are not yet married, nor will we ever be, if you continue to behave like a savage."

With a steely note of warning in his eyes, he watched her move farther away from the bed. "Did you not learn anything in the hall just now? I won't be pushed, nor will I tolerate a disobedient wife."

"And what are you going to do with me if I defy you? Beat me? Kill me? That won't get you the child you want."

He regarded her with increasing interest. "There are a dozen ways I could have you on your back in an instant, lass, whether we're married or not, and none of them will be gentle or chivalrous—so I suggest you mind that sharp tongue of yours."

She turned to the window, feeling desperate again. "Haven't you had enough violence for one day? Besides, wouldn't it be more pleasant for you if I were willing, and eager?"

God help her, she was scraping the bottom of the barrel now.

He strode forward, slowly. "Now *that* sounds intriguing. How eager would you be? Give me an example."

He was too clever, too intuitive, for he must have known she didn't have the slightest clue how to convey "eagerness" once he began the dreaded deflowering. The question knocked her off balance completely.

"Come now," he said. "Don't be shy. How eager will you be when I begin to unlace you?"

She wet her lips and felt her insides begin to tremble again. "That depends on how merciful you are."

She was rather proud of that shrewd deflection of the question.

"And how gifted an actress *you* are." He strode closer, his heavy broadsword bouncing lightly against his hip, and she had to steel herself against the daunting impact of his approach. He was tall and mighty, and the perfection of his golden features had a way of distracting her from his more degenerate intentions. She found herself gaping up at those soft full lips and intense blue eyes, and wondering how such perfection was even possible in the human form—villainous or otherwise.

"I'll be frank with you," he said, touching her cheek with the back of a finger. "Merciful or not, I'll be having you in my bed, so you may as well part with any foolish hopes that I'll be easily manipulated or deterred by your precious innocence, or your feminine charms, bountiful as they may be. I won't be sympathetic to any begging or pleading, either. You'll not weaken or outwit me, nor will you soften my heart with these futile attempts at distraction. There's not really much of a heart there to work with, you see, so don't bother to waste your time. Just submit, and accept that this is the way things are.

I'll not be rough or cruel to you—as long as you remember not to cross me—and you may even find you enjoy certain things."

"Certain things? Like what, precisely? Your knife at my throat each night?"

Something flickered in his eyes—something she had not seen before—and she wondered if he was amused.

"That's a bit dramatic," he said. "I think you might be making too much of my weapons. But don't be troubled, lass. I'll put them away when I make love to you."

"Make love? Is that what we're going to call it?"

"Would you prefer I use another turn of phrase? I'd be more than happy to, though you don't strike me as the type who likes to say 'shag' or 'f—'"

"Enough! Please!" She backed away, and stumbled over her feet. "Let's just not . . . Let's not call it anything. I'd prefer not to speak of it at all."

His eyes glimmered with renewed interest as he followed her across the room. "Why not?"

"Because there's no way to speak about it without being lewd or vulgar."

He strolled toward the bed in a predatory swagger, and leaned a broad shoulder against the bedpost. "I beg to differ. Some men can be anything *but* vulgar when seducing a comely lass like you. I'm not one of them, but if you like, I could try to romance you with a sonnet."

"Now you're mocking me."

"Aye." His eyes were cold and forbidding. "I told you before, I'm not the romantic sort."

She lifted her chin. "As if *you* would know a sonnet, anyway."

"Mm, you're right. On top of everything else, I'm an

illiterate brute. All I know how to do is conquer. And plunder, plunder, plunder."

Her vision began to blur as he strode toward her. She backed up and said, "If I could, I would summon my father from the grave to run you through. And he would do it, too. This was his bedchamber, you know, and he was a great warrior."

The closer he got, the more desperate she became.

"I'm sure he was, and I admire your devotion to him, lass, but it's discipline that wins the day, not ghosts."

"And how do you plan to discipline me? Will you throw me onto the bed like the wild, savage beast that you are, and ravish me against my will?"

"Are you *trying* to get me excited?"

She sucked in a breath. "Or will you beat me, and keep me locked up forever?"

He backed her up against the wall and let his hungry gaze travel from the top of her head, slowly, all the way down to her toes. "Neither holds much appeal to me at the moment. I've had enough fighting for one day. All I want is your soft naked body under my own, and I'm surprised we're still standing here discussing it. You ought to be proud of yourself, lass, for causing such a delay."

Her hands tightened into fists. "Why don't you find yourself another woman to satisfy your lust? I am not willing."

"You're a bit of a shrew, aren't you?"

His lips brushed over her cheek. He was so close, she could smell the masculine fragrance of his skin.

"If it displeases you, then yes, I am."

Without the slightest warning, he scooped her up

into his arms and tossed her onto the bed. Before she could utter a single word of outrage, he was on top of her, pressing her into the feathery softness of the mattress—so deep, she thought she'd never find her way out.

"Maybe I should just take you now and complete the invasion," he said in a low voice as he slid his hand up under her skirts to caress her thigh. "Why wait for our wedding night?"

"But we had an agreement. In the hall . . . You promised . . ."

"Maybe I was just toying with you." He brushed his nose over the tip of hers, then across her cheek to her ear, while his broad palm slid under her backside and pulled her hips tight up against him.

Gwendolen remembered her earlier vow to be brave, no matter what he did to her, and tried to focus on some dignified response to this sudden brutish pillaging of her innocence. "I may be forced to submit my body to you," she said, "but I will never submit my soul."

He laughed in her ear. "Enough with the theatricals, lass. Do you know how comical you are? It's like something out of a bad play. What have you been reading lately?"

She was both infuriated and mortified. Every part of her body seemed to be throbbing and flaming with unbidden heat, and she felt completely exposed. "It was not my intention to provide you with entertainment."

"And yet, I am spellbound. If I didn't have to hold you down, I'd be applauding your performance, and throwing roses up onto your stage."

His mouth found hers, and the intimacy of the connection was too much for her to take. Her lips, burning and aching, soon gave way to his plunging advance and softened to the irresistible stroke of his tongue.

Oh, how would she ever navigate her way through this sacrifice?

Although "sacrifice" was becoming less and less the proper word to describe what was happening here, for she was floating away rather quickly on an intoxicating haze of sensation.

He laid soft, wet kisses across her eyelids and along her forehead, and inched his body upward, thrusting against her with smooth, gentle undulations that reminded her of the sea. A moment later, the kisses found their way to the sensitive, tingling flesh at her neck. His tongue pushed into the hollow of her throat.

Gwendolen focused on her breathing, working hard to remain resistant—or at least give the appearance of indifference.

She looked up at the crimson canopy overhead and chastised herself for this swift surrender, when she had been so determined to fight and die an honorable death today, alongside her clansmen who had battled so valiantly. Instead, she was melting like warm sugar cake in her conqueror's arms.

She told herself that it was only because she had never been kissed before today, and she lacked the experience necessary to use sex for power, as her mother would have done—quite effectively—had she been here in Gwendolen's place.

On the other hand, she had a feeling that her mother might have fared no better. She would probably be melting like warm sugar cake, too.

All at once, Onora's face flashed in Gwendolen's eyes. "Please, I must ask you one thing," she said breathlessly. "Is my mother safe? Tell me you have not harmed her."

Angus kissed the side of her neck and thrust his hips. "How badly do you want to know?"

"Badly," she replied. "I promise, if you tell me that she is alive and well, I will not cross you again. I will do whatever you ask."

A smug grin graced his lips as he kissed the edges of her neckline. "Ah, lassie—you've shown me twice today that you have a very soft and pretty Achilles' heel. Just the sort of thing a ruthless warrior looks for in a situation like this. A chink in the armor, a crack in the gate . . ."

"What are you saying?"

His lips brushed over hers. "You make it almost too easy. You're taking all the fun out of it."

"Fun for *you,* perhaps. Not for me."

The Lion rose up on both arms and looked down at her in the shimmering morning light that was streaming in through the windows.

"You and your precious, holy virtue," he said. "You really ought to give it up."

Gwendolen struggled to think straight. "Wait . . . What do you mean, a chink in my armor?"

He kissed her on the mouth again, and never had she imagined a man's lips and body could evoke such delirious sensation. It was like drinking liquid fire, or falling from a cloud.

"What did you mean?" she repeated, and he rolled to the side.

He rested his cheek on a hand, and his eyes chilled over with frost. "What I was trying to say, lassie, is that if you cross me one more time, it's not *you* I'll be locking up. It will be your beloved mother."

"I beg your pardon?"

He spoke with malice. "You're too easy to read, and far too self-sacrificing. I believe you would have died for your clan if I'd pushed you too far in the hall. And look at you now, playing the part of a willing bed partner, opening to me like a soft spring blossom, when we both know you'd rather shoot me dead than let me slide my hand up under your skirts."

"No," she replied ridiculously, "that's not entirely true."

He slid off the bed and tucked his shirt back into his kilt, then pulled the knife from his boot and pointed the sharp blade at her.

"We had an agreement," he said, "and I'll honor my word. I'll not claim your virginity until we are wed, and your mother will have her jewels and sit at our table. I'll give equal rights to all MacEwens who pledge allegiance to me tonight, as long as you hold true to your end of the bargain."

Gwendolen leaned up on both elbows and struggled to control the ragged pace of her breathing. "And what did I promise . . . exactly?"

Lord help her, she couldn't remember. Her brain was addled. Her thoughts had been stomped on, like grapes to wine. She felt completely inebriated.

"You gave me your word that you would be amiable toward me from this day forward. You will not defy me, nor will you resist or dispute my authority over Kinloch. You will support my rule, both publicly and privately. And when your brother returns, your loyalty will rest with *me*, as your husband. Not him."

And this meant he would not bed her? He would not force himself upon her? It was the only condition she seemed able to focus upon.

"Are we agreed?" he asked.

She quickly nodded.

"Good. Obedient at last. Now get your skinny bones out of that bed, woman. You're needed in the bailey. There are wounded men to attend to." With that he turned and walked out the door.

Gwendolen sank back down onto the bed and exhaled sharply. He had read her like a book just now, and used all her fears and weaknesses against her. Clearly, he was not an ignorant brute. He was clever and cunning, and had a quick mind for strategic warfare, even in the bedroom.

But she, too, was an intelligent woman. Her father, God rest his soul, had encouraged her to use her brain. She would therefore spend the rest of the day thinking about what he had shown her. He, too, would be a book she would read—and by tonight, she would have him deciphered and decoded, and then she would begin her own strategic battle for survival.

Chapter Four

The Great Hall that evening pulsed with the laughter of men, underscored by the spirited music from a fiddle player who wandered about the room, his bow dancing merrily across the strings. The colorful gowns of the MacEwen women lent a festival atmosphere to the gathering, and the aroma of fresh bread and seasoned roast mutton, with the promise of sweet pastries for dessert, made it seem as if there were something to celebrate.

Not so for Gwendolen, however. She entered the hall in a plain gown of gray silk, feeling as if she were descending into the searing hot flames of Satan's dining room.

All the MacEwen heraldry had been taken down. There was nothing left of it, except for what was carved into the stones over the hearth. Everyone seemed happy enough on the surface, she supposed, but for the Mac-Ewens, this smiling civility toward their invaders was nothing but a mask they wore to cover their fear and loathing.

Fear, mostly, thanks to their new leader.

She ventured more deeply into the hall and roamed through the crowd. Having spent the day tending to the wounded on both sides, she was physically and emotionally spent. For those who had survived the battle, their injuries were mostly light. Some were here this evening, patched up, but still ready to drink and make merry, although one clansman—Douglas, her old friend—had suffered a painful end when the surgeon tried to remove a musket ball from his shoulder.

Hence, the music and tempting aroma of the feast did little to improve Gwendolen's mood. She knew she must hide her grief, however, for the people of her clan would need her confidence and encouragement in the coming days.

She spotted her mother on the far side of the hall, looking radiant in a sage-colored gown that highlighted her auburn hair. Gwendolen was at least pleased to see that Onora was wearing her best jewels, which meant Angus had kept his word and not deprived her of her status.

Gwendolen glanced around the hall for her future husband, whom she had not seen since the morning, but recognized only the darkly handsome warrior who had escorted her to her father's chamber—the one named Lachlan. He had caught sight of Onora, however, and set out on a determined path toward her from across the room.

Gwendolen hurried to join her mother, and like the third point of a triangle, she arrived just as they all connected in the center.

"And who, may I ask, do I have the pleasure of addressing?" Onora asked, when Lachlan handed her a goblet of wine he had picked up from a passing servant.

"I am Angus's cousin," he said with a heavy Scottish brogue. "Lachlan MacDonald, Laird of War. My father, before me, was also Kinloch's Laird of War, cut down in battle when your husband invaded here two years ago." He gazed at her with a masculine, but somehow playful, arrogance.

Gwendolen's mother, also playful and never daunted, awarded him a dazzling smile. "What an honor to meet such a brave and heroic man. I am charmed." She held out her hand.

He bent forward and kissed it, never taking his eyes off hers, and Gwendolen felt rather invisible.

"You have soft lips, sir."

"And your eyes, madam, are as elegant as your jewels."

Gwendolen stepped forward to interrupt. "We met earlier this morning," she said.

He straightened and turned to her. "Aye. Miss Mac-Ewen."

"And where is our great conquering laird this evening?" she asked. "I hope he will soon grace us with his presence."

He smirked at her blatant show of sarcasm. "As do I, because I have no interest in occupying his chair this evening. I have other plans."

Onora touched a finger to the brooch at his shoulder, and adjusted his tartan. "And what might those plans be, sir?"

"Don't know yet, madam. I'm just now getting re-acquainted with the lay of the land."

"Well." Her eyes sparkled. "If you need help finding your way around the castle, you must come to me first. I would be delighted to assist. If there is *any* way I can be of use to you. *Any* way at all . . ."

Gwendolen cleared her throat. "If you will excuse us

please, Lachlan. I would like to have a word with my mother."

He bowed to them, and backed away toward a group of warriors who were knocking their pewter tankards together, spilling ale onto the floor, tipping their heads back to guzzle.

Gwendolen led her mother to a quiet corner. "Must you idly flirt with every last member of the enemy clan? Can you not behave yourself for just one night?"

Onora shook her head. "First of all, I never flirt idly. That one was Laird of War. Now tell me what happened this morning when the ferocious Lion locked you in your father's chamber. I heard it was difficult. Are you all right?"

"I am fine, Mother. I spent the day tending to the wounded."

Onora led her deeper into the shadows. "I don't care what you did all day. I want to know what happened in the bedchamber. You can tell me anything, darling. In fact, tell me everything. What happened?"

Gwendolen looked around to ensure no one was listening, then leaned close and spoke in a whisper. "It was difficult, indeed. He used the threat of sex to bring me under control and trick me into submission, because he knew I did not want it."

Onora drew back slightly. "Only the threat of it?"

"Aye. Well . . . He did toss me onto the bed, and he joined me there, and took . . . certain . . . liberties." Her body trembled at the mere memory of it.

"You didn't try to fight him off?"

"Of course I did, but he's very strong."

"Mm. I did observe that."

"You've met him?"

"Aye. He visited your bedchamber this morning to have a brief word with me after he saw you. He came through the door, bold as a bull, and informed me that he was the new laird. He then told me to return to my own apartments, and that I could keep my jewels."

"What did you say?"

"Nothing. He walked out before I had a chance to speak. He didn't seem interested in hearing what I had to say anyway. He was very impatient. Appeared to be in a great hurry."

A hush fell over the crowd just then, as the great Lion entered the hall and took a seat in her father's chair at the head table, which was draped with a white cloth and adorned with pewter bowls of fruit and flowers. A servant brought a jewel-encrusted goblet of wine and set it down in front of him. He picked it up and reclined back in the chair.

Onora watched him with interest. "I learned today that he was banished to the Hebrides for the past two years, and while he was there, he had an oracle for a lover."

"An *oracle*?" Though Gwendolen did not wish to know anything about his past lovers, she could not deny that this particular piece of information fascinated her. "Was she genuine? Did she predict things?"

"Apparently so. She told him he would succeed in his quest to regain control of Kinloch, and that his time would come, that he would achieve all his dreams. You know—the sort of thing that encourages a man's passions." Onora twirled a lock of hair around her finger. "Perhaps *I* should call myself an oracle."

Gwendolen ignored the silly remark. "Where is this oracle now? Please do not tell me that she followed him here."

"No. He left her behind in the Hebrides. From what I understand, she was a crafty little witch. And I mean that in the worst possible way." Onora sipped her wine and watched Angus over the rim of her glass. "How was he, when he came to you?"

"How do you mean?"

"Was he a good lover?"

Gwendolen sighed with discontent. "How would I know? It was the first time anything like that ever happened to me, so I am in no position to make such an assessment. And can we please talk about something else? The man is my enemy. I do not care if he is a good lover or not. It won't matter."

Her mother took another sip of wine. "I think you may discover that it matters very much. Even more so, *because* he is your enemy."

Gwendolen watched her future husband converse with a MacEwen warrior, who stood just below the dais, seeking to make a good impression, no doubt. "I don't understand you."

"No, clearly you do not, but you will eventually, and you may come looking for my advice—at which time you will have a world of wisdom at your fingertips. Then we shall see who brings whom under control. You may be surprised to discover you have the upper hand." Onora raised the goblet to her lips again and watched Angus carefully while she took a long, slow drink. "At least he's handsome. Imagine if he had the face of a boar."

"Mother."

She turned her sparkling eyes to Gwendolen. "Promise that you will at least try to charm him. You know what they say—you can catch more flies with honey . . ."

"I don't want to catch him. I want him to leave.

Which is why we must send word to Murdoch and tell him what has occurred. The sooner he returns, the better. If he could come with an army . . ."

"Mm," her mother said. "I suppose that is the responsible thing to do."

Gwendolen looked around the room with dismay. "Sometimes I wonder why I am so devoted to you."

Onora beamed a smile at her. "Because I am your mother, and you adore me."

Ten servants entered the hall carrying platters of warm bread, fresh out of the oven, which they placed on the long trestle tables. The hum of conversation and laughter in the room died away as the clansmen and women moved to find seats at the benches.

"I suppose it's time we joined our enemies," Gwendolen said. She made a move to leave, but her mother caught her arm.

"Wait." She spoke in a more serious tone. "You should know, Gwendolen, that Angus has ordered his men to refrain from helping themselves to any of our women, especially those who lost husbands in the battle today. The women are all to be given time to grieve. Only then will the MacDonald clansmen be permitted to make wives out of them."

"Why are you telling me this?"

She shrugged. "I thought you might like to know. And perhaps such information about your future husband will make it easier for you to do what you must do. The first time is never easy."

She regarded her mother with understanding and a whisper of quiet gratitude.

"I appreciate what you are trying to do," she said, "but I don't think anything is going to make this less difficult. Let us just pray that it is over as quickly as possible."

Angus leaned back in his chair when a servant came to refill his goblet. His attention was diverted, however, by the image of his future wife crossing the hall to join him at the table.

He marveled at his unexpected good luck—that the woman he'd claimed for a bride did not have the face of a turnip. Even in that ugly gray frock, she outshone every woman in the room, for there was something intangible and strangely ethereal about her beauty, something radiant that burned in those keen brown eyes. Her complexion was ivory-white, while her thick, sable hair was an exotic and striking contrast of darkness. To top it all off, those cherry-red lips were supple and full, and the effect of her presence as a whole was enough to make his head spin.

But as he watched her approach—and felt a carnal urge to rise up from the table and drag her by the hand to his bed—he began to wonder if he had been cursed, rather than blessed, for he had no interest in becoming infatuated with anyone, much less a wife.

He had seen what romantic obsessions did to men. He had watched his closest friend, Duncan MacLean, lay down his sword and give up his warrior life for the mad love of a woman.

An Englishwoman, at that. Angus had been so frustrated by the affair—and by his own inability to talk sense into Duncan—that he'd gone a little mad himself. Mad with rage and unthinkable treachery. Eventually mad with shame.

"You look lost in thought," Lachlan said, sitting down

beside him and tearing off a hunk of the warm, crusty bread. "Can't blame you. She's a prize, that one."

Gwendolen stopped to speak to an older woman in the crowd.

Angus picked up his goblet and frowned. "Aye, she's fetchin', to be sure, and has the fire of a fighting Scot in her blood, but make no mistake about it. The real prize is Kinloch."

Lachlan leaned back in his chair. "Aye, but what is Kinloch, if not for its people? Without them, it's just stones and mortar."

Angus regarded him irritably. "Stones and mortar, Lachlan? Were your brains addled during the battle this morning? Without these walls, there is no home. There is nothing."

He could testify to that. He had been two years banished, living in the cold, damp outer reaches of the Western Isles in a thatched hut with Raonaid—another outcast like himself. A gifted devil of a woman who had been banished for her unearthly talents, and had no other place to go. The entire time, he'd felt like he was bobbing about in a frigid sea with no sign of land or even a mucky bottom to set his feet upon. He had never felt more lost or nonexistent. He had not known it was possible to feel like a living ghost.

He took another sip of wine and watched Gwendolen over the rim of the goblet. She and her mother—another dangerous beauty—were still chattering with the woman, who wiped a tear from her cheek. Gwendolen offered her a folded kerchief from inside her sleeve.

"Your future mother-in-law seems like a champion vixen," Lachlan said in a low voice, leaning close. "You ought to keep a close eye on her. I learned today that she took her dead husband's steward to bed on the day of the funeral, and has been pulling the man's strings ever since."

"Aye, but there's more," Angus replied. "She's been having him in her bed for over a year, ruling Kinloch from behind closed doors the entire time. Her husband was a puppet, too."

Lachlan sipped his wine. "I confess I am not surprised, having just met her. Does the daughter know?"

Angus studied Gwendolen from across the room. "I cannot be sure. It's difficult to imagine she didn't know what was going on. She's clever and strong-willed. Yet she seems too virtuous to condone such a thing."

He thought about the softness of her skin beneath his roaming hands, and how she had responded to his touch with such repressed desire. He wondered if she was like her mother, and it was all a clever act to make him believe he'd succeeded in conquering her—to give him a false sense of power and confidence—or if she had truly been aroused by his kiss and would prove malleable in the future.

"And what did you learn about the son today?" Angus asked, redirecting his thoughts to a different matter. "My future wife believes he will come home at any moment and seize back what he believes to be his."

"That, I am afraid, is no lie. News was sent to him about his father's death, but there has been no response, so he could arrive at the gates tomorrow for all we know. I also learned that his departure was not friendly. He and his father quarreled for weeks before. Some say it involved a woman he was not permitted to marry, which explains his absence at his father's deathbed, for they were estranged."

Again, Angus thought of his friend Duncan's romantic obsession with a woman, and how such passions could distract a man from his purpose as a warrior and leader of men.

"Does Murdoch have the power to raise an army?" he asked.

"He has the support of King George. It's why Kinloch was lost to the MacEwens in the first place."

"Because of my father's undying Jacobite passions." Angus sipped his wine and remembered all the politics and campaigning for the Stuart Crown, and how it had ended in defeat on the battlefield at Sherrifmuir.

Lachlan tore off another hunk of bread. "Your father raised an army to dethrone a king, and reigning monarchs don't take kindly to that sort of thing, Angus. King George will no doubt be watching you very closely in the coming months, for any secret maneuverings."

"I have no such intentions," Angus replied. "At least not presently. I want peace at Kinloch. I've seen enough bloodshed for a while."

Lachlan studied his profile. "I never thought I'd see the day when Angus the Lion was not hungry for battle."

"Nor did I. And that's not to say I won't get an itch I'll want to scratch one day in the future. But for now, I have a duty here—to restore Kinloch to the people of my clan and provide stability."

"A wife and child ought to bring that about."

"Aye, and in light of that, we need to annihilate the possibility of any further invasions from another ambitious MacEwen chieftain."

Lachlan leaned forward. "I thought you said you were tired of bloodshed."

"Aye. I am," Angus replied. "And I'd prefer it not come to that. I don't think my intended bride would take kindly to it. He is her brother after all."

"What is to be done then?"

Angus spoke in a hushed tone. "Send a man to find Murdoch, and make him an offer of land and status. If he wants peace, he will accept."

"And if he doesn't?"

Angus glanced soberly at Gwendolen, who began to make her way toward the table. "Do what is necessary to ensure peace. There can be no more invasions."

Lachlan nodded and sat back. "I understand. I'll put a few hunters on his trail at first light."

The noise and laughter in the hall subsided as Gwendolen stepped up onto the dais. Angus rose to his feet and held out his hand. She hesitated and eyed it with suspicion before she slipped her tiny fingers into his palm and faced the members of their clans. The hall fell silent and remained so, until Angus and Gwendolen sat down together to eat.

Chapter Five

Gwendolen looked down at the bowl of soup that was placed before her, and breathed in the rich, steaming aroma of meat, swimming in a thick, seasoned broth. In the center of the table, a whole roast pig, golden and crisp, rested on a platter, waiting to be sliced and devoured. She gazed around despondently at the urns of fruit, the shiny candelabras, and all the servants moving about the hall with trays of food, and felt a pounding chaos inside her head that simply would not die.

"I heard rumors," Angus said, "that you were helpful in the surgery today. That you worked tirelessly, devotedly, and that you were kind and compassionate. It sounds like you were an angel of mercy."

Gwendolen strove to remind herself that she had promised to be amiable toward him. "I did what I could, though some losses were inevitable. And very great."

"The men of your clan fought bravely," he said. "You should be proud."

"Perhaps that is true, but my pride will not bring that woman's son back from the dead." She gestured toward Beth MacEwen, Douglas's mother, to whom she had just been speaking.

Angus gave her a sharp glance. "Nor does my triumph

today restore my father to this chair, lass. Rather it is I who must take his place."

She recognized the note of displeasure in his voice and took some time to allow the heated moment to cool before she replied. "I am sorry for the loss of your father. It is never an easy thing. As you know, I lost my father, too, and my grief is very recent."

He inclined his head. "Is this a competition? Do you think that because my father died two years ago, you suffer more?"

"No, I did not mean that—"

"I learned of my father's death one month ago. For two years, I have lived in exile with no knowledge of it. I was not here to fight at his side, and for that, I will always live with regret."

She sat quietly, dipping her spoon into the broth. "I'm sorry. I did not realize." After a brief moment of silence, she added, "I suppose that means we have something in common."

"And what is that?" he asked impatiently.

"Grief. Four weeks old."

He studied her profile for a moment, then turned his head the other way to say something to Lachlan, who sat to his left.

Similarly, Gwendolen turned her attention to her mother, who sat beside her, praising the food and the wine as she conversed with the MacDonald clansman who sat to her right.

"Are you learning anything?" Onora discreetly asked Gwendolen, while reaching for a bright red apple.

"I am trying my best."

"Keep trying, darling. You must discover how this man can be brought to his knees."

Under any other circumstances, such talk about a man would have offended Gwendolen, who believed in truth and honesty between the sexes—not this strategic posturing and game playing. But this impending marriage was hardly a natural one. It was forged from bloody battles and a quest for power, so she could not afford to be so righteous or romantic, nor could she retreat from her duty.

"I don't know what to ask him."

"Find out if he plans to follow in his father's footsteps and raise another rebellion for the Stuarts. If that is the case, we may find ourselves on the wrong side of the law when King George learns of it. He awarded this castle to our clan as a gift of loyalty. We cannot be branded as Jacobites. You must discover Angus's intentions."

Gwendolen turned to her future husband, but Onora touched her arm. "Wait. First, try to find out if he is the Butcher of the Highlands. Knowledge like that could be invaluable. The Butcher is the most sought-after rebel in Scotland, and if we were to reveal his identity and turn him in, the King would be in our debt."

Recognizing the simple brilliance of that plan, Gwendolen turned to Angus and strove to be inconspicuous as she brought up the subject of his past. "May I ask you a question?"

"Aye."

"Why were you gone from Kinloch for so long? And why did you ever leave, if you love this place so much?"

"Have you not heard the rumors?" He glanced at her with a thin sheen of ice over his eyes.

Determined not to shy away from the question, she met his gaze head-on. "I have heard some, yes, but I don't put much stock in them. Especially when they surround a man like you, who attracts gossip like the plague."

"I don't seek such attention," he told her.

"Nay, but it finds you, nevertheless. And you still have not answered my question."

"Nor have you told me what rumors you've heard."

She took a sip of wine. "There are a few different stories. Some say you are the infamous Butcher of the Highlands—the notorious Jacobite rebel who disappeared two years ago after escaping from an English prison. No one has seen or heard from him since. His identity is still a mystery, and many think he is secretly gathering forces to raise another rebellion. Is that what this is?" she asked him directly. "Have you taken Kinloch to create a garrison for the Jacobites?"

He was quiet for a long time. "Nay. I don't want to raise a rebellion. I want to live in peace."

She glanced at his face, searching for the truth in his eyes—whatever it was—but everything about him was hard as steel. There was nothing readable in his expression, no hint of vulnerability, no chink in *his* armor.

"You wouldn't tell me anyway, would you?" she said. "Even if this was to become a Jacobite stronghold, you would guard that secret with your life, for you know my political opinions."

"Aye."

"But would you tell me if you were the Butcher?" she asked. "Because I would like to know if I am about to marry someone so . . ." She was about to say "murderous," but thought better of it. "Famous."

Angus glanced at her knowingly, as if he knew exactly what she was going to say the first time. "Did you follow his escapades, lass?"

"Aye, and although I did not agree with his politics or his savage approach to achieving his goals, I was intrigued and strangely moved by his passions. They say he did everything to avenge the death of his beloved, that he loved her so much, he could not exist without her."

Angus slowly sipped his wine. "I would expect you to condemn him for his methods, not praise him for his motivations."

She dipped her spoon into her soup. "I am not praising him. I simply found the situation intriguing. That is all. As you know, I am a proponent of peace, and indeed his methods were inexcusable."

Angus turned in his chair to face her. "But sometimes violence is the only way to achieve peace. Do not forget that your own father attacked this castle in the name of it. Many clansmen were forced to fight, and many died that day."

Gwendolen nodded, for he was correct on that point.

"And I am not the Butcher of the Highlands," he added. "You have my word on that."

She was pleased to hear that she was not about to marry that particular murderous rebel, whose reputation was even more notorious than Angus the Lion's—but then she reminded herself that if he *was* the Butcher, King George's army would have marched here straightaway and liberated her clan from the clutches of that Scottish fugitive in an instant.

"Do you believe me?" he asked.

She looked up at him and nodded.

But his eyes turned cold. He picked up his wine.

"Good. Because I couldn't possibly be him. I never had a great beloved, nor am I even capable of such passions where a woman is concerned. That sort of thing clouds a man's judgment and makes him weak."

She looked him squarely in the eyes, realizing that he was again working to put her in her place, to make sure she understood that she would never be able to control him or influence him with her femininity. She was a mere lamb to him. She was not a threat.

"You prefer it when people fear you," she said.

He reclined against the tall chair and looked at her with a renewed sexual hunger that seemed to come out of nowhere. "I'm glad to see you're catching on."

Her heart began to pound, for there was nothing weak or cloudy about this man's passions. He wanted to bed her in order to slake his lust, and he was fully confident that he would do so, without impediment, when the appropriate moment arrived.

She was offended by the notion of simply providing him with an outlet for his sexual impulses. He might be an unromantic, coldhearted warrior, but she was more sensitive than that. Before this invasion of her home, she had dreamed of a great love match for herself. She'd imagined a chivalrous Scotsman who would devote himself to her passionately until his last dying breath.

She was a romantic at heart, she'd always known it, but it seemed the time had come to accept a harsher reality. Soon she would be married to a ruthless warrior without a tender bone in his body, and it filled her heart with dread.

They did not converse during the rest of the meal, and only when dessert was served, did Gwendolen realize he still had not answered her question about why he left Kinloch two years ago.

"Are you ever going to tell me why you were gone for so long?" she asked, without looking at him. "Or do you intend to use the mystery of your absence to keep me guessing about your ferocity?"

He swallowed his dessert whole, then wiped his mouth with a linen napkin. "My father and I had a disagreement," he told her. "I did something deceitful and will probably burn in hell for it. He told me I was no longer his son, and he ordered me to leave and never return. I abided by his wishes until Lachlan found me after a two-year search, and informed me of my clan's defeat, and the loss of Kinloch to your father."

Gwendolen regarded him with a persistent curiosity. "What deceitful thing did you do to deserve such a punishment?"

She waited, breath held, for a description of his offense.

"I betrayed a friend."

"Why? Did he do something to you? Did you quarrel?"

"Aye, we quarreled a number of times. Let's just say I did not approve of his choice of a wife, and I was adamant in my opinions."

She mulled over his reply. "Were you in love with her yourself?"

"*God,* no! Did you not hear a word I said earlier?"

Gwendolen supposed she had become somewhat flustered since she sat down. "Pardon me. I wasn't thinking."

He picked up his goblet and held it on his lap. "I despised her, if you must know. If I'd had my way, she wouldn't have survived long enough to bewitch him into marrying her."

"Good heavens, would you have killed her?" The horror poured out of Gwendolen like a flash flood.

A muscle clenched at his jaw, and he spoke with a dark and quiet foreboding. "What do *you* think?"

Gwendolen leaned back in her chair. "That is why you betrayed this friend? Because he chose her, over you?"

He glanced the other way. "Aye."

"I can hardly blame him," she said. "Love should always triumph over evil."

Remarkably unperturbed, he leaned very close. "You think I'm evil, do you?"

"You said yourself that you would burn in hell for your actions."

"That I did. And I'm certain I will."

A fiddler passed in front of them. He sang a lively tune in Gaelic, distracting them for a moment, then moved on down the table.

"Did you ever try to reconcile with your friend?" Gwendolen asked, reaching for her goblet.

"Nay."

"Why not?"

"Because I still think he was wrong."

She pushed her plate away. "Is he still with the woman you warned him against?"

"Aye."

"And are they happy?"

He tapped the tip of his finger impatiently on the arm of the chair. "I don't know, and I don't care. I haven't seen either of them for two years."

The fiddler finished the tune, and Angus rose to his

feet. A hush swept over the room like a breezy chill, for everyone knew it was time for all MacEwens to pledge their oath of allegiance to their new laird.

Feeling a ripple of apprehension, Gwendolen sat back and considered all that she had learned about her future husband in the last hour.

None of it made her feel any better about her situation.

That night after the feast, Gwendolen lay in bed, still contemplating the disturbing conversation she'd had with her betrothed.

He claimed he had no intentions of using Kinloch in another Jacobite rebellion. She wasn't certain, however, that he was telling the truth.

He also did not believe in romantic love. Not that she had any fanciful notions that their marriage would be anything other than a political arrangement, but she'd hoped that somewhere in his past, he might have cared for a woman, or at least understood the emotion in others. With every word or gesture, however, he confirmed her initial impressions of him—that he was an instrument of war, a steel-edged blade, and his heart was made of stone.

Although . . . There was one thing she had learned tonight which suggested a hint of compassion somewhere in the dark abyss of his soul. He had insisted the MacEwen widows be given time to grieve for their dead husbands before any MacDonald clansmen could make advances upon them.

Had that order come from him directly? she wondered. Had he felt some sympathy for their plight? Or had the idea come from his cousin Lachlan?

At least *that* man seemed attuned to the feminine mind. He had been understanding of her fear when he escorted her from the hall that morning, and he had certainly known how to go about charming her mother.

Angus, on the other hand, had no interest in charming anyone. He was more like a sledgehammer when it came to getting what he wanted.

A knock sounded at the door just then, and she sat up in bed, startled as she peered through the darkness. "Who's there?"

The door creaked open, and without waiting for an invitation, her fiancé entered the room, carrying the silver-plated candelabra from her father's chamber.

Although it belonged to Angus now. Everything did. Including her.

He set the candles down on the chest, closed the door, locked it behind him, then slowly approached the foot of the bed.

Gwendolen watched him in uneasy silence. "What are you doing here?" she asked.

He strode casually around the bed, while the candlelight picked up the golden tones in his wavy hair.

Chapter Six

Gwendolen fought to suppress her alarm. "You promised to leave me alone until our wedding night. Please go."

"Nay, I promised to let you stay a virgin. I didn't promise to leave you alone. I'm here now, and I am staying, whether you like it or not."

She frowned. "If I am to be your wife, you could at least *try* to win my affections."

"I have no interest in your affections, lass. That's the last thing I want from you."

He truly was a heartless man, interested in only one thing—power over others. And perhaps a little debauchery on the side.

"No, you just want me to satisfy your vulgar desires. But I am a woman with independent thoughts and feelings. I am not a dog you can command."

"You'll be my wife soon, lass, and you *will* obey me, for I am laird and master here."

"You are laird of Kinloch, not laird of my body. And I am not yet your wife, so I will say it again. Please leave my bedchamber."

He moved around the side of the massive bed and began to tug at the coverings. She squeezed them to her chest, refusing to let him tear them away.

"I think *you* are the one who's forgetting the promises we made to each other today," he said. "You gave your word that you'd be amiable toward me until our wedding night. Yet here you sit, insulting my character, calling me vulgar." He tugged harder at the bedclothes.

"Let go," she said through gritted teeth.

He used both hands, as if it were a frivolous game of tug-of-war and he was determined to win it. They pulled back and forth for a few seconds until Gwendolen knew it was pointless to continue. His hands were too big, his legs too strong, braced firmly on the floor. Sure enough, before she could voice a protest, the covers were whisked off the bed and tossed behind him.

Clad only in her shift, Gwendolen hugged her knees to her chest.

"That's better," he said, gazing down at her heatedly. "I don't like it when you hide from me."

"Well, you'd better get used to it, because I have no intention of simply offering myself to you on a silver platter."

He sat down on the edge of the bed.

"Why are you here?" she asked. "Why can you not just leave me be?"

"I couldn't sleep."

"Neither could I, but that does not give me the right to go traipsing about in other people's bedchambers, forcing them to share in my wakefulness."

He was always so serious, so somber, angry and threatening. She had yet to see him smile or show any warmth. Even if she closed her eyes, she could not imagine it.

"Traipsing about," he said. "Is that what I'm doing?"

"Aye."

He casually looked about the room, which was lit only by the candles he'd brought with him and a small square of moonlight shining in through the window. "This was my bedchamber once, before I was sent away."

Taken aback by this news, she tucked her bare toes under the hem of her shift. "I was not aware. I assumed . . ."

"What?"

"I don't know. I just never thought about which chamber was yours."

Had he slept here as a lad? She could not imagine that either.

Her heart was beating very fast, and when he said nothing more, she felt compelled to ramble on. "We changed the linens," she told him. "Other than that, everything is the same. The furniture, the rug . . ."

He glanced at the braided rug and the bedclothes lying in a heap on top of it, and continued to sit in silence.

What in the world did he want?

"Of course, I could move to another room if you wish to have this one back," she suggested, wondering if that was why he had come. "There is a chamber just below this."

"Nay, that was my sister's chamber. I occupy my father's quarters now."

"You have a sister?" That was a surprise.

"*Had.* She's dead now."

Struck by his gruff tone, Gwendolen softened hers. "I am sorry to hear that. How long ago?" she carefully asked.

"A few years." He looked the other way.

Still struggling with the flutter of nervous butterflies in her belly, Gwendolen sat very still, hoping that he might simply grow bored with her conversation and decide to leave on his own.

She was not so fortunate, however. Slowly, he swiveled on the bed and stretched out on his back beside her. He crossed his long, muscled legs at the ankles and tossed an arm up under his head, while resting the other at his side.

She took note of the fact that he was not armed. No swords, knives, or pistols hung from his belt. But that only made her more aware of his enormity, for her eyes were free to travel the full length of him from his large booted feet and thick thighs beneath the kilt, to his muscular torso and chest. The position of his arm, bent to cradle his head on the pillow, accentuated the incredible brawn of his biceps and the sheer breadth of his shoulders.

Every nerve in her body was humming with the same mixture of fear and fascination she had felt that morning. And the fact that he was lying here quietly, without touching her or threatening ravishment, was not lost on her. She was attuned to every breath he took, every movement he made, while she strove not to do anything to attract his interest or arouse his lust.

Perhaps he simply wanted to see his childhood room in order to prove to himself that he had indeed reclaimed his home. Despite everything, she was sympathetic to that. She hoped it was the reason for his presence in her bed, and that once he satisfied that curiosity, he would leave.

A full quarter of an hour must have passed while she

sat upright on the bed. The stars outside the window proved a useful distraction, until the steady sound of Angus's breathing alerted her to the fact that he had fallen asleep.

She gazed down at him with surprise, for the sight of this battle-hardened warrior, sleeping peacefully beside her, was like staring into the shifting fog of a dream. It did not seem real. Angus the Lion could not possibly be this man in her bed, who had been a small boy once, sleeping in this very room, cradled perhaps in the arms of his mother.

She leaned closer to study his face. There was nothing vicious about him now. The steely eyes were closed; his expression was serene. Her eyes drifted to his neck, then across his broad shoulders to the silver brooch pinned to his plaid. She glanced down at his kilt and knew what was under there. One day he would use that part of himself to claim his husbandly rights over her body. He would lie naked on top of her, and she would be forced to relent.

Feeling a sudden rise of panic, she set a hand down on the bed to steady herself, and realized this was an unexpected opportunity. Her conqueror was asleep and vulnerable beside her. Was it not her duty to take some kind of action against him? He was reputed to be invincible, but she knew those stories were nothing but fireside tales and legends.

Nevertheless, could she actually succeed in killing him if she tried? Would she have the courage?

Gently and carefully, she rolled to the edge of the bed and reached down to feel for the knife she had placed beneath the mattress that morning. Her fingertips located the grip, and she wrapped her whole hand around it. Slowly, she rolled back toward Angus. He had not moved, nor had his breathing changed in the last few seconds. It was entirely possible that she could plunge this knife into his chest, or slit his throat, and succeed at freeing herself and her clan.

She looked down at him in the candlelight, at his bare, vulnerable neck. She could see the throbbing of his pulse. A crashing wave of nausea overcame her. She had never killed anyone, and was not sure she could do it now, despite the fact that he was her enemy and she had watched him slaughter dozens of her clansmen that morning.

Would she not go to hell for murdering a sleeping, unarmed man in cold blood? It was not a fair fight, but it *was* self-defense—if one could stretch the definition to include generalities, such as the need to protect herself from an unwanted marriage . . .

Suddenly his eyes opened. In a lightning flash of movement, he seized the knife and flipped her over onto her back. The sharp blade was now pressing against her throat, and she was pinned to the bed, unable to breathe, her heart racing with white-hot terror.

"You should have done it when you had the chance," he said in a dangerous whisper. "You could have ended my life and spared yourself the horror of your deflowering."

She stared up at him in shock. "I've never killed anyone before. I couldn't even do it to *you*. I am no warrior."

She was a complete and utter coward.

His blue eyes focused on her lips, then he pressed the dull edge of the blade up under her chin. Terror pulsed through her veins as she faced his newly awakened wrath, felt the tight grip of his hand on her shoulder. His body was heavy, pressing her into the bed. After a long, agonizing moment, he leaned over her and set the knife on the bedside table.

"Don't turn yourself into a killer," he said, "unless it's absolutely necessary, and even then, think carefully about the damage to your soul, and whether or not it's worth an eternity in hell."

She tried to sit up, but he pinned her arms over her head. "Was it worth it for you? All the killing you did?"

"My soul was damaged early in life, lass, so I had little to lose. Now give me your mouth. I didn't come here to talk about killing."

He let go of her wrists and slid his hands under her behind, pressing his hips tightly to hers. The sweeping physical sensation made her body arch and burn. Her mind careened with fear. Her limbs went weak and tingly as his hands stroked the side of her hip, and his own hips thrust against her in a steady, potent rhythm.

Then he kissed her. Her mouth opened instinctively, and it was hot and wet and searing.

He had promised he would not rob her of her virginity, yet this was surely just as depraved. She could feel her innocence slipping away, sliding into a strange world of need. She had been more than capable of resisting such feelings earlier in the day, but now all she felt was relief over the fact that she had not killed him. Which made no sense. Because she hated him—*she hated him*—and she did not want this.

But what was it about the darkness that made touching him feel like a hallucination? She was slowly pulling away from her rage, and had to work hard to remember that he was her enemy. All she felt now was a heady desire for his touch, and it was somehow delicious. He was a virile man with greedy hands and cunning lips, and he possessed the ability to turn her body to liquid fire.

"I don't understand why you're here," she said in a breathless whisper, fighting to subdue the throbbing rush of heat that was traveling from her belly to her thighs. "You can't make love to me. You promised. Yet that seems to be what you are doing."

"I can make love to you without rupturing your maidenhead, lass, and you, in turn, can pleasure me tonight, and still be a virgin in the morning."

"How?"

He drew back slightly. "You *are* an innocent, aren't you?"

She tried to push him away, but her arms had turned to limp rags. His lips found hers again, and the damp thrust of his tongue plunging in and out of her mouth made her quiver inwardly and yearn for something more, when she did not want to feel any such thing. If only she was built of steel, like he was.

He spread his fingers down the side of her leg and tugged at her shift, lifting it up over her trembling thigh.

"Please don't," she said, grabbing hold of it and yanking it back down to remain as a barrier between them, even while she was tempted by the danger and fear of the unknown.

Surprisingly, he removed his hand from her leg and cupped the back of her head instead, kissing her more deeply, while thrusting his strong body into hers.

She had not known how restless a person could become in such a situation, and found herself responding to every touch, every kiss, each incredible, erotic sensation.

"Ah," he sighed. "That's it, lass. Do you know how appealing you are?"

"You need not flatter me," she said harshly. "I am your prisoner. You have control over me. I must therefore pleasure you, regardless of my own objections."

His head drew back again, and he looked at her in the candlelight. "But you are warming to me. I can feel it in your kiss, hear it in your voice."

"You hear only what you want to hear, for I am *not* warming to you, Angus. I assure you."

She was surprised by the hatred she managed to convey in those words, even while she was melting with desire and a strange bliss she had never known to exist.

But she was even more surprised by the severity of his reaction. He frowned at her with pointed anger and sat back on his haunches.

She wasn't sure if the anger was directed at her, or at himself.

"What's wrong?" she asked, more fearful now than she had been a moment ago when he was attempting to slide his hand up her leg.

He slid off the bed. "I've lost interest in this."

Shocked, and ridiculously humiliated by his sudden withdrawal, she sat forward. "You're leaving?"

"Aye. I have things to do."

"In the middle of the night?"

He offered no explanation as he strode to the door, walked out, and swung it shut behind him. The flames on the candelabra flickered wildly in the draughts from the corridor, then everything went still.

Gwendolen flopped down on the bed and exhaled with relief, for she was still in possession of her virtue and had not disgraced herself by surrendering in a delirious fever to the Lion's seductions, when there was so much more to this than mere physical desire.

She struggled to regain her sanity, knowing that she must keep her head and remember where her loyalties lay. She had to resist the wanton urge to give him free rein over her body, for her brother might soon return, and when he did, she must be ready to reclaim her freedom, and the independence of her clan.

She could not succumb to this temptation.

Chapter Seven

The next morning, Gwendolen woke to bright sunshine beaming in through her window. It was no surprise that she had slept late, for she'd been awake half the night recovering from Angus's presence in her bed, and all the different ways he had touched her, and the shock of how pliant she'd become in his arms. It was quite a stroke of luck that he had left the room when he did, otherwise she might very well be an experienced woman this morning.

Stretching her arms over her head, she sat up and reached for her robe, then hurried to her dressing room, for there was something important she had to do that morning, before the women of the kitchen left for the village market.

She was going to attempt to send word to Fort William, the nearest English garrison, to inform them of yesterday's attack. The governor at the fort was obligated to report all Jacobite activities to the Crown, and surely he would wish to know that the son of a Jacobite rebel had just taken over a castle of Hanoverians and declared himself chief. It was information the governor would value, and perhaps he would recognize the threat to England and send assistance.

She considered going to Gordon MacEwen, the castle steward, to share her plan with him, but decided against it, for she was not sure who could be trusted. He had been manipulated by her mother in recent weeks, so it was obvious that he was easily seduced. And God only knew how long that affair had been going on. Her mother was no saint.

Gwendolen washed up and donned a striped skirt with a blue bodice, and quickly braided her hair. She hurried down the curved stone staircase and made her way through the vaulted passageways to the kitchen, where the smell of bread baking in the ovens caused her mouth to water.

"Good morning, Miss MacEwen."

She whirled around, realizing how very taut her nerves had become. "Mary. You surprised me. Good morning to you, too. You're just the person I was looking for. Are you going to the village market this morning?"

"Aye. Last night's feast drained us dry. We're in need of everything." She gave a sigh of annoyance. "I'll have to take two wagons, and I may make a few of those hungry MacDonald clansmen get in the harness instead of the mules, because they're the ones who cleaned us out, and they certainly have full bellies this morning."

"That's a perfect idea."

Gwendolen glanced around to make sure no one was watching, then took Mary by the hand and led her into a dark corner of the kitchen, out of sight. "Can you do something for me?"

"I'll do anything for you, Miss MacEwen. You know that."

"Aye. It's why I came to you." Gwendolen reached

into her stays and pulled out a sealed letter. "Can you see that this is delivered to Marcus MacEwen, the wine-maker, and tell him to give it to his brother, John. They'll know what to do with it." She slipped the note into Mary's hand.

"I cannot read, lassie, so you know I won't pry into your personal affairs, but can you tell me what it's about?"

"No, Mary, it's best if you do not know. The only thing you must do is keep it secret and make sure no one sees you handing it over, and make sure it's well hidden when you leave the castle, in case you are searched."

Mary stuffed it into the depths of her generous bosom and patted down her frizzy hair. "You can trust me to do your bidding, Miss MacEwen. The winemaker and I go way back. He'll be more than happy to accept the message. I'll lead him behind a haystack and take a few naughty thrills for myself while he searches my underthings."

Gwendolen touched Mary's arm. "You are a very good friend. I appreciate your sacrifice, but please be careful."

She returned to the busy kitchen, where the others were kneading balls of dough on worktables. "May I have some breakfast? I am famished."

Mary directed her to the tray of oatcakes, fresh out of the oven, and a bowl of fresh cream.

A short time later, Gwendolen was passing through the Great Hall on her way to her mother's chamber, when she heard her name called out from the head table.

Angus's deep voice echoed off the ceiling timbers, stopping her in her tracks. She shut her eyes, took a breath, then turned around to face him. He was seated at the table alone, eating his breakfast.

"Here I sit," he said, spreading his arms wide, "in my father's chair again." He leaned back casually. "And I have no one to talk to but that little bird overhead."

His eyes lifted, and he gestured toward the swallow, perched on a beam over the door.

Gwendolen looked up. "She's still here. After yesterday, I thought we might never see her again. Clearly she is unaware of her peril."

He inclined his head. "Now why would you say such a hurtful thing, lass? Do you think I am such a monster, that I would prey on a small, defenseless creature such as that?"

"You have preyed on my entire clan, and me as well. In the dead of night, may I remind you?"

"Your clan is hardly small," he replied. "And *you* are hardly defenseless—neither by day, or night. Do you forget the knife you held at my throat?" His shrewd eyes raked over her from head to foot, then he wiped his mouth with a napkin, tossed it lightly onto the table, and stood.

Gwendolen's stomach clenched tight as he hopped down from the dais and approached her. She couldn't keep from backing away from him, which set a certain tone for their encounter. He was the predator, she the nervous prey.

In a belated attempt to assert herself, she halted on the spot and straightened her posture.

"Tell me, lass," he said, as he reached her with brooding curiosity. "What are you up to this morning? You look rather . . . *sly*."

Her eyebrows flew up. "Sly? What is that supposed to mean? I have no idea what you are referring to."

He cupped her chin in a big hand, lifted her face slightly to examine it from all angles. "Now you're blushing. Your cheeks are turning red."

"Maybe that's because I don't like your hands on me."

He pondered that. "Nay, that's not it."

"It most certainly is!"

Letting go of her chin, he leaned his golden head closer. She felt his hot, moist breath on her cheek. "I think you like my hands on you very much, and that's what has you so desperate to dash out of this hall right now, praying that you'll be rescued before the grand thrill of our wedding night."

"That's not true," she said.

She sensed the tiniest hint of a grin on his face and turned her head quickly to look at him, wishing she could catch it, but it was too late. He stepped back, looking dangerous again.

"I suppose I owe you a debt of gratitude," he said.

"Good Lord, for what?" She couldn't begin to imagine.

"For not butchering me last night. Part of me wanted you to, and I might have let you, if you'd put more effort into it."

She studied his pale blue eyes. "Why would you want that? You just achieved a great victory and reclaimed your father's castle. One would think you'd have reason to celebrate."

"One would think so . . . if I was a happy sort of man." He turned from her and headed for the door.

"Wait!"

He paused and faced her. She wanted to ask him why he was unhappy, but something about that question seemed too personal, too caring, and she did not wish to care for him.

"Nothing," she said.

He stared at her for a tense moment that seemed to go on forever, then returned to her, as if he had peered into her soul and heard every private thought and emotion, and wanted to interrogate her further about why she looked so *sly*.

"We'll dine in the hall again tonight," he said. "It's important that the clans feel united. You'll see to the arrangements?" He eyed her expectantly.

"Of course." Heaven help her—her heart was slapping uncontrollably against her rib cage.

"And don't wear that ugly frock you wore last night," he said. "Wear something colorful. This place needs a bit more cheer."

"Then you might try smiling once in a while."

His eyes narrowed, then he took a step closer. "Would you like that, lass? Would it help you warm to me?"

She thought carefully about how to answer that, then decided that this time, *she* would be the one to walk away first. She turned around and headed for the door. "No. It would take considerably more than a smile to warm my heart where you are concerned."

She was distinctly aware that he remained where he stood, watching her cross the vast distance of the hall. It brought a tiny smile of satisfaction to her face.

Angus found Lachlan in the bailey, supervising the rebuilding of the front gate, which they'd smashed to bits during the invasion the previous morning. The crack of hammers pounding on wooden pegs echoed off the castle walls, while a number of clansmen worked together to saw through fresh timbers and carry heavy planks of wood to the bridge outside the tower.

"Mornin'," Lachlan said to Angus, while leaving a crew of three men to continue about their work. "Did you sleep well, back in your own bed at last?"

"I didn't sleep a wink," Angus replied, "for it's my father's bed I must occupy, not my own—and I swear that his ghost was pacing about the room, shouting at me."

Lachlan chuckled. "And what did his cranky spirit say?"

"He told me I disobeyed him by coming home, and he slapped the back of my head with a book."

Lachlan scoffed. "That's bluidy ridiculous, Angus," he said. "Your father hated reading."

"Aye, but the MacEwen chief left a novel on the bedside table."

"Maybe it was *his* ghost who whacked you in the head. That would make more sense, would it not?"

Angus looked up at the bright blue sky, then let his gaze travel along the battlements from one corner tower to another. "Have someone keep an eye on the comings and goings out of the kitchen today, but be discreet about it."

"Anyone in particular you're concerned about?"

He regarded his cousin coolly. "I'm concerned that my food will be poisoned, for one thing. Replace the head cook with a MacDonald, but leave the rest of them where they are. And make sure a MacDonald goes along to market today. Send someone observant."

"Understood."

Angus turned to go.

"Where are you off to now?" Lachlan asked.

"To the treasury. I need to examine the records and find another, less influential position for that puppet steward, Gordon MacEwen. I'll need a MacDonald there as well." He strode with purpose toward the entrance to the hall, but shouted one last important order over his shoulder. "Keep working on the gate, Lachlan, and make it stronger than before."

"Why? Are we expecting company?"

Angus merely waved a hand.

Knowing it was important to carefully choose her battles with her future husband, Gwendolen decided to obey him in the small matter of her choice of gown for the evening. He had told her to wear something colorful, so she selected a crimson gown of silk and velvet, with gold trimmings across the brocade stomacher, and tiny sprays of white flowers along the hem of the skirt.

She entered the Great Hall and spent some time conversing with members of both clans, while going over in her mind what she had accomplished that day. She wondered how long it would take for her message to reach Fort William, and if the English army would even come. It seemed to be her only hope, for she had no idea if Murdoch even knew of their father's death, much less the MacDonald invasion. They'd had no word from him in over three months, and he could be dead for all she knew.

Her mother approached and fingered an errant lock of hair that fell across Gwendolen's forehead. "You look lovely this evening, darling, but do try to keep up a flawless appearance. Sloppiness will not do, now that you are the laird's wife."

"I am not yet his wife," Gwendolen reminded her.

"No, but you will be soon enough. You may as well start playing the part now. Why wait?"

Gwendolen frowned. "This is not a theater, Mother. If I am to be his wife, I will take my position seriously, and I will use it to serve my clan."

Onora glanced the other way. "Did you find out what his plans are for Kinloch? Does he intend to use it as a base for another Jacobite uprising?"

Gwendolen lowered her voice. "No. He says he has no interest in rebellion. He wants to live here in peace."

"And you believe him?"

"I'm not sure."

Onora shook her head. "Use your brains, Gwendolen. He is a warrior at heart. He won't know what to do with himself once the smell of battle wears off his shirt. He's a hot-blooded Highlander. He'll be looking for another fight."

"Perhaps not. Perhaps he's already experienced enough violence to last a lifetime."

Her mother shot her a frustrated look. "He's a man, Gwendolen. They thrive on violence. Even if they are quiet for a while, they will eventually feel the need to roar." She smiled at a MacDonald clansman who walked by. "Besides that, he could simply be lying to you. If he were planning something, he certainly wouldn't trust *you* with it. At least not yet. Which is why you must try harder to capture his heart."

"He is not capable of that sort of thing."

Her mother rolled her eyes. "His *lust,* then. Whatever you wish to call it. I fear you are a very slow learner, Gwendolen. You have no concept of the power you could have over him, and others as well."

She sighed irritably. "I don't want power over my husband. All I ever wanted was love and respect. I wanted to be my husband's equal, his supporter, and perhaps occasionally his adviser."

Her mother cupped her daughter's chin in her hand. "Darling, you must get your head out of the clouds. We are women, and love will get us nothing. We're not the equals of men, therefore we must protect ourselves by being quietly cunning."

Gwendolen felt a great wave of melancholy move through her. "Sometimes I believe you speak the truth, Mother, but other times, I want something more. I want to have influence, but through honest means. I want to earn my husband's respect, so that he can rely on me. I do have an intelligent mind. I can offer insight."

They were quiet for a few minutes, then her mother's eyes softened with a show of sympathy. Gwendolen was surprised to feel the touch of her hand at her back. "Perhaps you are not such a slow learner after all. Perhaps you are faster and more ambitious than all of us. I am just not sure that you are realistic."

Her future husband entered the hall just then, and Gwendolen wondered if she was indeed a dreamer. Of all the men in the world, this one was least likely to bend and allow anyone to wield power over him. He'd already told her in no uncertain terms that romantic love made a man weak, and that he wished to avoid it at all costs.

He seemed just as determined to avoid feminine manipulations of a sexual nature. When it came to the bedroom, *she* was the one who was seduced into a puddle of dazed surrender—and that did not bode well for her future influence as Mistress of Kinloch.

* * *

It was a fine night for a feast, Angus thought as he entered the Great Hall and was arrested on the spot by the sight of his future bride on the other side of the room, dressed in a bloodred velvet gown that accentuated the curve of her hips and heightened her full, luscious bosom. The gold trimming transformed her into a priceless trophy, and her purity somehow mixed sensuously with the red-hot color of the gown against her ivory skin and glossy black hair. It was hot sex and sweet innocence combined, all wrapped up in one tempting, pretty package, and it aroused a rough and unruly restlessness in his core.

Someone knocked into him and apologized, then engaged him in conversation. Yes, it was a fine night for a crowd. He needed the diversion, for he'd had trouble during the day concentrating on more important matters, like the management of Kinloch, now that he was chief.

He'd spent many hours going over the record books in the treasury and had found everything in order—perhaps even better managed than it had been when his father was laird. Revenues were up in all areas, and a number of useless, miscellaneous expenses had either been decreased or removed from the accounts entirely. As a result, he decided to allow Gordon MacEwen to keep his position as castle steward, with one of his own men to take on the role of assistant, and keep a watchful eye.

A chorus of laughter from the interior of the room drew his attention. He found Lachlan in the center of it and led him away to discuss the matter with him, but was again preoccupied by the attendance of his future wife, who was moving about the room with effortless charm and a smile more dazzling than the sun.

He realized at that moment that this political marriage was going to be a problem, for he was completely out of his element. He was an experienced warrior who faced lethal deathblows on the battlefield and struck back with ferocity. When he fought, he fought fearlessly, but he was not on a battlefield now. This was foreign territory, and he had no idea how to "conquer" a proper wife. She was not a woman of loose morals, like his usual sexual partners, who were more than happy to lift their skirts for the famous Scottish Lion. He certainly couldn't challenge her to a swordfight. Nor could he bed her against her will. Life experience prevented that sort of thing.

So if he could not take her by force, he would have to seduce her into wanting it—which was proving to be more difficult than he'd anticipated. Because he did not wish to be intimate with her. Not now. Not ever. Love and intimacy made a man weak. It led him down a path that made him believe happiness was possible, and that he could forget all the evils in the world.

Angus could not afford to rely on someone else for his happiness. Nor could he forget certain evils. He simply could not let down his guard. He could not become weak.

"I find it odd," Gwendolen said to Onora that night after the feast, "that Angus has not forced himself upon me. He has had two opportunities, and it was hardly necessary for him to negotiate my terms of surrender. He simply could have bent me over the table in the hall and claimed me as his property, right then and there."

They moved through the torchlit corridor to her

bedchamber. She unlocked her door, entered, and sat down on the edge of the bed.

"I learned something about him tonight," Onora said, as she removed her shoes and placed them together on the floor. "His cousin Lachlan is quite a charmer, and with a little persuading, he was willing to indulge me when I asked some delicate questions."

Gwendolen swiveled on the bed to face her mother. "What exactly did you learn?" She wasn't sure she had ever craved information with such fervor before.

Onora sat down on a chair. "He told me that Angus's younger sister was raped and killed by English soldiers a few years ago. It's part of the reason why he was banished. He went absolutely mad with vengeance against the English and betrayed a close friend who married an Englishwoman, and it was all very ugly in the end. Lachlan is not surprised that Angus is waiting until your wedding night before he beds you. He said Angus cannot bear to see any woman cry or plead, for it makes him think of his sister's final moments. It's why he has ordered his men to stay away from our MacEwen women. He wouldn't stand for any raping or pillaging."

Gwendolen pondered this with a rather morbid curiosity, and not without some sympathy. "And yet, he told me he wanted to kill that Englishwoman."

"But he didn't kill her, did he? And Lachlan said he had plenty of opportunities." Onora rose to her feet. "From what I understand of the situation, that friend he betrayed is now married to that woman, and they are very much in love. They have a son and another child on the way."

Gwendolen pulled the pins from her hair. "He told

me about his friend, and that he betrayed him, but he didn't tell me why. I had no idea it was because of what happened to his sister."

Onora shrugged. "Well, at least it has given him reason to spare you for a week or so. You'll have time to prepare yourself for your first encounter. It won't be so terrible, darling. You'll see."

Rising from the bed to undress, Gwendolen wondered if she would ever truly be prepared for it. And despite everything her mother had just told her, she was still amazed that Angus had shown such mercy toward her and her clan. Bitter, brooding vengeance was blatantly visible in his eyes. His deep anger and contempt for the world was obvious, and it never ceased to unnerve her.

No, she was not yet ready to lie back and give herself over to him without fear. He was a dangerous man, and though he could be merciful in some ways, he did not seem capable of genuine tenderness or love. She was still very much afraid.

Chapter Eight

Angus lay in bed, tossing and turning. There was no point in visiting Gwendolen's bedchamber again, he told himself, over and over. He'd given his word that he would not bed her before marriage, and he'd drunk too much wine tonight. In his present mood, a single moment alone with her could turn him into a liar, or worse.

Nevertheless, when sleep continued to elude him, something compelled him to rise. He lit a candle, donned his shirt and tartan, and quietly ventured out of his father's chamber. He walked through the chilly castle corridors toward the East Tower and hesitated there. The torch at the bottom of the stairs had gone out, so he used his candle to light it again, climbed the twisting staircase, and stopped, disconcerted, outside Gwendolen's door.

He felt like a dog that had caught the scent of something juicy and couldn't resist rummaging around. Reaching into his sporran for the key to her room, he inserted it into the lock, carefully turned it and entered, with the full intention of merely checking on her.

Moving closer to the bed, he raised the candle high over his head and observed her sleeping form. The flame cast a dim golden glow across the gentle curve of her body. She had pushed the covers aside and was stretched out on her belly with one leg bent, her shift tangled around her voluptuous hips and bum. Her hair was splayed out around her like rich ribbons of black silk. The soft ivory flesh of her thighs gleamed erotically in the candlelight.

His blood quickened, and he was forced to confront the uncomfortable truth that his capacity to be patient with her was fading fast. For two years, he had lived apart from society with the oracle, Raonaid—a beautiful but unfeeling woman, who was, in a way, his mirror image. There had been nothing innocent or vulnerable about her. She was not tender, and she regarded the world with antagonism and ill will.

For a time, he'd believed she was his perfect match, for she required very little from him. He could be distant and uncommunicative with her, and she offered no complaint, for she was just as distant in return. He really knew very little about her past, except for the fact that she had visions.

This woman, however—his future wife—was his opposite in every way, for she was innocent and pure of heart, noble and self-sacrificing. Some long-forgotten part of him wanted to touch that purity. A more familiar part of him wanted to pilfer and consume it—even when he knew he did not deserve to be in the same room with it. What he deserved was to rot in hell with a woman like Raonaid, who would not dare to judge him for his rancor, for she was the same.

Gwendolen breathed deeply and rolled to her side. She cupped the pillow in her arms, brought her knees to her chest. A chilly draft caused the candle's flame to dance wildly on the wick, so he set the brass holder down on the table and pulled the covers up over her shoulders.

A moment later, she tossed the covers aside with agitation and rolled onto her back. The sweet-smelling perfume of her body touched his nostrils and awakened his senses, just as she opened her eyes and blinked up at him innocently.

A dangerous, passionate stirring of desire overwhelmed him. It was unlike any other desire he had ever felt for a woman. It was beyond sexual. He felt dazed, restless, and ravenous. In that moment, he was not sure he had the strength to keep the promise he had made to her, for he had never been a calm or patient man. He was a warrior at heart, and when he wanted something, he wanted it with violent, blinding fury.

And tonight—bargain or no bargain—he wanted *her*.

Gwendolen had been dreaming of the lion again, and when she opened her eyes and saw Angus standing over her bed like a beautiful creature of the wild, she wasn't sure if she was awake or still floating in a mindless slumber.

A candle flickered in the room, and his enormous shadow loomed on the wall behind him. He smelled of musk and leather. His golden hair fell in blustery waves onto his broad shoulders—just like the lion's mane in her dream—and her flesh tingled when his hungry gaze roamed over her body.

Was she still dreaming? Her body felt warm and languid, remarkably calm, as she squirmed lasciviously on the mattress.

He crawled up onto the bed and positioned himself

above her on all fours. His hair touched her cheek like the soft teasing tip of a feather, and she breathed deeply, realizing at last that he was not a figment of her imagination. He was true flesh and blood, and he had come to her bedchamber again, perhaps to break the promise he had made. Or perhaps he was here merely to explore and test the limits of her resistance.

Without uttering a word, he found her mouth in the hush of stillness between them, and her quivering lips parted instinctively. His tongue, constantly moving, circled around hers in a rush of damp heat, while her blood began to pulse through her body in a sweltering torrent of sensation.

His hand moved to her breast, and she gasped faintly at the light pressure of his thumb over her tingling nipple. She was surprised at herself—that she was not fighting his advances—but he had awakened her at the worst possible time, when she was aroused by the dream and did not feel so innocent.

Angus lowered his heavy body to hers. Her shift was bunched around her hips, for she had tugged it up during sleep, and she could feel the soft wool of his tartan against her bare inner thighs. His hands came to rest on her hip, while his tongue continued to swirl erotically around hers.

He had said nothing since the moment he entered the room, and she suspected that if she voiced even the smallest note of resistance, he would retreat, and for once, that was something she did not want. At least not yet.

His hands explored her body in smooth, graceful motions, and she grew bold enough to touch the corded muscles of his back through the fabric of his shirt. She gathered his tartan in her fists, desperate to squeeze and tug at his clothes.

A moment later, he dragged his lips from her mouth and kissed the side of her neck, moaning softly, as if he were devouring something succulent. She moaned in response, and his hand slid up under her shift and found the throbbing ache between her legs. His mouth moved quickly to her breasts, while he pushed her collar out of the way to gain better access. Gwendolen found herself squirming under the twin pleasures of his fingers stroking her womanhood and his tongue caressing her sensitive, pebbled nipple.

His erection pressed against her thigh, and the room seemed to spin in circles. He would have her eventually, she knew, but somehow, full knowledge of his manhood at this moment seemed incidental to the overwhelming intensity of her emotions and her desire for more. Whether it happened now or later did not seem to matter. It was going to happen at some point. She could not stop it. She didn't *want* to stop it, at least not now.

Using the heel of his palm, he continued to stroke between her legs until she could barely endure the pleasure. Then he slid one long, slick finger inside her. She stiffened and bucked slightly at the shock of the invasion.

He paused, drawing his head back to look at her. "Am I hurting you?"

They were the first words spoken since he entered the room.

She shook her head, rather frantically.

"One finger won't make a difference," he whispered. "You'll still be a virgin in the morning."

He kissed her neck and breasts, as she lay panting, her chest heaving.

"You must think me a child," she said.

"Nay, I don't think that." He was still sliding his finger in and out of her with a slippery ease that made her shiver with delight. "You're all woman, and I'm surprised that you're mine."

"I'm not yours yet," she reminded him, feeling overwhelmed by the pleasures. They made her feel wild and out of control. "I could still change my mind."

He regarded her intently, then rolled to the side and rested a cheek on a hand, while still stroking her down below with the other. "Why would you say that now, when I'm doing everything I can to please you?"

"Because you invaded my home," she replied, feeling breathless and distracted, barely able to think through the violent flow of sensation.

"From what I heard," he said, leaning close to her ear and teasing her with his voice, "you almost put a bullet in my brain while I was completing the invasion. What stopped you?"

"I couldn't get a clear shot." She bit her lower lip and arched her back, while he continued to study her face.

"Do you want me to stop talking?" he asked.

She could only nod, grateful for the opportunity to focus on the increasing flood of pleasure that was moving through her body.

He lay beside her with his cheek still resting on a hand, while he continued to plunge his finger in and out of her pulsing, scorching depths. She was impossibly wet down there, and the ever-increasing tension begged for release.

Needing to hold on to something, she grabbed his forearm, closed her hand around the firm bands of muscle, and thrust her hips upward to meet each of his deep, slick penetrations. At last, the tension seemed to burst out of her. Pleasure racked her brain, and she tossed her head on the pillow, feeling as wild as an animal. A moment later, her heart slowed its galloping pace, and she shuddered inwardly as each exhausted throb of relief vibrated through her.

He bent close to kiss her neck, lifted her shift and his kilt out of the way, and rolled on top of her. Her legs parted to accommodate him, and he swiveled his hips and touched the silky tip of his erection to the place where his hand had just been. The connection lit her on fire. She wrapped her legs around his hips, and wondered if he would claim her now.

"Why did you not resist me tonight?" he asked, rising up on both arms to look down at her in the candlelight.

"I don't know."

It was the honest truth. Though perhaps it had something to do with the dream.

"I'll need you to be willing when I make love to you."

"You're not going to do it now?"

He paused. "Nay."

"Why not?"

"Because I gave my word, and I can't expect you to keep yours, if I don't keep mine."

"I see." He wanted her loyalty. Especially when her brother came. *If* he came.

Angus drew himself away and sat back on his heels at the foot of the bed, looking at her.

She leaned up on her elbows. "You should know," she said, "that I understand why it's important to you that I am willing. I know about your sister."

He sat for a long time with his eyes downcast, then

ran a hand through his hair. He climbed off the bed and fingered the brooch at his shoulder to straighten his tartan.

Gwendolen crawled across the mattress and hugged the corner bedpost. "I'm very sorry that such a thing happened to her."

He twisted slightly to arrange the belted section at the back. "I don't talk about it."

"Not ever?"

He shook his head. "Nay. I have to go now."

The candle flickered as he picked it up and carried it to the door. "Good night, Gwendolen."

"Good night," she replied, feeling rather bewildered by his swift, yet strangely polite exit.

There had been something very different about him tonight. He had treated her with a certain degree of courtesy, for one, and his hands had been surprisingly gentle. She was still reeling from the pleasure she had never expected to feel with him.

She watched the door close behind him, then flopped back onto the bed and strove to recover from her astonishment.

Chapter Nine

Construction of the new gate began the following day in the open bailey, the clansmen pounding away with their hammers, and groaning as they raised heavy planks under the warm sun. Gwendolen worked hard from the kitchen, supervising the luncheon preparations, for the men required their sustenance.

Late in the afternoon, she ventured through the Great Hall with a group of servants to deliver a cart of ale. She crossed the sunny bailey, her feet tapping lightly over the packed earth while the servants followed with the wheeled cart. When she reached the gate, she breathed in the sweet-smelling scent of freshly cut timber. Wood shavings from the lathe littered the ground, and the crack of hammers echoed off the castle walls.

Then Gwendolen caught sight of Angus. She had not known he'd joined the laborers, and her thoughts clogged her brain as she watched him drag a long wooden plank across the bailey. The heavy length of wood rested on one broad shoulder, and he leaned forward into the task, the muscles of his thighs straining as he took one heavy step, paused, then took another. His shirt clung wetly to his back. Perspiration dampened his hair. He had rolled his sleeves up to the elbows, and she could see the muscles in his forearms, flexing and contracting with each strenuous step.

She stood watching him until the clansmen recognized what was in the cart and began to crowd around it. She helped serve the ale to the thirsty workers, while Angus reached the bridge beyond the gate tower, stopped, and twisted his body to set the plank down. It bounced heavily as it landed, and sent a cloud of sawdust swirling into the air.

He straightened and tipped his head back, closed his eyes as if to drink in the sun's warmth. A drop of perspiration trickled down the side of his sun-bronzed face, and he wiped it away with the heel of his hand.

Gwendolen stood transfixed, holding a tankard of ale, waiting for him to notice her. At last their eyes met, and she held out the drink.

Striding toward her, he accepted the ale and tipped it back. His throat, shiny with sweat, pulsed as he guzzled. The liquid cascaded over the sides of his mouth and down his damp, muscular chest, disappearing under his shirt. Gwendolen followed the path of the ale with rapt eyes, as he wiped an arm across his mouth and handed the tankard back.

She grew flustered by the intensity of his stare as he waited for her to take the empty container. When she reached out, their fingers brushed lightly together, and the brief contact created a lingering havoc in her brain.

"Thank you," he said.

"My pleasure. How is the new gate coming?"

"It's coming." He gazed at her briefly with those ice blue eyes, then turned to resume his work.

She set about collecting the empty drinking vessels from the other clansmen, realizing with some unease that she was beginning to look forward to her wedding night, and was thinking about it far more than she should.

But what did that say about her loyalties to the Mac-Ewen clan? she wondered uncomfortably, then quickly swept the question from her mind.

For three days, and three excruciatingly long nights, Angus refrained from visiting Gwendolen's bedchamber, for he did not think he could manage another session of foreplay that didn't end in full-scale, outright, bed-smashing intercourse.

Instead, he spent those days exhausting himself on the construction of the castle gate, deliberately choosing tasks that tested his body, in order to distract himself from thinking about Gwendolen. Currently, he was at the top of a ladder, pounding on a wooden peg.

He also took steps to get their wedding celebrations under way as quickly as possible. Naturally, if he could drag her to the chapel that afternoon and be done with it, he would. He would marry her and bed her without delay, and rid himself of this hunger for which there was only one cure. But the two clans needed something to celebrate, and he wasn't marrying Gwendolen to satisfy his lust. He was doing it for Kinloch—so it had to be a first-rate spectacle with a bounty of food, dancing, drinking, and applauding.

And then, by God, there would be sex. Lots and lots of sex.

He pounded harder and faster on the wooden peg, and accidentally smashed his thumb with the hammer.

The following day, Angus entered his bedchamber in the middle of the afternoon, locked the door behind him, and sank into an upholstered chair by the window. He was drenched in sweat after testing the gate, which was now complete, but required a few minor adjustments. He was tired of working on it, however. His thumb was still swollen and throbbing, so he came here to rest a while.

He lounged back, closed his eyes, and stretched his long legs out in front of him. He rubbed his stinging eyes with the heels of his hands. It felt like the insides of his eyelids were coated in dust. He hadn't enjoyed a good night's sleep in days.

He pushed himself out of the chair and practically crawled to the bed, where he flopped onto his stomach and thought of his forthcoming wedding night. An unwelcome rush of lust stirred his blood.

He was not accustomed to satisfying his own needs. Raonaid, over the past two years, had always been eager, but it had been two months since he left her, and Gwendolen was still, as of yet, unavailable to him. He might do better if he just took the edge off a bit. At least one fist still worked, and that's all he needed.

He rolled onto his back and stared up at the canopy above, feeling riled and annoyed that he had been reduced to this.

A knock sounded at his door just then, and he sat up abruptly. *"Fook off!"*

"Fook off, yerself," Lachlan replied from the corridor. "Open the door."

"I'm busy."

There was a pause. "Too busy to receive Colonel Worthington, the governor of Fort William? I thought you might like to know that he's outside, pounding at the gate. He seems agitated."

"Dammit, Lachlan," Angus said in a low voice, as he vaulted off the bed. "I'll show you agitated."

He'd always known that passion for a woman made a man weak, and here was the proof. He had been caught off guard, distracted by the persistent merrymaking that was going on under his kilt.

He flung the door open. "If you tell me he's here with the full force of the English army, I'll be throwing you over the castle walls."

Lachlan stood in the corridor with feet braced apart, loading a musket. "Nay. It's just the colonel himself and ten redcoats. But he's getting impatient. I think you ought to let him in." Lachlan poured powder into the pan, charged the weapon, and rammed down the cartridge.

Angus pushed past him, heading for the staircase. "Tell the guards to open the gate," he ordered. "Bring the colonel to the solar. I'll wait for him there. And offer drinks to his men."

He quickly descended the curved staircase, aware of how quickly the threat of an attack could douse certain fires in a man's blood, and light others that were equally hot.

His passion for Kinloch was immense.

He swept all thoughts of Gwendolen from his mind.

Gwendolen leaned over the battlements and looked down at the small company of mounted soldiers on the bridge, led by the great Colonel Worthington himself.

It was hardly an army of liberators with archers and cannons, appearing over the horizon for a surprise attack. To the contrary, the soldiers, in bright red uniforms, looked lethargic and bored. While they waited on the bridge for the gates to open, the horses nickered and tossed their heads. One soldier sneezed three times into his hand and complained about the dust, and another suggested that he sniff strong vinegar into his nose each morning to take care of the problem.

Clearly there would be no heroic battle today.

Colonel Worthington removed a folded linen handkerchief from his pocket and dabbed at the perspiration on his forehead, while insects buzzed incessantly in the meadow beyond.

At last the enormous new gates swung open, and they all trotted into the bailey. Gwendolen moved to the other side of the roof to watch.

The redcoats were greeted cordially by Lachlan MacDonald and a few other MacDonald clansmen, who took charge of the horses and led them to the stables. The soldiers were taken into the hall, while Lachlan escorted Colonel Worthington to the North Tower.

Gwendolen's heart began to pound. What would happen when the colonel spoke to Angus? Would he take her side, and command Angus, under order of the King, to restore Kinloch to the MacEwens? Or would he recognize Angus's right to rule Kinloch and inform him that he had learned of the invasion from someone inside the castle walls? Worst of all, would Angus discover who had sent the dispatch?

Chapter Ten

Gwendolen sat in her private chamber, feeling as if she were waiting to be escorted to the executioner's block. Every sound outside her door caused her to jump, as if it were the ominous approach of the hooded axe man. By the time someone actually climbed the stairs and knocked, she had worked herself into such a state of anxiety that she kicked over a stool in her haste to answer the door.

Standing outside in the corridor, it was—as she had expected—the conqueror of her clan, looking grim.

He had not visited her chamber since the night he carried a candle into the room, woke her from her dream, and joined her on the bed. She experienced a flash memory suddenly—of his body pressed tightly to hers, his mouth on her neck, her legs wrapped around his kilted hips—and shivered with a mixture of sexual arousal and fear.

How strange that she would think of such things now, when there were far more pressing matters to worry about—like the fact that in his hands, he held the letter she had written to the English colonel at Fort William.

Angus's eyes were cool and mistrustful. Not knowing what to expect, and feeling guilty and convicted before he even spoke a single word, Gwendolen invited him inside, while her stomach turned over with dread.

He entered and glanced around the room, as if looking for more evidence of treachery, then glared at her directly. God help her. He knew she had sent the letter. She had broken her vow to him, and may have cost him his ultimate triumph.

"You have something you wish to say to me," she said, deciding it would be best to confront the issue head-on.

She glanced down at the small rolled parchment in his battle-scarred hands, which was tied with a black ribbon that had come from her own dressing table, and felt transfixed by the sight of those long fingers. He ran a bruised thumb along the length of the dispatch.

"Did you write this?" he asked.

She knew she had to say something, but couldn't seem to find her voice.

His eyes lifted, and a muscle flicked at his jaw. "*Did* you?" he repeated, causing her to jump.

Gwendolen strove to remain calm. She looked him in the eye and nodded, for she certainly couldn't let Mary take the blame for it. The poor girl couldn't even read. This was her own doing, and she would claim full responsibility.

Bracing herself for the oncoming storm of the Lion's wrath, she wondered if he would beat her. Or drag her to the prison.

He looked down at the dispatch again, and she was forced to stand and wait, while he decided what to do with her.

Slowly, he moved to the window and stood with his back to her, saying nothing for the longest time. Gwendolen grew more desperate to explain herself. She wanted to apologize, because she had indeed broken her word, while he had kept his side of the bargain. He had not harmed or mistreated her, nor had he robbed her of her virginity before marriage. He'd treated her mother with respect as well, and had permitted her to keep the jewels that once belonged to his own mother, years ago.

As much as it shocked and pained Gwendolen to admit it, Angus the Lion, savage warrior and sworn enemy of the MacEwens, had been merciful.

"You lied to me," he said at last, in a low voice that made her wonder if those days of mercy and kindness were over.

"Aye. But if you will let me explain—"

"Do you think you deserve that opportunity?"

"Please, Angus—"

He faced her and took a very long time to consider her appeal. "All right," he said at last. "I'm listening."

Somehow, she managed to speak in a steady voice. "I sent it the morning after you invaded Kinloch and claimed me as your wife."

His eyebrows pulled together in a frown, but she forced herself to continue.

"Please understand that I was afraid of you and I felt a responsibility to my clan. Kinloch belonged to the MacEwens. My father had been dead only a month, and already we had lost it. I didn't know what to expect from you. All I knew was that you were a ruthless warrior and you claimed me for your own political gain, and I am still unhappy with your tyrannical methods and the life you have forced upon me, without ever asking."

He eyed her with his usual menace, and she spoke even more passionately while stepping forward.

"Angus, you are a warrior. Surely you cannot blame me for fighting for my freedom and what belonged to my family. It was my father's greatest achievement, and now that he is gone—*because* he is gone—Kinloch means everything to me. I was only trying to save the people of my clan from your cruelty."

She stopped herself, realizing she had just insulted him. But there was no other way to put it. It was the truth.

"You think I came here to be cruel?"

"That is how you are perceived," she told him. "You took our home by force. You crushed us, swiftly and brutally. You left me no choice but to rebel."

His eyes had a burning, impassioned look in them. "Is this explanation supposed to make me overlook your treachery?"

She considered the question carefully, then lifted her chin. "Aye, it is. I admit that I violated our agreement, but I was frightened, and you can hardly blame me. You are an intimidating man. It seemed my only option at the time."

He strode forward with narrowed eyes. "At the time . . ."

"Aye."

"You were frightened . . ."

"Aye."

"Are you frightened now?" His eyes were forbidding, his voice husky, as he ran a rough knuckle across her cheek.

Gwendolen backed away and bumped into the bed. "Very much so."

"So you'd do it again if you had the chance? You'd

call on some other army to come and remove me by force? Or kill me?"

Her body trembled as she strove to get air into her lungs. "That depends."

"On what?"

"On what army it was. I wouldn't call in the French. They'd probably take your side over mine."

Angus held the tiny rolled dispatch in front of her face. "I should beat you senseless for this betrayal, and teach you a lesson you would not soon forget."

He stood before her, waiting for her to speak.

"I'm sorry," she said.

Angus's chest was heaving. He wet his lips.

"Will you at least tell me what Colonel Worthington said?" she asked.

"What are you hoping to hear? That he threatened me and ordered me to leave Kinloch? That if I disobey, King George will return with an army of redcoats and drop an anvil on my head?"

"Now you're mocking me."

He backed away. "It was pointless to send this message, lass. The English have more important matters to contend with than a disagreement between two clans. Colonel Worthington said so himself. He doesn't wish to become involved. What were you thinking? That they'd come and defend your dead father's claim to this territory?"

She moved away from the bed. "I don't know. I thought that our loyalty would mean something to him. We are Hanoverians and we defeated an army of Jacobites two years ago. I thought the King would defend our lawful possession of these lands, which we earned in defense of his Crown."

Angus palmed the hilt of his sword. "You know nothing of politics and war, la's. The Whigs wanted my father dead, and your father took care of it for his own personal gain. He was offered Kinloch as a prize, and that's why he invaded. It had nothing to do with honor or loyalty to any Crown. It was about land and power, nothing more. That's what it's always about, when one man tries to take another man's home." He crumpled the dispatch in a fist and walked to the window. For a long time he looked out at the surrounding countryside. "I have taken back what belongs to me, and Colonel Worthington has no interest in challenging my rule here. He made it clear it's a clan issue, nothing more."

"He's not worried that you will try to raise another rebellion?"

"I gave him my word that I will live here in peace."

"And he believed you?"

Angus swung around to face her. "You seem to take promises very lightly, lass. Does a man's word mean so little to you? And do you have no care for your own?"

She was overcome suddenly with shame. She walked slowly to a chair and sat down. "My honor means everything to me."

"But you broke the promise you made to me when you negotiated terms of surrender. You promised to be loyal."

She bowed her head. "Does this mean our agreement is annulled?"

Perhaps he would not even wish to marry her now. If he felt he could not trust her, he might imprison her. Or perhaps simply banish her. And then what? She would be forced to leave her home and the members of her clan, while they would remain here to be ruled by a

MacDonald. As things stood presently, she at least had an opportunity to rule beside him and petition for the rights of her own people.

Perhaps her mother had been right all along. Perhaps she should cease these futile efforts to oppose him, and find a way to submit and exert some influence, through her position as his wife.

It was not as if it would be wholly unpleasant. Heaven help her, she had been anticipating their wedding night with a surprising degree of curiosity and desire. And from what she'd witnessed from his behavior thus far—especially today—it would not be a life of beatings and torment. He had every reason to punish her after what she'd done, but he had not done so. At least not yet. He'd proven himself over the past week to be a fair chief. And he was handsome. Despite everything—she was attracted to him.

Acutely aware of his movement across the room, even while her eyes were downcast, Gwendolen awaited his decision. He approached and stood before her. His kilt brushed against her knees, and her heart began to race. His presence was overwhelming to her in ways she could barely comprehend, and she found herself hoping that he would not call off their marriage.

He cradled her chin in his callused hand and lifted her face. Her heart pounded erratically while he looked down at her, as if he was trying to decide whether or not he could ever trust her again.

She gazed into his eyes and spoke with straight-forward sincerity. "I was wrong to betray you, but if you will give me another chance, I promise it will not happen again. I have learned my lesson, and I will pledge myself to you now, if you like."

He slowly brushed his bruised thumb over her lower lip, and his touch caused something inside her to tremble with unease. Or perhaps it was desire. She couldn't seem to make sense of her feelings.

Without responding to her apology, he backed away. There was a grim shadow of resentment in his expression. Was it possible he no longer wanted her as his wife? Perhaps there was not even a single shred of hope for a second chance.

Not yet ready to give up, she took hold of her skirts and moved forward off the edge of the chair to her knees. "I, Gwendolen MacEwen, pledge loyalty to you, Angus Bradach MacDonald, as Laird of Kinloch. I promise to serve you faithfully and devotedly, and provide you with heirs."

A raven flew past the window, screeching noisily. Gwendolen waited through the rush of her anxiety for Angus to say something.

"What about your brother?" he curtly asked. "If he returns, will you honor this pledge to me?"

She met his clear blue eyes. "I give you my word that if he comes, I will not betray you, and I will do my best to encourage peace between you. You once said you would offer him land . . . ?"

"Aye."

"Then I will hold true to my pledge. I will do my best to convince him to accept your offer."

Something dark continued to simmer in his expression, but his words delivered another message. "Then I accept your oath."

Profoundly relieved, she gathered her skirts in her fists and stood. "You still wish to marry me?"

"Aye. We'll exchange vows in four days."

She blinked. "That soon."

"There's no reason to delay."

He stood motionless, staring at her, then looked down at the crumpled dispatch he still held in his hand. For a moment he seemed lost in thought, then he moved to the desk, lit a candle, and held the parchment over the flame.

"No one knows you are the traitor who sent this," he said, as her letter slowly turned to black ash and disintegrated before her eyes, "except for the woman in the kitchen. Can you keep her quiet?"

"Of course."

"It's best if the clans believe that you are a faithful bride of Kinloch. To behave otherwise is to encourage rebellion, and I want peace here."

"I want that, too," she assured him.

He lifted his eyes briefly and glanced at her.

Gwendolen suspected he was not yet convinced of her trustworthiness. He would be watching her very closely in the coming weeks.

The flame devoured the dispatch, and when it was gone, Angus blew the ashes off the desktop and wiped it clean. "We will not speak of this again," he said, making his way to the door.

"Angus . . ." She followed him into the corridor, where he stopped at the top of the stairs with his hand on the wall. "After what I did, will you still honor the original terms of our agreement?"

With cold, seething eyes, he returned to her. She backed up and hit the wall. He braced both arms on either side of her, trapping her there.

"If you're asking whether or not I intend to wait until our wedding night to make love to you . . ." He paused, considering it. "It's very tempting to ignore the terms, since they've already been breached." She sucked in a breath, and he took his time to peruse her face. "Do I make you nervous, lass? Are you afraid of me?"

"No, I am not afraid." But she was. Heaven help her, she was.

He looked down at her lips, then leaned in for a deep, wet, demanding kiss that tested the genuineness of her surrender. One arm slid around her waist and pulled her close, while the other remained braced against the wall. The texture of his tongue sent all her nerve endings into a buzzing state of awareness, while a shock of pleasure rippled outward from her lips down to her belly. His spiky whiskers rubbed against her chin, and she marveled at the strangely gratifying pain.

Slowly, he backed away. Her eyes fluttered open.

"Don't work yourself into such a tizzy," he said. "I'll honor my word. You can keep your precious virginity for a few more days."

"Thank you."

"Save your gratitude for our wedding night," he said, as he turned to leave, "because I suspect you'll want to thank me then. Repeatedly."

He disappeared quickly down the curved staircase, and Gwendolen exhaled sharply with relief.

Chapter Eleven

Four days later, after speaking vows before God in the chapel and pledging herself, body and soul, to the leader who had conquered her clan, stolen her home, and claimed her as his bride, Gwendolen followed Angus into his bedchamber.

Dozens of candles had been lit. A hot fire blazed in the hearth. The room smelled of rose petals and wine, but not even those extravagant luxuries could calm the storm of her anxieties—for she would soon be lying naked in bed with the great Scottish Lion.

He turned and shot a threatening glance at the drunken MacDonald clansmen who had followed them up the stairs, teasing and heckling. The men halted on the spot, then backed away and stumbled into one another as he shut the door in their faces.

He twisted the key in the lock, then turned toward Gwendolen, who stood in front of the window, uncertain about what to do next. Remembering the promises she had made—to be a devoted and dutiful wife—she raised a slightly trembling hand and pulled the pins from her hair, then shook it down her back, determined to do her best to please her husband tonight. If he was happy with her, she might eventually gain his trust and secure a more comfortable, influential role for herself, where she would not fear him quite so much.

He strode forward, his eyes fixed on hers as he slid the tartan off his shoulder. He unbuckled his leather belt, along with his dress sporran, and tossed everything onto a chair. Next he pulled his shirt off over his head, and stood before her, naked.

Gwendolen's lips parted, and she strove to control her breathing as she regarded his beautiful, gleaming body in the candlelight. Firm, thickly muscled, and marked with battle scars, he was an extraordinary image of strength and virility. Her curious eyes took in the contours of his chest, and the ripples of sinew across his torso. Down lower, he was copiously aroused, and the sight of his full male genitalia made her tremble with shock and apprehension. How was she ever going to survive this? How would she know what to do? She felt a strange heat from within, while her mind catapulted with nervous tension.

For a long while, they beheld each other, saying nothing. But what was there to say? Gwendolen knew what was expected of her on this night, and she had done everything she could to prepare herself.

Determined to relax and heed her mother's advice—which was to embrace and enjoy this experience—she lifted her hair and piled it on top of her head, then turned her back to her husband, waiting for him to unhook her gown.

He took his time undressing her. He removed one article of clothing at a time, then lightly tossed each piece to the floor—the stiff brocade stomacher, the skirts and petticoats and wide, whalebone hoops. Gwendolen raised her arms over her head while he removed the linen chemise, then at last he stepped back to take in her naked form in the dim candlelight.

She blinked up at him timidly.

"Do not fear me, lass. I give you my word, I'll do my best to be gentle."

"I cannot help but fear you," she replied. "Not long ago, I watched you fight a battle in the bailey and kill dozens of my clansmen. I saw how you claimed what you wanted—by force."

She shivered in a sudden draft, and he held out a hand. "You're cold. Come. Get into bed. You'll feel warmer soon enough, and less fearful of me, I hope."

He led her to the canopied bed and pulled back the thick covers. She climbed onto the luxurious feather mattress and slid her legs between the sheets.

Angus blew out all the candles in the room, then got in beside her. Now, there was only the firelight to illuminate his face. Gwendolen marveled at his handsome features—his unfathomable blue eyes and strong, chiseled cheekbones. She could barely wrap her mind around the fact that the great Scottish Lion, Angus MacDonald, was her husband and she had pledged herself to him today before her clan and under the eyes of God. Tonight he would seal that sacred union. He would make love to her, and perhaps put a child in her womb.

Slowly, he inched closer and laid a large, heavy hand on her belly. Closing her eyes, she thought of the lion in her dreams. Powerful, exotic, sensual, he had come to her in a meadow, rich with colorful wildflowers and thistledown that floated in bright shafts of sunlight. In the dream, she was engulfed by humid summer warmth, and never felt afraid. She longed only to stroke the lion's thick mane. She held out her hand and lured him closer.

He licked her wrist, and his tongue soon found the sensitive flesh at her neck.

Gwendolen opened her eyes when Angus settled himself on top of her, his skin hot against her own. She slipped her arms around his waist and felt the solid bands of muscle at his lower back.

"Are you still afraid?" he asked, his voice husky as he kissed behind her ear. Her body responded in a tingle of gooseflesh.

She thought of the dream again and remembered how it felt to be completely unafraid and aching to touch the lion, but dreams were not the same as reality. Her belly was tied up in knots. Her heart was pounding wildly.

"Aye, but I can't seem to do anything about it."

He looked into her eyes. "I'll only take you when you're willing, lass, so give me a chance to make it so. Can you relax for me?"

She nodded.

"I'll not rush you," he whispered, as he touched his lips to hers and swept his tongue inside, while the heat from his body was surprisingly comforting and made her sigh in unexpected content.

He bent his head and kissed her cheek, and sure enough, his reassurances began to calm her nerves. His palm slid up her rib cage, and his thumb settled on the pebbled tip of her breast. He flicked it back and forth, while he kissed her collarbone with parted lips and a probing tongue, sending tiny waves of eroticism shimmying down her spine. Her legs parted, and he settled himself more comfortably between her thighs.

She trembled at the desire racing through her body, while her hips began to pulse. He laid kisses across her shoulder and down to her breasts, where he licked and suckled tirelessly for such a duration that the minutes began to blur into one exquisite path of rapture, leading her somewhere unfamiliar and thrilling in its promise of adventure.

A flaming heat began deep inside her. She cupped his head in her hands and let out a tiny moan.

He paused and gazed down at her. She felt suddenly lost in a feverish delirium and wondered if she'd had too much wine during the celebrations, but no . . . that was not the case. This delirium was something else. It was erotic and emotional, and she suspected she was in fact going to enjoy herself more than she ever imagined she could.

He held her in his gaze as he slid his hand between her thighs and began to stroke her. The memory of what he did to her five nights ago still burned in the fires of her imagination, and the intensity of his expression filled her with courage and daring, and a genuine desire to please him.

She reached down and wrapped her hand around his manhood, and was amazed by his size and stiffness. "Show me how to touch you."

"You're doing fine, lass. You need no instruction."

With growing passion, she stroked him, measuring her success by the intensity of his responses—the catch of his breath in his throat, the movement of his hips, and the passion in his kiss.

Keen to explore, she squeezed down lower, but he lightly seized her wrist. "Not so aggressive with that part of me, lass. It requires a softer touch."

"Did I hurt you?" She was mortified.

"I've survived worse."

He lowered his mouth to hers again, and they each resumed their explorations. Angus rubbed and stroked her until she was drowning in wetness, then at last he shifted and positioned the swollen tip of his erection against her tender maidenhead.

"You're ready for me. Can you feel it?"

She nodded and braced herself, for he would now claim her as his wife. She would belong to him. No other man would ever receive what she was about to give him.

He pushed forward, hard up against the delicate barrier of her virginity, and paused. "Am I hurting you?"

"A little," she replied, "but don't stop."

He thrust forward again, more deeply this time, and the pain was significant, for he was incredibly large.

"Are we almost there?" she asked, clutching at his shoulders, biting her lower lip.

"Aye."

He gave one final thrust, all the way in, deep to the hilt, easing himself into the confines of her virginity, until it existed no more.

Her body stiffened at the painful invasion, and yet she wanted it.

Angus gave her a moment to grow accustomed to the feel of his body inside of hers. He lay very still. "Are you all right?"

A bewitching fever was overtaking her senses. She didn't feel like herself. Whatever pain she was experiencing seemed trivial compared to the raw need to drive her hips forward. Erotic sensation flooded through her body, and his initial penetration soon became a series of them, creating a rhythm of rapture that left her breathless. She clung to his shoulders and wrapped her legs around his hips, matching each of his deep, smooth, pounding thrusts, measure for measure, delighting in the pain that still lingered with the friction.

His body grew damp with perspiration. She cried out and tossed her head back on the pillows. She was slick with moisture as he worked deftly in and out of her.

She was his now, it was done, and she knew that when he finally spilled his seed into her womb, their union would be sealed forever.

Her mother had been right. This was indeed something to enjoy.

She dug her fingernails into his buttocks, and pulled him all the way in, as deep as he would go.

Angus held still for a moment, acutely aware of the shocking notion that Gwendolen had finally surrendered to him. She had not resisted this most intimate invasion, but instead had placed her body, her life, and her future in his hands, which was an astounding occurrence—for no woman, and certainly no virgin, had ever given herself over to him like this before.

Another part of him, however—the darker, more cynical side—tensed at her unguarded abandon, for he had never desired passion or intimacy with any woman, much less a wife. Sexual release, yes. Power, definitely. But passion? It was not something he had wanted when he shouted from the rooftops that he would claim a MacEwen daughter as his bride.

But this was not the time for soul-searching, he knew. All that mattered now was his hunger for her body. Slowly, he began to resume their coupling. He drove in and out of her with a primal, reckless need, and it wasn't long before he felt the hot rush of an oncoming orgasm and was compelled to move faster and faster—until it became some kind of wild sexual frenzy.

It had been years since he'd experienced such a buildup of pleasure, and he had to work hard to rein it in and stall his orgasm, but in the end, it was no use. He felt as if he were making love for the first time—but he supposed he'd never been with a virgin before.

He couldn't think, couldn't even stop to consider Gwendolen's pleasure. He climaxed in a compulsive rage and exploded into her with a groan of blazing heat. He bucked and pushed, and she dug her fingernails into his back. It was rough, wild, and extreme—and it took some time to get his breath back before he collapsed onto her soft body with an immense sigh of satisfaction.

"That's not what I expected," she said, still clinging to him.

"Nor I."

In fact, he felt a sudden impulse to get up off the bed and exit the room. He resisted the urge, however, and rolled off her to stare up at the canopy overhead.

"Did I please you?" she asked—in that sweet, innocent voice that made him realize how very different they were.

"You were fine," he replied without meeting her eyes.

She paused. "I'll do better next time. I promise. I was nervous, that's all."

He turned his head on the pillow and looked at her. "You did nothing wrong."

It was a lie. She had held him too close, enthralled

him too quickly, and he was reacting to it now with a sudden rush of uneasiness.

He rose from the bed and crossed to the fire. For a tense moment, he stood naked before it, staring into the red-hot lure of the flames. He reached for the iron poker and pushed the logs around. Sparks exploded and snapped and escaped up into the chimney.

He set the poker back on its hook and went to pick up his shirt, which he had tossed on the chair earlier. He pulled it on over his head while Gwendolen watched. She was sitting up now, hugging the covers to her chest.

"Are you going somewhere?"

He picked up his tartan and wrapped it around his waist. "Aye. Down to the hall for some ale."

"But why? Don't you want to stay in bed? You can have me again if you like. You could teach me how to do all the things that please you."

He tensed in response to her provocative proposition, and had some trouble with his tartan. He couldn't seem to locate the brooch in all the folds, and was beginning to reconsider his decision to leave, for he was keenly aware of her naked form on the bed, and her enticing suggestions were still reverberating in his brain. Would it be so wrong to stay and teach her a few things?

"How long will you be gone?" she asked.

He found the brooch and turned his back on her. "I don't know, but don't wait up. You can return to your own chamber if you'd be more comfortable there."

He didn't let himself look at her, but he didn't have to. She was hurt by his wish to leave. It was their wedding night after all.

"I would prefer to stay here," she informed him,

with less innocence and more of that proud defiance he had witnessed on the day of the invasion.

"I may be a while." He sat down on the chair and pulled on a boot. "And I'll likely be drunk."

She sat up on her knees, still covering herself with the sheet. She crawled across the bed toward him. "Is that supposed to cool the fires of my lust?"

He glanced up at her in shock, and couldn't help but laugh. "Honest to God, woman! I don't know what to make of you!"

"How so?"

He pulled on the second boot and stood up. "Sometimes I wonder if there's a sharp-toothed tiger under all that virtue and purity. Who the blazes did I marry?"

She frowned at him. "Perhaps you'd understand me better if you didn't feel the need to leave every time we make love."

He strode forward and raised an eyebrow at her. "*Every* time? We've only done it once, lass."

"You know what I mean. The other time . . . when you came to my bed . . . You didn't stay very long."

He felt suddenly as if the walls were closing in around him, so he started for the door. "I'll not explain myself to you. I am laird here. I'll do what I want, and leave a room when I please."

He yanked the door open.

"Even if you leave your wife unsatisfied?"

He halted abruptly in the doorway, seething with a mixture of fury and arousal, which had not abated since the moment she'd offered to let him have her again.

He turned and reentered the room. She stared at him with wide eyes—terrified, probably, that she had crossed a line, which she most definitely had.

He kicked the door shut behind him and strode back to the bed—for he had something important to prove to her: Angus the Lion never left any woman unsatisfied. Especially not his wife.

Gwendolen sat frozen in shock as her husband approached, for she was baffled by the stormy nature of her emotions. One minute she was overcome with desire and enraptured with her new husband. The next minute, she was shouting insults at him across the room and bracing herself for his sexual retaliation.

She had not intended to rouse his anger, but he couldn't just leave her like that. This was their wedding night, and he had just put an end to her life as a virgin.

He advanced to the side of the bed and pointed at the mattress in front of him. "Right here."

She moved to the place where he indicated.

"Now lie back."

She did as he commanded, and he wrapped his arms around her thighs and dragged her to the edge of the bed. He placed his hands on her knees and looked down at her. Her legs stretched wide, opening for him.

Feet still on the floor, he leaned over her and laid hot, openmouthed kisses on her breasts. His callused hands stroked up and down her sides, over her hips and down to her calves, then he used his mouth to blaze a trail of kisses down her flat, quivering belly. He probed her navel with his tongue.

She grew weak with yearning and the excitement of the unknown, as he kissed her hips and made her squirm with delight.

"How's this, lass?" he asked in a low, seductive voice. "Is this what you want from me?"

She could do nothing but nod earnestly as he knelt on the floor and brushed his lips across her inner thighs. A soft gasp escaped her when his mouth and tongue plunged into the sensitive core of her womanhood.

She'd thought she'd experienced everything earlier when he claimed her virginity and poured his seed into her, but this was something new and unimaginable. She had not known how intimate the marriage act could be—or how satisfying. He was driving her to the brink of madness.

She bucked and writhed on the bed as he pleasured her, and soon she was plunging down that raging, foamy river of sensation. When it finally came, the orgasm was excessive to the point of excruciating. She clutched the bedcoverings in both fists and cried out, while he continued to thrust his tongue into her, until her arms fell open and she was faint with exhaustion.

Angus rose to his feet and rested his fisted knuckles on the bed on either side of her.

Her eyes fluttered open. She felt groggy. Drunk. And very happy.

"Are you satisfied now?" he asked.

She could barely think through the sexual fog that was clouding her brain, but somehow she managed to nod her head.

"Good. Now maybe I can have some peace and quiet."

He stalked to the door, but halted before he opened it. *"Bluidy hell,"* he whispered.

She leaned up on both elbows, wondering dazedly what he was going on about. He swung around to face her.

"I can't go down there like this." He was aroused

again. His kilt wasn't hanging right. "Are you willing to have another go?"

"Oh yes," she answered breathlessly. "And since I'm already well satisfied, there's no need for foreplay."

Her ferocious Highlander returned to her, and with a fiery glint in his eye, said, "Are you sure, lass? Because I'm feeling energetic. This might last a while."

"I'm absolutely sure." All she wanted was to feel him inside her again.

He braced his feet apart on the floor, then slowly slid into her soaking depths with glorious ease this time. He made love to her while standing up, and he made it last a good long time, working inside her with smooth, plunging meticulousness that left her reeling with amazement. When he climaxed, she felt it as if it were her own. He finally collapsed onto her with a groan of deep satisfaction.

A moment later he climbed onto the bed—explaining that he was too exhausted to make it to the door. He stripped off his clothes, then fell onto his back like a tremendous toppling oak.

He did not leave the bed again until morning, and by that time, Gwendolen was feeling somewhat addicted to her new husband's sexual expertise.

And quite thoroughly schooled in the enticing act of lovemaking.

Chapter Twelve

Angus strode in circles around the Great Hall, swinging his sword through the air in wide, sweeping arcs, waiting impatiently for Lachlan for arrive.

He had not had breakfast yet—it was still too early for that—but he felt a great need to work his body into a lather and ease some of the tension he was feeling, for his wedding night had been more complicated than he'd expected. Gwendolen had drained him dry, and he needed to prove to himself that he was not entirely sapped of strength and vigor, otherwise he might have to lay down some boundaries.

At last Lachlan appeared under the wide, arched entrance and leaned a shoulder against the wall. His face was shadowed with dark stubble, his eyes rimmed with red. He watched Angus lunge and strike at the air, then he ambled forward, yawning.

"Is there a reason you dragged me out of bed on this, of all days, when you should still be shagging your pretty new wife? Bluidy hell, Angus, I only got to sleep an hour ago."

"And what were you doing all night?" Angus asked irritably.

"Ah, you know. The usual. Drinking. Singing. Shagging."

"I told you to stay away from the MacEwen women for a while."

"Not to worry. My little friend last night was a MacDonald from the village, and a bonnie one at that."

Lachlan drew his sword. They paced back and forth, eyeing each other intently.

Suddenly, Angus swung hard, and the heavy clang of steel against steel did wonders for his mood. He needed to feel like he was still the same man he had been on the day he stormed the gates of Kinloch. He needed to know that his desire for his wife was not going to consume him.

A particular memory flashed through his brain as he ducked under Lachlan's aggressive attack. He remembered wiping a tear from Gwendolen's cheek, just before dawn. She'd looked up at him and told him she was happy, and he had done the unthinkable and gathered her into his arms.

Lachlan came at him suddenly.

Angus shouted a fearsome war cry and defended himself against his cousin's impressive overhanded swing.

"Is there a reason you're so keen to fight this morning?" Lachlan asked, moving quickly to deflect another blow. "She didn't hold out on you, did she?"

"Nay."

They fought hard and fast for a few more minutes.

"That's it?" Lachlan said, as he turned away and circled the room. "That's all you're going to say about your wedding night?"

"That's all I'm going to say."

Lachlan came at him again. There was a piercing ring of steel against steel.

"No regrets then?" Lachlan asked. "You're pleased with your wife?"

"Stop talking, Lachlan, and fight me!"

Later, when they were both dripping with sweat and breathing heavily, they sat down on the dais. Angus threw Lachlan a towel.

"You know," Angus said, wiping his face, "I never imagined I'd end up married to a woman like Gwendolen MacEwen. I always believed that only foolish men took beautiful wives because they were thinking with their knobs instead of their heads."

"And love makes a man weak," Lachlan added. "So you've always said."

Angus looked up at the swallow's nest in the rafters, but the bird was not there. "Has there been any word from her brother yet?"

"No news, but I sent five men out to hunt him down, so one of them should be able to discover something. It might take a while, that's all. In the meantime, I'm extracting all kinds of interesting facts and opinions from Onora. She's an easy flirt and a fountain of information about Kinloch, and the people in the village."

Angus wiped the towel over his face again. "Do you ever feel like you'll burn in hell for using her like that?"

Lachlan chuckled. "Nay, because she's using me, too. She's quite the seductress. And it's not as if I'd ever bed her."

"Just keep your wits about you." Angus wiped at his arms. "And don't forget your first priority—to maintain a strong defense. Position the most reliable men at the battlements and keep sending out the scouts."

"I've got it all under control."

"Has anyone been out yet this morning?"

"Not yet."

"I'll go myself, then."

Lachlan regarded him keenly. "Are you sure? Don't you have a pretty young bride waiting in your bed?"

"Aye, but she took advantage of me last night. I need to refill my well."

Lachlan threw his head back and laughed.

A short time later, Angus strode across the rooftops to check on the sentries. He looked toward the horizon, then went to the kitchen, grabbed an apple and crunched into it on the way to the stables. He told the groom to back off and mind his own business while he saddled a horse for himself, then departed from the castle through the main gate.

Galloping fast across the bridge, he relished the hollow sound of the hooves clopping over the planks, then trotted across the dewy field to the forest. As he delved deeper into the wood, the dappled shade cooled his body, and he stopped a moment to breathe in the fresh scent of the pines and listen to the sound of fast-rushing water nearby. A squirrel chattered overhead.

He was pleased to be home at last, after two years on a distant, windswept island. He felt at peace here—something he had not thought possible for himself. Not in this lifetime. Yet here he was.

At the same time, he knew that if he was going to maintain control over Kinloch, he would have to be exceedingly careful. He could not allow himself to become distracted by a beautiful wife. Until Gwendolen's brother was found, the possibility of an invasion would be a constant threat. Angus would have to stay focused and remember why he married Gwendolen in the first place—to improve relations between his clan and hers and provide stability at Kinloch.

He also needed an heir, and for that reason, he would continue to bed her. It was his duty, and he would fulfill it. With luck, the fires of his lust would diminish over time and these persistent thoughts about her would fade. Perhaps when she was with child, his passions would cool.

But she was not with child yet . . .

Turning his mount back toward the castle, he wondered if she was awake and imagined how she would respond if he slid back into bed beside her. He galloped through the wood, hungry for her body, and failed to notice the MacEwen clansman who was crouched low in the bushes, watching him with sharp and vigilant eyes.

After a record number of days of sunshine, it rained buckets in the Highlands for a month. Despite the wet weather and muddy terrain, the Kinloch scouts continued to scour the surrounding forests each day, and the sentries paced back and forth on the rooftops, providing security against the threat of attack.

Angus placed his trust in Lachlan, his devoted cousin and competent Laird of War, and poured a great deal of energy into the important task of providing Kinloch with an heir.

He and Gwendolen spent the afternoons indoors, ignoring the weather outside and alternating each night between her bedchamber and his.

"Has Lachlan always lived here at Kinloch?" Gwendolen asked, late one morning, as they lay naked in Angus's bed with a fire blazing in the hearth. His chamber was warm and they were cozy beneath the covers. Angus lifted his head on the pillow to look down at her, for they were at opposite ends of the bed. She was resting her head on the footboard. He was massaging her feet.

"Aye. We grew up together," he told her. "We used to compete in everything. I was a faster runner, but he had better aim with a musket."

"What about swordplay? Which of you prevailed?"

"We were equally skilled, and to this day our sessions almost always end in a draw."

She rubbed her toe over his shoulder and down the length of his arm. "How many of these scars did you get from your childhood competitions with Lachlan? Surely they were not all earned in battle."

"I'd wager more than half came from friendly fights, when one of us was not paying attention, or was too drunk to be wielding a weapon in the first place."

Her eyes flashed with excitement. "Could you teach me how to fight with a claymore? It might prove useful one day. You never know when you might need your wife to protect you."

"Protect *me*?" He pinched her hard on the bottom.

"Ouch!" She kicked him under the covers.

Ducking beneath the sheets, he slid down to join her at the foot of the bed. "Are you carrying my child yet?" he asked.

"I can hardly answer that question," she replied. "We've only been married a month."

"But we've shagged so much, lass, it seems more like a year."

Gwendolen was tempted to kick him again, but

couldn't seem to do anything but gaze into the brilliant blue of his eyes.

"Is this normal?" she asked. "Do all married couples spend this much time in bed?"

"Don't think so. I believe we are strange."

She huffed. "I know for a fact that *you* are. Are you aware that you grind your teeth in your sleep?"

His eyes narrowed. "How would you know that? Do you stare at me in the night?"

"Occasionally."

"Why?"

She ran a finger over his lips and spoke with quiet seduction. "Because I am fascinated by your beautiful mouth and all the wonderful things you do with it."

"And I am fascinated by the smell of your skin." Smoothly, he rolled onto her. "Especially this shoulder." He brushed his nose down the inside of her arm. "And your wrists . . . Your hands . . . And lovely little titties."

He took a nipple into his mouth and began that slow, succulent licking that never failed to bring her to the heights of trembling desire.

Gwendolen relaxed her body and let her eyes fall closed, accepting the fact that she was becoming rather obsessed with her brave, passionate lion, even when she knew that he did not return her feelings, for there was always something distant about him, even at times like this, when he was making love to her.

He wanted a child. She knew that much, and it was important to him that she was amenable in bed, so he did what was necessary to make it so. She suspected, however, that this was just a temporary interlude for him, a pleasant diversion from his warrior life, and the moment it was confirmed that she was expecting, he would retreat, and she would not see him again until the time came to conceive another.

It was not so for her. All her life, she had wanted a marriage built on intimacy and love, and she was frankly surprised that this first month had been so passionate, considering that they had begun as enemies. She still could not forget the fury she had felt when she watched him storm the castle gates and kill her clansmen, and often wondered what her father would think if he could see how infatuated she had become with his enemy.

Two nights ago, she had dreamed about their first-born son on his wedding day. Angus—proud and loving as any father could be—presented him with his prized claymore as a gift. She woke from the dream feeling elated, and wondered if some dreams did come true. It was possible, she supposed, for many of hers had found their way into the reality of her life. The lion, for instance.

A moment later, her husband slid into her with exquisite ease and looked down at her face, while he braced himself above her on both arms. She gazed up at him in the silvery morning light and prayed that, one day, something more than sexual desire would exist between them. She was coming to realize that she wanted a deeper, soulful connection with her husband. For she could not live for duty alone. Not with him.

The knowledge of that fact terrified her.

Chapter Thirteen

On her way to the solar one afternoon, Onora rounded a corner in one of the vaulted passageways and collided unexpectedly with Lachlan MacDonald.

"Well, well, well," she purred, taking hold of his tartan and pulling him into the shadows of an alcove. He followed her up against the wall and rested an arm over her head.

"Have you been following me, Mrs. MacEwen?" he asked. His eyes were playful, his voice seductive, and she quivered with pent-up desire.

Heaven help her, she had not yet recovered from her conversation with him the night before, when he crossed the Great Hall, whispered hotly into her ear, and teased her with sweet flatteries. He was a captivating man—the kind who knew just how to charm a woman onto her back in two minutes flat. Onora would be more than happy to volunteer to become his next conquest, even though she was ten years older and a woman of vast experience and reason.

"Certainly not, sir," she replied, rubbing a finger down the center of his chest and wishing she could do so much more. "Perhaps you are the one who is following me."

A glimmer of interest lighted his eyes. "And what if I was? Would you call the castle guards and have me reprimanded?"

She shook her head at the outrageousness of it all, for she had never been one to let any man affect her this way. It was usually the other way around. Her lovers often became obsessed with her, and perhaps, because of that, she had grown overconfident in recent years.

But Lachlan MacDonald was not like other men. He was extraordinary—darkly handsome and divinely muscled—and his devastating smile promised sexual fulfillment with a teasing confidence that drove her mad with longing.

Men like him ought to be outlawed, she thought petulantly, as she fiddled with the tartan that was draped over his shoulder—for they committed the worst kind of offense. They turned strong women like her into pathetic, pining fools.

"Will you come to my chamber later tonight?" she asked, frustrated that she had to ask, when he should be the one making the proposition.

He glanced up and down the passageway, making sure there was no one about, then gave her a brilliant smile and spoke teasingly. "Tsk-tsk, Onora. You are, without a doubt, a stunning and desirable woman, but we are practically related."

"Not by blood," she replied, with a spark of mischief in her eyes.

He ran a finger from the bottom of her ear, along the line of her jaw to her chin, and focused on her lips. "Nevertheless, you shouldn't tempt a man so. It's terribly cruel. You'll break his heart."

Her body burned hotly with need. How was it possible that he could turn a rejection into the most thrilling, intoxicating form of flattery? The man was too charming for words.

"But Lachlan, I can promise you a night of wicked pleasures, and make all your fantasies come true. It's the least I can do, to reward you for your superb efforts as our new Laird of War."

He smiled again. "Your offer is very tempting, madam. You know exactly how to make a man suffer." Then he backed away with a seductive glimmer in his eye and left her standing there breathless, almost faint with desire. "I'll see you later in the hall," he said casually over his shoulder, as he continued down the passageway.

"Perhaps," she called after him. "Though I cannot guarantee I'll be there early, for I'll be enjoying a hot bath, while rubbing sweet-smelling perfumes over my naked body . . . thinking of you, of course."

He disappeared around the corner.

Onora continued in the other direction, then stopped suddenly and sank onto a bench against the wall. Frustrated with herself, she squeezed her hair in both fists and let out a near feral growl.

Flirting with Lachlan MacDonald was supposed to be about power and strategy, not fluttering hearts and girlish crushes. If she was going to accomplish anything here, she would have to work harder to control her impulses, for this was a volatile situation that required a cool head and a steady hand. She could not afford to become infatuated.

She stood up, smoothed out her skirts, and hurried to the stairs.

* * *

That evening, after the music and dancing had begun, Angus lounged back against a stone column in the Great Hall. He used his knife to cut into an apple, one slow slice at a time, and placed each juicy sliver into his mouth on the edge of the blade.

He watched his wife across the crowded room, dancing a reel with other members of both clans. The music was lively, the spirit of the room infectious with laughter and merriment, but it was all he could do to watch Gwendolen with narrowed, ravenous eyes while he absentmindedly ate his apple.

A young MacEwen lad with red hair and bony legs encouraged her to dance a second time. It put Angus in a foul mood. The mere idea of any man touching her or bringing a smile to her face sent his thoughts into a storm of possessive hunger.

He finished the apple, slipped his knife into his boot, and strode with purpose to the center of the hall, where she was still dancing the reel. All it took was one look, and her smile transformed into a shared sexual awareness that burned in her eyes. When the dance ended, she placed her hand in his, and he led her out of the hall toward the stairs to her bedchamber in the East Tower.

He had never known such desire could exist—and for the first time, he didn't care if he was distracted by it. All he wanted to think about was kissing his wife and burying himself in her soft, heated depths.

Everything else, he could lay aside until morning.

Onora watched Angus stalk through the crowd toward Gwendolen.

It was lost on no one that the great MacDonald chief

had become infatuated with his wife and was growing more obsessed with her each day. He looked at her like she was something delicious to eat, and he was a starving man.

Gwendolen responded in kind. They were two young lovers overcome by fresh passions, which was an astounding turn of events, to be sure—for on that first day, Gwendolen had loathed their conqueror with such intensity, she'd wanted to see him hanged.

Onora's gaze traveled across the hall to Lachlan, who was taking a young MacEwen clanswoman onto the floor.

Though one could hardly call her a woman. What was she? Seventeen? Eighteen? She was slender and blond and looked as stupid as a bag of hammers, but Onora nevertheless felt a harsh pang of jealousy in the pit of her stomach.

Was he attracted to such youthful innocence? she wondered irritably. Would he set his sights on seducing that trembling young lass tonight, instead of coming to her bedchamber for a more advanced and sophisticated program of activities?

"What has you lookin' so melancholy, Onora?"

Startled by the interruption, she turned toward Gordon MacEwen, the castle steward. His belly was round, his head bald, and there was a film of greasy perspiration on his nose.

She had taken this man to her bed many times when he was master of Kinloch in all but name. But now, after flirting with a brawny champion like Lachlan MacDonald, she felt rather disgusted by Gordon.

"Nothing of any permanent importance," she replied. She sipped her wine and regarded him congenially over the rim of her glass, for she would never be so foolish as to allow her passions to get the better of her. She had to keep all options open. She might find herself in need of Gordon's assistance in the future.

"I see that your daughter has found some contentment in her marriage," he said.

"Indeed."

"No doubt, she has been greatly conflicted by it," he added. "It's been such a short time since her father's passing. She's barely had time to grieve. And her brother . . . Well. He will certainly regret his absence when he learns of her personal sacrifice to Angus the Lion."

Onora pondered her daughter's happiness over the past few weeks and decided it was not turning out to be such a terrible sacrifice after all. The passion Gwendolen felt for her husband was genuine, and no political differences of opinion could change it. She was falling in love with the great Highland Lion, and despite her own personal loyalties, Onora was happy for her.

"I suppose they won't return to the hall tonight," Gordon remarked.

"Probably not." Onora felt a hand on her shoulder just then, and found herself gazing up at Lachlan's dark and handsome eyes.

"Am I interrupting?" he asked.

"Not at all." She handed her glass to Gordon, so that Lachlan could lead her onto the floor.

A thrill of anticipation shimmied up her spine.

"He's too old for you," Lachlan said with a smile, as they began to dance.

"He's exactly my own age," Onora replied. "If anyone is too old for anyone, I am the one who is far too worldly for you."

"But I, too, am worldly," he told her, leaning close. "I am an experienced man of war who has seen things most virtuous young lassies like yourself couldn't even begin to imagine."

" *'Virtuous young lassie'?*" Onora laughed out loud. "Are you drunk?"

"Does it matter?"

She smiled at him appreciatively, while an emotion she did not welcome began to grow inside her.

It was a feeling of affection, she supposed.

Or perhaps desperation.

Either way, it worried her.

"First you must learn how to select a sword," Angus said, as he unsheathed his claymore and held it out, point up, for Gwendolen to admire.

She had convinced him to teach her something about swordsmanship by telling him she would not remove her gown until he satisfied some of her curiosities.

"The basket-hilted broadsword is the best weapon for battle," he told her, "but even the mightiest blade is useless in the hands of a man—or woman—who is not calm or lacks judgment on the field."

"May I hold it?" she asked.

"Aye." He moved to stand behind her, and she reveled in the sensation of his body brushing up against hers. "Take it in your right hand like this. That's it. Now left foot forward."

She let him guide her into the proper stance.

"If I had my shield," he said, "I'd show you how to hold that, too, but since I don't, we'll just have to use our imaginations." He closed his hand around her left fist and lifted her arm. "You would hold it right here, like this, close to your face at an angle, or lower, to protect your sword arm, depending on what your opponent was doing. If you were charging into a bayonet line, you'd keep it low to guard your belly."

"Good Lord." She turned her head slightly to look up at him. "How in the world would you charge a bayonet line and live to tell about it?"

He moved around to face her again, and the instant he let go of her sword arm, the heavy point dropped to the floor.

He sat on the footboard of the bed, curling his big hands around it. "It's a sophisticated technique, lass. Only the strongest, most able of men can manage it."

She was both amused and aroused by his confidence. "And I suppose *you* fall into that category?"

"Aye. I'm the best there is."

"Is that a fact?" She leaned the sword against the wall by the door and smiled at him cheekily. "Why don't you describe to me the details of your supreme talents? I long to know them."

He inclined his head at her, then moved into position to demonstrate. "It goes something like this. You approach the bayonet line at a run, then dip low with the left leg, thrust the bayonet upward with your shield, then move ahead with your other foot, strike the soldier to the right with your sword, while you dirk the front-ranked man in the chest."

All her muscles went weak as he showed her the complex maneuver.

"That's it?" she replied, however, folding her arms at her chest. "Sounds simple enough."

In a flash, he scooped her into his arms and carried her to the bed. She shrieked with laughter and sighed when he came down upon her, kissing her deeply on the mouth.

"If you're not impressed by that," he said in a husky voice, "I will impress you some other way."

"I have no doubt that you will."

He tossed her skirts up and settled into a very different sort of charge that displayed an equally supreme set of skills.

For hours they made love without inhibitions, and each stroke of a finger, each kiss, each whisper of endearment, lifted their passions to new heights.

Gwendolen fell asleep in his arms, exhausted and satisfied. But not even the blissful haze of her dreams could diminish the terror she experienced when she woke up to an explosion of feathers beside her head, as a steel blade came slashing through the air and cut deep into Angus's pillow.

Chapter Fourteen

Instantly awake, Angus rolled off the bed just in time to avoid the strike. He leaped to his feet and strained to see through the darkness as the intruder sliced through his pillow and nearly took Gwendolen's head off in the process.

The prospect of her death hit him like a punch in the gut. It was followed by a wild fury of rage—and a debilitating dread that was completely unfamiliar to him, for he had never experienced a fear like this in any previous hand-to-hand combat. But he was not just thinking of himself tonight. There was another to protect.

Naked and unarmed, Angus backed away on agile feet to draw the man away from the bed. The enemy clansman was already spinning on a heel to swing his blade.

"Angus! Take this!"

Gwendolen tossed a dagger at him—the same one she had used to defend herself against him when he first came to her bed.

He caught it by the grip and tossed it into the air, then caught it again in an overhanded hold. Dropping to the floor, he rolled to avoid another swing of the intruder's sword. A pulse beat later, he was plunging the dirk into the Highlander's side.

The man crumpled forward with a raspy groan and fell to the floor, dead at Angus's feet.

He immediately disarmed the intruder, while Gwendolen scrambled across the bed and dashed into his arms.

"Are you all right, lass?" he asked. "Are you hurt?"

"I'm fine. Is he dead?"

"Aye." He crouched down to turn the Highlander over. "Go light a candle. I need to see this man's face."

Gwendolen moved to the table, fumbled with the flint, then struck a flame. She brought the candle closer and held it over the dead man's body.

"It's the MacEwen tartan," she said.

"Do you know him?"

"No, I've never seen him before. What was he doing here? How did he get in? The door was locked."

Angus searched the man's sporran, belts, and scabbards, then stood up and donned his own shirt and kilt. "He doesn't have a key on him now. Someone must have let him in." He belted his sword around his waist, then went to the door, which was slightly ajar, and looked up and down the corridor. "How many keys are there to this room, and who has access to them?"

"Besides the one you carry, there is only one other key, and my mother keeps it."

He looked at her fiercely. "Would she want me dead?"

"Of course not! She encouraged our alliance from the beginning."

He came back inside, and Gwendolen regarded him in the strangely sinister light from the candle. She felt as if she were falling headfirst into a nightmare. He had that look about him again—the ice-cold fury she had seen in his eyes on the day he invaded Kinloch. It was a callous bloodlust, and it sent a chill down her spine.

Nothing of the lover she had known since their wedding night existed in the man before her. Here stood a dangerous warrior, filled with fury, and she was frightened by his intensity.

"You cannot stay here tonight," he said. "You'll come to my bedchamber. I'll put a man at the door to watch over you."

"Where will you be?"

"I'll be looking into how this enemy got into my castle in the first place." He glared at her with steely wrath and held out his hand. "Come."

She put her hand in his and let him lead her out of the room, but first she had to step over the dead man on the floor.

His eyes were still open. Her stomach rolled with nausea.

Angus banged repeatedly on Lachlan's door until it opened. Gathering a loose gray blanket about his shoulders, Lachlan squinted through the flickering torchlight and stepped into the corridor.

"Get dressed," Angus said.

"Why? What's happened?"

"I woke up to the blade of an assassin."

Lachlan's eyes narrowed with concern. "Bluidy hell, Angus. Are you all right? Where's Gwendolen?"

"She's fine, but I must speak with Onora."

A few minutes later, he pushed his way through his mother-in-law's bedchamber door, and Lachlan followed him in. Onora sat up in bed and pulled a sheet up to cover her breasts.

"Have you been in here all night?" Angus asked.

"Of course," she replied. "Why? What is going on?"

Angus paced around the room like a tiger. "A Mac-Ewen warrior just entered your daughter's bedchamber and tried to murder me in my sleep."

"Good Lord!" She tossed the covers aside and rose to her feet, where she stood naked before them. "Is Gwendolen all right?"

He regarded her shrewdly, looking for signs of deceit or treachery. "She's safe. The assassin got into the room by way of a key. Gwendolen said you are the only other person at Kinloch, besides me, who keeps one."

"Aye." She hurried across the room to a cabinet with heavy doors, which contained a small chest. She carried the chest back to the table where a candle was burning, then opened the lid and sorted through a number of trinkets, mostly jewels and hair ornaments.

"It's not here," she said. "Someone must have taken it."

Angus strode around the bed and seized her by the wrist. "If you are lying to me . . ."

"I'm not!" she shouted.

He had half a mind to drag her to the dungeon and employ more ruthless tactics to draw the truth out of her, because something told him she was keeping secrets.

He glared at her in the dim candlelight, while she wet her lips and took in a shaky breath.

Lachlan laid a hand on his shoulder and squeezed gently. "Let's take a minute to think about this," he said in a relaxed tone. "Anyone could have stolen the key."

Angus let go of Onora's wrist, backed away and crossed to the other side of the room. Resting his hands on his hips, he bowed his head.

His temper was getting the better of him. He knew it. Lachlan was right. Neither the cabinet nor the chest was locked. Anyone could have come in and taken it. And he was sure to have many enemies bent on revenge. He'd killed a number of MacEwens during the invasion. Frankly, it was astonishing to him that there had not been an attempt on his life before now.

He turned and faced them both. Lachlan was standing with his arm out, handing a robe to Onora.

Angus realized suddenly that for the first time in his life, he had let his passion for a woman take precedence over his desire to fight and defend. When he was with Gwendolen, the whole world seemed to disappear into quiet waves of sensation, and nothing existed for him outside the pleasure they experienced together.

What astounded him most of all, however, was the fact that he had no desire to reverse it. All he wanted to do at this moment was use every skill and talent he possessed to discover who was behind this murderous attempt and ensure it never happened again—because nothing mattered to him more than Gwendolen's safety, especially now that she could be carrying his child. The drive to protect her was consuming him like a fever, and perhaps that was the most dangerous threat of all.

Late the next morning, Onora knocked on Gwendolen's door. Gwendolen invited her in and sent her maid down to the kitchen to bring back a light lunch.

"What is the latest news?" Gwendolen asked.

Onora sat down. "Angus and Lachlan both believe that Gordon MacEwen is the most likely suspect behind the assassination attempt, and I must say I concur."

Gwendolen sat down as well, and digested this news with concern. "Did you confess that you and Gordon were lovers?"

"Aye." Her mother began to chew on a thumbnail. "But they already knew it."

"How?"

She shifted uncomfortably and waved a dismissive hand through the air. "Oh, I might have said one or two things about it to Lachlan. I can't remember. We've been flirting for the past few weeks, and I seem to consume a lot of wine when I am in the same room with him. At least I think it's the wine that makes me so giddy." She shook her head. "But that is another matter. Your husband questioned me relentlessly this morning. He is positively ruthless. I must look a fright." She stood up, moved to the looking glass, and pinched her cheeks.

"You look fine, Mother. And yes, my husband is ruthless. That should come as no surprise to you. It's why everyone fears him, and why they do exactly what he tells them to do, the very second he commands it."

"Even *you*?" Onora swung around and regarded her with accusation.

For some strange reason, Gwendolen was overcome by a ridiculous urge to laugh. "I *want* to do what he asks," she replied. "Not out of fear, but out of loyalty. I know you wanted me to find a way to wield power over him, but it is the complete opposite between us. He has power over *me,* but not because I fear him. I want more from him, and I am beginning to believe that I would do anything to please him and win his affections. Anything."

Her mother gazed toward the window and resumed

chewing on her thumbnail. "You don't need to explain it, Gwendolen. I understand." She cleared her throat. "Do you have anything to drink in here? Whisky perhaps?"

Gwendolen noticed that her mother's hands were shaking. She went to pour a dram from the decanter on the table, then returned and handed it to her. "Did he hurt you?"

"No, it's not that. It's just . . ." She took a deep swig from the glass. "Suddenly I feel as if my world is spinning out of control. Nothing is the same as it was before the MacDonalds invaded. I have lost the powers I once had, and I feel confused and absentminded half the time." She looked away. "I am afraid I may be going a little mad."

"It's because of Lachlan," Gwendolen bluntly said. "You're falling in love with him."

Onora stared at her dubiously, then turned away. "No, I am not. He is far too young for me, and I am no fool. But this whole situation . . ." She poured herself another drink and swallowed it in a single gulp. "Your husband is a very frightening man, Gwendolen. There is something cold in his eyes. I half expected him to slit my throat this morning, without the slightest warning."

Gwendolen sat down. "I am sure he wouldn't do that."

But was she really sure? She had seen that look herself—that brutal, murderous contempt in his eyes. They could go from hot to cold in an instant.

When her mother finally seemed to regain her composure, she sat down also, and leaned back in the chair. "Gordon was implicated by the fact that he was the only person besides my personal maid who knew of the key's location. He denied any involvement of course, but he's being held nonetheless. They've locked up my maid, as well. Poor, sweet Madge. She's frightened out of her wits, and I cannot blame her. Something needs to be done, Gwendolen, but I was in such a hurry to escape the interrogation . . ."

"I will speak to Angus about it," she promised, "and ask if he will consider releasing her." Gwendolen paused. "Unless you think that she—"

"Oh, good gracious, no. Madge? She would never go behind my back to steal a key, or anything else for that matter. She is as loyal as they come."

"Not even if Gordon forced her, or bribed her?"

Onora considered it for a moment, then chewed on her thumbnail again. "I suppose one never truly knows who can be trusted. These are desperate times."

They sat in silence for a few minutes.

"Has anyone been able to identify the assassin?" Gwendolen asked.

"No. There was not a single MacEwen, or MacDonald for that matter, who recognized him. It was as if he flew into Scotland from some foreign land, like a migrating bird of prey." She took another sip of whisky. "Speaking of birds, I believe that tiny swallow in the Great Hall has departed for good. She flew out the door on your wedding day, and no one has seen her since."

"Is that right?" Gwendolen asked, hiding the fact that she already knew. She was extremely mindful of the little bird's whereabouts, for she had dreamed of her death in the jaws of a raven on the eve of their nuptials. Gwendolen had told no one about the dream, not even Angus, for it seemed like a bad omen, and now she was beginning to think that's exactly what it was.

She decided she would pay closer attention to her

dreams in the future. And perhaps she would tell Angus about them.

But for now, she would focus on getting Madge released from the prison.

Chapter Fifteen

Gwendolen lay in bed in the darkness, waiting for Angus. For a fortnight, she had seen very little of him. Not only did he continue to investigate the failed attempt on his life—and sometimes left the castle for hours on end to scout the surrounding forests and glens—he also worked with his army in the bailey to improve their fighting skills.

By the time he climbed into bed each night, he was exhausted and had no interest in the playful, extended lovemaking sessions she had grown accustomed to in the early weeks of their marriage. The man she had come to know on those rainy afternoons had disappeared and been replaced by the dark, brooding conqueror who had invaded her home and killed so many of her clansmen. He had retreated into that shadow of violence and cynicism, and had taken with him any hope she might have entertained that there could eventually be more intimacy or affection between them. She knew now that he was a warrior, first and foremost. That came before anything.

She did not complain, however, nor would she ever do so—for his leadership of Kinloch and the safety of its people was a primary concern. Deep down, however, she was lonely. Each time she remembered how it felt to be held in his arms at night, she felt a terrible sense of loss.

A key slipped into the lock, and the bedchamber door swung open. Light from the corridor spilled across the floor, and Gwendolen sat up on her elbows, squinting at her husband as he entered and shut the door behind him.

"Go back to sleep," he said, removing the pistol from his belt and setting it on the bedside table. Next he removed the powder horn that was slung over his shoulder, and last, his heavy belt, sword, and shield.

"Where were you today?" she asked. "Did you have any supper?"

"I just ate with the men." He moved to the chair before the fire, sank into it, and stretched his legs out.

Gwendolen tossed the covers aside. Slowly, she moved across the room and knelt in front of him. "Can I do anything for you?"

Perhaps he would ask her to make love to him while he lounged back in the chair—for already, her body was humming with desire. She ran her hands up and down his forearms, stroking the muscle and brushing her fingertips over his large, battle-scarred hands.

He tipped his head back against the chair and closed his eyes, shaking his head in refusal.

Wondering if he simply needed some soothing pleasures to inspire his passions, she slid her hands up under his kilt and massaged his muscular thighs, but he surprised her by lifting his head and grabbing hold of her wrists. His eyes were cold and gray like winter ice, his voice threatening.

"I said *no*." He tossed his head in a commanding

gesture that indicated the bed. "And I told you to go back to sleep. I'll have no defiance from you tonight, lass. Go. Leave me be."

She sat back on her heels, withdrew her hands from under his kilt, and frowned at him. "Did something happen today?"

"It was a day like any other," he said, "but I am weary. I'm in no mood to talk or do anything else. I've already said it once. Now *go*."

Hearing the sharp note of impatience in his voice, Gwendolen stood and worked hard to suppress the hurt she felt over this rejection—which was both sexual and personal. She had begun to hope that she would be a solace for him when the pressures of his position as laird grew oppressive. She wanted to ease the burdens he carried. She wanted to provide him with pleasures outside of the violence and hardships of battle, to be the one who welcomed him home at night, patched up his wounds, and built up his strength so that he could rise again the next day and fight.

But he did not want that from her—at least not tonight, when he saw her only as an extra chore that was making him irritable.

Her head throbbed suddenly with indignation, for she was no man's chore. She had only wanted to do something to ease his burdens.

"I'll leave you alone then." She stalked across the room. "I'll go back to my own bedchamber."

"Nay!" he shouted, leaning forward in his chair. "You'll do as I say, lass, and get back in this bed, here in this room. I'll not have you tiptoeing about the castle corridors at night."

"Fine!" She returned to the bed, climbed up onto it,

and shoved her feet under the covers. "I'll stay here, and I won't bother you with another sound!"

She wrenched the covers up, wishing she could be more docile, but there was no hope of that. She wanted certain things from this marriage—and his complete emotional withdrawal was not one of them.

Angus watched Gwendolen from the chair as she shot back into bed like a musket ball. He knew she was angry with him. Hell, it was as obvious as a bucking horse in the kitchen.

He also knew that he wasn't cut out for this. He'd thought he could manage this marriage when he'd claimed her as a wife. He'd thought it would be a simple matter of wedding her and bedding her a few times until she was with child. But the sex had proved far more intense than he'd imagined, and the wife more appealing and intriguing than any woman he'd ever encountered, and that created a problem. Keeping his mind on his duties—while she was wandering about the castle in her pretty frocks, smelling like roses—was like wading upstream through rushing water.

He bent forward, cupped his forehead in a hand, then raked his fingers through his hair. His desires made no sense to him. He wanted her, yet at the same time he wanted to send her away.

Turning in his chair, he looked at her gruffly. She was lying on her side with her back to him. She had the covers pulled up to her ears like an angry child.

He had offended her. She was making that abundantly clear. Was she crying?

Ah, bloody hell. What if she was?

He sat back and rubbed a hand over his face, then

rose from the chair and slipped into bed behind her. He snuggled close, tucked his knees into the backs of hers, and leaned up on an elbow. Brushing the hair away from her face, he said, "You want to kick me in the nuggets, don't you?"

"Aye," she flatly said. "You were very rude."

He was quiet for a minute. "I'm sorry, lass. It was a long day. I was tired and grouchy. What can I do to make it up to you?"

God! Was he really saying these things? Did she have any idea that it was bloody earth-shattering? Not once in his rough and hellish life had he ever groveled to anyone, except maybe his father when he was just a lad facing a beating.

But never to a woman. Not once. Not ever.

"There is nothing you can do," she replied, "because you already told me you are too weary for anything, and alas, I have disobeyed you sufficiently by not going straight back to sleep."

The ill-tempered mood that had festered inside him all day cracked a small, reluctant smile, and he shook his head at these unbelievable circumstances—for his pretty little trophy bride suddenly seemed to have him wrapped around her finger.

"Sometimes," he said, "you drive me so mad with frustration that I think I'm going to lose my mind, and it's almost comical. Do you know that?"

"You didn't find it amusing five minutes ago."

"Nay, and that's the shock of it. You're the only person in Scotland who can crush my wrath and mash it to wee bits in the space of a single minute."

She rolled over onto her back and blinked up at him with those big, beautiful brown eyes. Something inside him snapped at the sight of her wholesomeness. She was like a fluttering butterfly he wanted to catch and hold in his hands.

Then she pinched him hard on the shoulder.

"Och!" he shouted. "What was that for?"

"You deserved it."

He immediately rolled on top of her. "So I did. Does that mean we are even now?"

"No, we most certainly are not."

He began to slowly pump his hips. "Then I'll ask you again, lass. How can I make it up to you?"

She wiggled beneath him, and his erection increased sizably.

"You can make love to me, Angus. And do your absolute best to pleasure me greatly, and enjoy it yourself, as well."

"There will be no difficulty there," he replied. "I'm already having the time of my life."

"Well, I am not. I am still angry with you. You were a brute just now."

He kissed her softly on both eyelids. "Aye, but you'll soon forgive me when I slide into your warm, sweet pastry and make you tremble with rapture."

"My pastry? Good God, you are without a hope."

He reached down to move his kilt and her shift out of the way, slipped his fingers into the luscious damp haven between her thighs to ensure she was ready for him—which she most definitely was—then he thrust into her with extravagant, soul-gratifying ease.

She arched her back and closed her eyes. "Ah, yes, that is *perfect . . .*"

He moved slowly in and out, deeply and compellingly. "Do you forgive me now?"

She nodded, and he took his time over the next hour, making sure she did not change her mind.

When she finally drifted off to sleep, sated and restful in his arms, he wondered if he would ever be able to sleep like that—so soundly, without one eye constantly open, watching for danger, awaiting death in the night, and fearing the loss of her and everything else that he cherished. He was no stranger to loss, and he could not seem to escape the expectation of it.

And so, an hour later, he slipped out of the bed and left the chamber. He headed to the place where he went each night in search of solace. He had never found it before, and sometimes he wondered why he even bothered to try.

But something inside him felt different tonight.

Perhaps it was the awareness of hope.

Chapter Sixteen

Gwendolen sat up in the darkness when she heard the sound of the door open and close.

She was not surprised that Angus had left. There was a discord in his life and heart, and she could feel it in her own. She also knew that he had no interest in discussing it with her. Since the beginning, he had deflected most personal questions in an effort to keep her at a distance, and when he did not want her to press him, he either left the room completely, or reacted with anger and violence, frightening her into a corner. Sometimes he made love to her, which was always an effective distraction.

Tonight, however, for the first time, he had shown some remorse and had apologized for his harsh behavior. It had given her hope that perhaps one day he would open his heart to her more fully.

She lay back down and stared up at the canopy, but knew she would never be able to sleep. She wanted him beside her, and she wanted to understand why he had left in the first place.

Slipping out of bed, she found her shift on the floor, donned a shawl, and padded across the room. She peered out into the corridor and heard his footsteps at the bottom of the stairs, then hurried out to follow him.

She tiptoed over the cold stones, passed by flickering torchlights, and clutched at her shift to keep the drafts from blowing up under it. She ventured through the arched passageways to the chapel, where she finally found Angus kneeling at the altar, his head bowed low.

Of all the places she expected him to be, this was not one of them.

She stood quietly in the doorway, waiting for him to finish, but before she could think about what she was going to say, or how she would approach him, he spun instantly on his knee and drew his pistol.

"It's only me!" she shouted, lifting her hands as her panicked cry echoed up into the high, vaulted ceiling.

He stared at her for a few seconds, then shoved the pistol back into his belt and rose to his feet. He stalked down the aisle toward her. *"Have you got rocks in your head, lass? I could have killed you!"*

"I'm sorry! I didn't think of that. I woke and you were gone. I was worried."

He stopped cold, halfway down the aisle. "You were worried. About *me*?" He shook his head with disbelief, as if she were the biggest fool in the world.

For a long moment, he stared at her in the smoky candlelight, then his shoulders rose and fell with a defeated sigh, and he held out his hand. "Ah, lass, you'll be the death of me. Come in, then. It's drafty in the door." He glanced down. "Where are your shoes?"

"I'm not made of sugar," she replied. "I can survive a chilly floor." Though the bones in her feet were beginning to throb.

He led her to the front pew closest to the candles that were burning near the choir stall, and she crossed herself before taking a seat. He sat down beside her, told her to swing her legs up onto his lap, then proceeded to massage her cold feet in his big warm hands.

"You may be interested to know," she said, "that when my father was chief, he did not permit weapons in the chapel."

Angus lifted his eyes. "What's your point, lass?"

"No point. It just occurred to me now, and I thought you might care to know."

"Because I almost committed a terrible sin just now? *Thou shalt not murder thy wife in the chapel*'?"

"That's not a commandment," she said.

The corner of his mouth curled up in a sly grin. "Maybe not, but it should be."

She chuckled back at him. "Aye, I suppose it should. But if we're going to add that, we should also add: 'Thou shalt not murder thy *husband* in the chapel.' "

He continued to rub the arch of her foot. "Aye, I reckon that's only fair."

When he finished massaging her feet, she lowered her legs to the floor, and they both faced the altar, gazing up at the stained-glass window of the Virgin Mary.

"May I ask you something?" Gwendolen kept her gaze fixed on the window, but from the corner of her eye, she was aware of his eyes on her profile. He gave no answer, so she took that as a yes. "Why did you leave our bed to come here in the middle of the night? And I know this is not the first time."

He, too, looked up at the Virgin Mary. "To pray."

"For what?"

She waited patiently to hear his answer, but he seemed determined to take his time. At last, he bowed his head and pinched the bridge of his nose.

"Tonight I started with the usual prayer for my mother's soul, though I doubt she needs it. She was a saint. At least that's how I remember her. Then I prayed for my own sins, for the people of Kinloch who have entrusted me with their safety and prosperity, and when you walked in, I was just getting to my own treachery two years ago, and praying not only for God's forgiveness, but for my father's forgiveness as well."

Gwendolen turned to look at him. "Because you betrayed your friend." She remembered how he spoke of it at his triumphal feast. She had thought of it many times since then. "You did not approve of his choice of a wife."

"Aye."

"Do you believe now that you were wrong about that woman? That she was not such a bad person?"

"I never thought she was a bad person," he told her. "I just didn't agree with what she stood for. My friend was a loyal Scot, but she was English and betrothed to our enemy, a despicable redcoat who is burning in hell as we speak, and rightly so. I only wish I had put him there myself."

He glanced at her and seemed to realize that he had spoken out of turn, considering where they were sitting.

Gwendolen cared little about that. This was a place for forgiveness. "Why?" she asked. "What terrible crime did that Englishman commit?"

He faced front again. "He went on a bloody rampage up and down the Great Glen, burning out innocent Scots for their mere knowledge of the Jacobite rebellion."

"Are you referring to Lieutenant Colonel Richard Bennett?" she asked, her brows pulling together.

"You've heard of him?"

"Of course," she answered. "Everyone knows of him. He was a dreadful villain, and he was defeated and killed by the Butcher of the Highlands two years ago."

Angus stared at her for a long, tense moment, and again, she wondered if he was keeping something from her. On the night of his invasion, she had asked him if he was the infamous Scottish Butcher, but he had denied it.

"It was your friend, wasn't it?" she said, putting two and two together, and reeling inside with this new knowledge of her husband. "The man that you betrayed—*he* was the Butcher of the Highlands."

Angus immediately shook his head. "The Butcher is naught but a ghost and a legend. But even if I did know him, I would never say so. Not even to you, lass."

Gwendolen gazed into her husband's pale blue eyes and saw, for herself, the truth. She had guessed correctly—that he once rode with that famous Scottish rebel, and that he had betrayed him. She knew the story well. Someone had informed the English army about the Butcher's whereabouts, which was why he was caught and imprisoned.

This was why Angus was banished two years ago. *This* was why he harbored such guilt. He was the one who had revealed the Butcher's hideout.

Angus faced the window. "But I'm beginning to see now that what existed between that Englishwoman and my friend was something I did not understand, and I had no right to judge him."

She did not push him to confess any more than he already had, for that would only press him to betray this friend further, and she did not wish to do that.

"What has changed, to make you see that now?" she asked, believing she already knew the answer, but she wanted to hear him say it.

"Because since the first day I met you, I would have done anything to keep you safe and make you my own. I now know that what exists between us is the same as what existed between them. I was your enemy at first, and you were just a political pawn to me, but it wasn't long before none of it mattered." He turned his eyes toward the altar again. "It was the same for my friend."

"But you *tried* to make it matter with us," she said. "You are *still* trying. You don't want to care for me, Angus. Admit it."

"I am the son of a clan chief," he shot back quickly. "I was raised to be a warrior, for the purpose of serving and leading the MacDonalds, who have honored me by placing themselves in my care."

"Loving me will not change that."

She realized too late what she had said, and dropped her gaze to her lap. She should not have used the word "love." He did not want to love her. She knew that.

"You are a good wife," he said. "I have no regrets."

She felt a rush of heat in her cheeks. "Because I please you in bed?"

He leaned close and cupped her chin in his hand. "Aye, but it's more than that, and you know it. It's why I've become so irritable lately. Sometimes, I need you so bad, I just want to drop my sword in the middle of a training exercise and leave the men to their own devices, so I can take you to bed. But when I think about you coming to any harm, I want to pick up my sword again. You pull me in two directions, lass."

She shivered inwardly. "Maybe that's how your friend felt about you and the Englishwoman. He must have been torn between the two of you, and it was probably very difficult for him to choose her, when he knew you did not approve."

One of the candles danced in a draft, and they both turned to look at the door. There was no one there, so they faced front again, but it took a moment for Gwendolen's heart to slow down.

"Do you regret your lost friendship?" she asked. "And do you think it might help to contact your friend? You could send him a letter and apologize for what you did, and explain that you now understand the choice he made."

Angus shook his head. "There is no way to apologize. What I did was beyond forgiveness."

"Nothing is ever beyond that, not if you truly express your regret. God, at least, will be merciful."

He gave her a questionable look. "So I should write this letter, just to secure an invitation to heaven?"

She relaxed her shoulders. "Of course not. You should do it for the right reasons—to mend your friendship and honor this man with your apology. Perhaps he regrets the loss of your friendship, as well, and besides that, I would like the opportunity to meet him."

It was no lie. The Butcher of the Highlands was a famous Scottish hero.

Angus toyed with the hair over her ear, and the light touch of his fingers made her body tingle with gooseflesh.

"You are a wise woman, lass. I'll be sure to consider it."

"Will you come back to bed now?" she asked.

"Aye, after I say one more prayer."

She stood up, but still held his hand. "Do you wish to be alone?"

"Just for a short while," he replied. "I still need to pray for my father, so that if we meet again in the afterlife, he'll not thrash me senseless, like he did the last time he saw me."

Gwendolen gathered her shawl about her shoulders. "I am sure that if he is watching you from above, he is very proud. You reclaimed his castle after all."

Angus shook his head. "How can you say that, when your own father must be rolling over in his grave, seeing you wed to me? I am the son of his enemy."

She looked up at the cross over the altar. "I believe he would have understood why I accepted you—that I did it for my clan."

"You made a great sacrifice, lass."

"Perhaps. But it's turning out to be less of one than I first imagined." She turned to go.

"Wait for me here," he said. "I'll be brief, and I don't want you wandering through the castle alone at night. Someone might kidnap you and hold you for ransom, and I'm beginning to think I'd pay any price to get you back."

"*Any* price?" she replied, with a spark of hope.

"Aye. I'm your husband, lass. I'd die for you."

A tremor of emotion shook her, for she was unprepared for such a strong vow of commitment from him, and she found herself wondering: was it duty? Or was it something more?

For her, it was far more than duty that kept her bound to him.

"Let us hope it never comes to that," she said. She glanced uneasily at the pews directly across from him, then slid into one of them. "But perhaps, just to be safe, I will wait for you here and say my own prayers."

"And what will you pray for?" he asked.

She thought about it briefly, then cupped her hands together and rested them on the back of the pew in front of her. "I'll pray that one day, you will be reunited with your friend, and he will forgive you." She gave him a knowing, sidelong glance. "I'm sure the Butcher of the Highlands has committed enough of his own sins to forgive you for yours."

Her husband pointed a warning finger at her.

"Don't worry," she said with a mischievous grin. "I'll carry your secret to my grave."

The following day, Angus sat down at his desk, picked up his quill pen, and dipped it into the porcelain ink well:

September 13, 1718
Dear Lord Moncrieffe,

I wonder if you will even break the seal on this letter, once you recognize the Kinloch crest. Perhaps I am about to waste a quantity of ink, but I must make the effort, for I owe you that at least, and so much more.

It has been two years since we last spoke, and no doubt you learned of my banishment and my father's death soon after. While I was exiled, Kinloch fell to the MacEwen clan, but I have recently returned and reclaimed my father's home. I have taken a wife, the daughter of the MacEwen chief, in order to unite the two clans.

But I am certain you are well aware of my return, and the status of Kinloch. That is not why I write to you now. My only purpose is to express my heartfelt regret over what occurred when last we spoke.

Duncan—I was wrong in every way. I have spent the past two years repenting my unspeakable treachery, and will never forget, or forgive myself, for what I did to you.

My lessons are now even more deeply ingrained upon my tarnished soul, for I have found myself in a position not unlike your own, when you first encountered the woman who was to become your wife. I did not understand the complexity of your predicament, but I see the world more clearly now, and I cannot possibly express my remorse over the events of 1716.

I close in penitence and despair over my ruthless and brutal actions. I pray for you and your countess, and wish you every happiness. And let it be known that as long as I am Laird of Kinloch Castle, you will have allies here.

Yours truly,
Angus Bradach MacDonald

He took a moment to reflect upon the ache of regret that had settled in his chest two years ago, and resided there still. Especially now, as he wrote this letter.

There had once been a time when he was indifferent

to the pain of others, but he had taken that callousness too far. His closest friend was the Butcher of the Highlands, and he had revealed his hideout to the English army as a punishment for taking an English bride.

He'd had two years to think on it and contemplate his shame. Two years alone on the edge of the world, pummeled by wind, rain, and ice, and the harsh, biting spray of the ocean . . .

But that was another life. He was home now. Everything was different.

He sprinkled sand on the letter, blew it clean, sealed it, and rose from his chair. A knock sounded at his door, but when he answered, he discovered it was not the courier he had sent for twenty minutes ago.

"Lachlan. What are you doing here?"

His friend's cheeks were white as a sheet. "You have a visitor."

"A visitor? Who is it?" He tucked the letter into his sporran.

"It's that woman you kept in the Hebrides—the one who predicted your time would come, and that the MacEwens would hear your roar, and all that silly witchy babble."

Angus felt a rush of dread in his gut. "Raonaid is here?"

God! A sickening wave of nausea rose up inside him instantly. What was she doing here? There could be only one reason.

"Aye," Lachlan replied. "The oracle. But you better hurry. She's breaking all the crockery in the kitchen. The staff is scattering like rats, and the cook has locked himself in the wine cellar. It's not a good situation."

Angus headed for the stairs. "What the hell is she doing in the kitchen? Who took her there? You should have brought her to me straightaway."

"She was hungry," Lachlan explained. "And someone made the mistake of telling her you took a wife. That's when she started breaking things."

"Aye. That sounds like Raonaid. You better follow me, Lachlan, and stay close." He glanced over his shoulder when he reached the bottom of the stairs. "Is she armed?"

"Damned if I know. No one could get close enough to search her."

Chapter Seventeen

By the time Angus entered the kitchen—which was in a terrible shambles, strewn with shards of broken crockery and spilled milk—Raonaid was seated alone at a table, dipping a spoon into a bowl of steaming-hot stew.

Before he made a sound or uttered a word, her sharp eyes lifted, blue as the winter sea, and she regarded him with knowing intensity, as if she'd already sensed his coming. He felt the penetration of her gaze like a knife in the gut.

Slowly he approached, taking in her overall appearance, while avoiding the obvious reason for her arrival, which he was not yet ready to confront.

Her russet-colored hair was tidy and clean. It fell past her shoulders in rich, curly waves. If not for the tattered woolen gown of faded umber and the complete absence of jewels, she would look as proud and superior as any woman of noble heritage. Everything about her conveyed an impression of pompous arrogance, but it was all a pretense. A clever affectation. For her upbringing was anything but regal.

Having been born with an unnatural gift of sight, she had spent the whole of her life as a social outcast, living in a grubby thatched hut on the outer fringes of

the world. Her notoriety as a witch had even reached
the Scottish mainland. People feared and despised her.
Some said she had the mark of the devil etched on
her skin, while others pitied her and prayed for her mad,
tragic soul.

Her family origins were unknown. She was raised
on the Western Isles by an eccentric old woman who died
when Raonaid was eleven. Whether or not the woman
was her mother, no one knew—not even Raonaid, who
chose to remain on the islands after her caregiver's
death, seeking comfort in her strange collection of bones
and potions. Eventually she matured into a resourceful
young woman—attractive and sexually alluring—but no
man wanted her, nor did she offer herself to anyone.

Her only comforts and pleasures came from her visions in the stone circles. Sometimes she saw the future.
Other times she saw herself living a parallel life in a different world.

Until Angus entered her life.

He had not feared her, as others did.

Dabbing at her mouth with a napkin, Raonaid set
down her spoon. She slid off the stool and approached
him.

He had not forgotten how beautiful she was. A man
could stumble and fall into that lush cleavage and disappear for a year.

"It took you long enough," she said. "Do you know
what your guards put me through? They weren't even
going to let me through the gates."

Lachlan interrupted. "They won't make that mistake again, Raonaid. They know who you are now, and
won't soon forget you." He nudged Angus in the side.
"She told one of the guards that she was seeing his

future, and he should expect all his hair to fall out before Christmas."

Angus shook his head. "Raonaid, if you'd been patient, I would have come to greet you properly."

"Just listen to you," she said, with a snide look in her eye.

Returning to the table, she picked up her spoon and resumed eating.

Angus and Lachlan stood in silence, watching her.

"Is that it?" Lachlan whispered, leaning close. "After smashing half the kitchen to bits, that's all she's going to say to you?"

Angus watched her for a long, tense moment, then approached. "What brings you here, Raonaid? You said you'd never leave the islands, and you also said you were overjoyed to see the arse end of me when I left."

"I was," she replied, "and I don't want you back, if that's what you think. I came here because of what I saw in the stones."

A cold knot tightened in his stomach. Raonaid's strongest visions had always come from the standing stones at Calanais. She was often drawn to them by dreams. It was there she had seen his father's death, predicted Lachlan's arrival, and foretold Angus's ultimate triumph over the MacEwens at Kinloch.

He recalled also, however, a promise he had forced her to make—that if she ever saw *his* death in the stones, she would come to him.

"Are you here to fulfil your pledge?" he asked.

"Aye."

He swallowed hard, then spoke matter-of-factly. "When? How much time do I have?"

"Weeks. Maybe a month, at most."

He had often wondered how he would react to the knowledge of his imminent death. He'd imagined he would accept it with a sense of calm, for he was not without courage. He was a warrior, and had lived a violent existence. For that reason, he always imagined his life would end in an instant, and there would be no time to contemplate much of anything.

In this strange moment, however, he could think of only one thing—Gwendolen—and how he was not yet ready to leave her. He had only just found her, and what if he had put a child in her womb? He could not leave this world if he was about to become a father. He could not leave them alone.

A terrible panic erupted inside him, and he had to fight against the overwhelming urge to vault over the table and shake Raonaid senseless, to demand that she confess that this was a trick—a cruel joke for her own twisted amusement. But he knew she would never leave the Hebrides and journey across the Highlands for a mere moment's entertainment. She was not that easily amused.

"How much do you know?" he asked. "How will it happen?"

She slid off the stool and sauntered around the table. "You'll die by the noose," she told him.

Willing himself to remain calm, he rested a hand on the hilt of his sword. "Will I be taken to Fort William? Or Edinburgh? Will I be charged with treason as a Jacobite?"

"I cannot answer why. All I know is that it will happen here. I couldn't have told you that until I passed through the gates. I recognized it immediately—the four corner towers, the rooftop and battalions. I saw it all in the stones."

Here? No . . . It could not be . . . It had to be a mistake.

"Who is responsible?" he asked. "Is there a traitor here? Is it Gordon MacEwen?"

Raonaid rested a warm, slender hand on his cheek, and regarded him with an expression of pity.

That, he could not tolerate.

"Dammit, woman. *Speak!*"

"You are betrayed by your wife," she explained. "I saw that in the stones, too."

Angus slowly backed away from her. "Nay," he said. "It is another woman. Not her."

"It *is* her," Raonaid insisted. "Unless you are sharing your bed with someone else. Are you?"

"Of course not."

"Then it is her. The stones never lie. I saw you making love to her, and then I saw them drag you away."

"Who?" he asked in a threatening voice. "Who drags me? I must know."

"I wish I could tell you that, Angus. Truly I do, but your enemies have hid themselves well. They would not show their faces."

He took hold of her arms and shook her. "What of their clothes? Were they redcoats? Or did they wear the tartan of the MacEwens?"

"I told you, I do not know those details! All I know is that *she* disarms you. She breaks you down, weakens you, and invites them in. You must leave this place, Angus."

Lachlan grabbed hold of his arm. "Don't believe her. She's mad."

Angus shook him away. "I cannot ignore her prophecies. Too many of them have come to pass. I never would have returned to claim Kinloch if she had not seen my father's death, predicted your arrival, and promised me a great triumph."

"But we need you here," Lachlan argued. "You cannot let a witch drive you out, in fear of your own death."

Angus started for the door. "I fear nothing, and I have no intention of deserting my clan. But I will not accept that I will be dead in a month. I will do what I can to prevent it."

Raonaid followed him and offered a quiet piece of advice. "Practice with your sword," she said. "Stay strong. Be the warrior you were born to be. Do not let yourself become weak or distracted."

After Angus left the kitchen, Raonaid stood in the arched doorway watching him go, then turned and faced Lachlan. He stalked toward her and pulled her roughly up against him.

"I want you to listen to me," he said in a low growl, "and listen very carefully, witch. If you have come here to stir up deceit and treachery, I will not stand for it. I will hunt you down, wherever you are, and I will slit your throat."

Raonaid laughed in his face. "Go ahead and try," she spat. "But I won't die by *your* sword, Lachlan Mac-Donald."

"Nay?" His gaze dipped lower to her moist, full lips and ample bosom, then lifted again. "Tell me, then. Whose sword will end your sorry life, Raonaid? I'll want to congratulate the man."

She pushed him away, then hauled back and punched him across the jaw. He cursed and doubled over in pain.

"No man will ever have that honor," she said. "Because I will live a long and happy life. Then, when my time comes, I will die in my sleep—a very old and wealthy woman."

Lachlan wiped his bloodied lip with the back of his hand, and worked his jaw back and forth to ensure it wasn't broken. "You are insane," he said. "You always were."

She scowled at him. "You're just angry because I wouldn't lift my skirts for you that night in the tavern. I'm the only woman alive who didn't fall prey to your handsome face and teasing charms."

He glanced down at the blood on the back of his hand and headed for the door. "Thank God for small mercies."

Gwendolen whirled around when the door to the weaving room swung open and slammed shut. Angus walked in and looked around at the three MacEwen clanswomen. Two were seated at spinning wheels. The third was sitting by the loom.

"Leave us," he commanded. They took one look at the fire in his eyes, rose from their stools, and scurried out of the room while the wheels were still turning.

"What's going on?" Gwendolen asked.

He crossed toward her, scrutinizing her face and every inch of her body from head to foot. "Are you going to betray me?"

"I beg your pardon?" Her temper flared. "Of course not!"

"Swear it on your life," he said.

"Of course I swear it!"

The wheels finally stopped turning, and he glowered at her in the quiet stillness of the room.

"I don't understand," she said, as he began to pace.

"Why are you asking me this? I made a promise to you before our wedding day. I pledged my allegiance. What makes you doubt it?"

He picked up a ball of wool thread and tossed it into the air. "I have reason to believe that you want me dead, lass, and that you'll be responsible for my head in a noose, right here at Kinloch. Are you conspiring with Gordon MacEwen? Were you the one who told him where the key was?"

She couldn't believe what she was hearing, but her shock was short-lived as fury took its place. "You are insane. Who told you this?"

"Never mind who told me. Answer the question."

She moved around a spinning wheel and approached him. "I am not conspiring with Gordon MacEwen. How could I be, when he is locked up in prison? I am loyal to *you*. I don't want you to die. I want you to live. Especially now that . . ."

She stopped. She couldn't say it. Not now. This was not how she'd imagined it.

"Especially now that what?" he asked.

She shook her head and deflected the question. "I don't understand you. Is it because of what happened a fortnight ago, when that man tried to kill you? Has there been some development?"

"Nay."

"Then what is it? You know you have my loyalty, Angus. Don't you? Can you not feel it?"

He watched her with dark, threatening mistrust as she moved closer to him. "Are you like your mother?" he asked. "Are you some puppet master who uses sex to turn a man into a blathering idiot?"

Panic rose up inside her. "No! And I don't understand where this is coming from. Why do you suspect me of these things? If someone has said something to smear my name, then they are trying to sabotage this marriage and the union of our clans. Do you not see that?" She took his face in her hands. "I have come to care for you, Angus, and we have shared many pleasures together. All I want is to live a long and happy life with you, here at Kinloch. You must believe me. I will never betray you."

He stared into her eyes with ice-cold bitterness.

"You don't believe me." She backed away. "Someone has turned you against me. Who has made these accusations? You owe me the truth, at least, if you intend to brand me as a traitor."

A muscle clenched at his jaw, then he walked to the window. "Raonaid is here."

Her belly began to churn. "The oracle? The woman who shared your bed in the Hebrides?"

What in the world had she said to him? And *why* did she come here? What did she hope to achieve?

"Aye," he replied, "but she shared more than my bed, lass. She shared her visions, as well, and I saw that they were real. She foretold my father's passing, and Lachlan's arrival, and my triumph here at Kinloch. When I left her, I made her promise that if she ever saw my death, she would come to me and warn me of it." He faced her squarely. "She has seen it, lass, and she has held true to her word. That is why she is here."

Not yet ready to believe this, Gwendolen moved to stand before him. "What exactly did she see?"

"My head in a noose. She also told me that a woman would betray me." He scrutinized her expression closely. "That woman will be you."

Gwendolen digested this information. *A noose. A woman would betray him . . .*

"When did she see this?"

"Weeks ago, at Calanais."

She worked over the details in her mind and clung to the absolute certainty that she would never betray her husband. Raonaid was wrong.

"Perhaps she was seeing the dispatch I sent to Colonel Worthington at Fort William," Gwendolen suggested. "In it, I wrote that I wanted him to come and take you away by force, and hang you at the gallows. I wanted it very badly at the time. I have no excuse, but you already know this, because you read the letter yourself. You burned it, remember?"

He regarded her with suspicion.

"I confess that when I wrote it," Gwendolen continued, "I was sincere in my wish to see you hanged, but afterward, I faced your wrath and regretted my actions. I meant it when I pledged my allegiance." She moved closer to him and laid her hands on his chest, willing him to believe her. "Since then, we have spoken vows before God to unite us as man and wife. I have given my body to you willingly." She paused. "Surely what Raonaid saw was a moment out of the past. That is all. I do not fault her for coming here. I would have done the same, but Colonel Worthington came here and met with you, and he did not do what I asked him to do, and thank God for that, because I do not want you dead. I want you to live. I *need* you to live."

He took hold of her hands and held them away from him. "How do I know I can trust you? You betrayed me once before, after you gave me your word that you would be loyal."

"Things were different then." He did not seem convinced, so she made another desperate attempt to prove to him that she could be trusted. "And today, they are different yet again."

"How so?"

She placed a hand on her belly, and felt a strange mixture of joy and anguish. "Because I was ill the past three mornings. I've had no flux."

For days, she had been anticipating this moment. She'd hoped to tell Angus the news in the Great Hall in front of the clans. She knew how pleased he would be, and imagined him gathering her into his arms, perhaps lifting her into the air.

He did none of those things now. The ice in his eyes grew more frigid than ever.

"How do I know this isn't a trick meant to distract me from some other treachery?"

"Is that what you think?" Sudden tears of rage pooled in her eyes. "Do you truly believe that I would lie about something like this?"

"I don't know what to believe. Raonaid has never been wrong before."

"So you'll believe her over me?"

She wanted to hit him, to scream at him, punch him, and demand that he take her side. She was his wife, and that woman was known all over Scotland as a mad witch!

He took hold of her arm and dragged her out of the room. "Come with me."

"Where are we going?"

"Back to your chamber, and I'll send for a midwife to examine you. I want to know if you're telling me the truth."

"Angus, how dare you!" Besieged by anger and disbelief, she struggled to pry his fingers off her arm, but he possessed an iron grip.

"I need to know, lass. There can be no lies between us."

"There are none!" she shouted. *"And I will never forgive you for this!"*

He dragged her down the stairs and through the stone passageways of the castle. "I'll believe you about the child when the midwife tells me it is so."

"I suppose it'll be a MacDonald midwife," she retorted, "and not a MacEwen?"

"Aye, and I'll be choosing the woman myself. At least that way, I'll know I'm not being deceived again."

He shoved her into the room and looked at her harshly, before he shut the door in her face and locked her in.

Chapter Eighteen

The midwife arrived within the hour to examine Gwendolen and confirmed that her womb was enlarged. Given her symptoms, it was therefore almost certain that she was expecting a child.

Gwendolen thanked the woman and escorted her to the door. "Will you inform my husband of the happy news?"

She spoke with cynical, false delight, but the midwife failed to recognize her mockery. Her eyes danced with joy. "Aye, madam, but he's waiting just outside the door. Perhaps you'd like to tell him yourself?"

"No, I want *you* to deliver the news. I doubt he'll believe it, coming from me."

The stout woman grinned. "He'll think it's too good to be true. Is that it? Well, I'll tell him myself, if that is your wish."

"Indeed it is." Gwendolen opened the door and found Angus waiting in the corridor.

The midwife approached him. "Congratulations, sir. Your wife is expecting."

His cool gaze lifted, and he glanced across at Gwendolen, who was leaning against the doorway with her arms folded at her chest. She tilted her head at him and raised an eyebrow.

"I see," he said to the woman, without looking at her. "You may go now."

The midwife's smile vanished immediately, then she lowered her gaze and hurried to the stairs.

"It is true, then," Angus said.

Gwendolen backed into her room and rested her hand on the edge of the door. She was so angry with him, she could have spat. "Of course it's true. I am surprised your precious oracle didn't inform you of it already, but maybe she doesn't always see the whole picture. Why don't you go climb into bed with *her*, and ask if she forgot to mention that she saw your firstborn child in my womb?"

He took an anxious step forward. "Gwendolen—"

"*No,* I don't want to hear it. I am too angry with you." She slammed the door in his face.

Leaning close to it, she listened, half expecting him to pound a fist against it, or come barging in to teach her a lesson or two about such bold acts of defiance. But all she heard was the sound of his breathing, slow and steady on the other side of the door until, at last, he turned and walked away.

She listened intently, waiting for his footsteps to disappear at the bottom of the stairs, then, very quietly, she opened the door and peered out.

The corridor was empty. He was gone.

"You ought to send her away," Lachlan said, as he followed Angus across the hall toward the bailey. "Send her back to the dark cave where she came from. She brings nothing but poison."

"She doesn't live in a cave," Angus replied. "She has a cottage, and she let me live with her for the better part of a year when I had nowhere else to go. I'll not send her away."

They entered the bailey. The sky was overcast, and a thick white mist hung over the four corner towers. Angus looked up at the clouds, barely able to comprehend what the midwife had just confirmed—that Gwendolen was with child. He was going to be a father.

It should have come as good news. He should be celebrating, but all he felt presently was a raw, blinding terror, which was completely unfamiliar to him, for he had never feared for the future. But now, everything was different.

Because of his marriage to Gwendolen. It had done something to him.

"Raonaid will destroy what you've built here," Lachlan said, keeping up with Angus as he quickened his pace across the bailey. "She'll wreck it with all her grisly omens and prophecies of disaster."

They had to stop and let a donkey and cart pass in front of them. The rickety wheels left deep tracks in the muck. Angus stared down at the tracks and watched them fill with water.

"And don't tell me you believe in her curses and spells," Lachlan continued. "She's a lunatic. It's nothing but folly."

"She doesn't cast spells," Angus said. "She has visions, and she predicts the future. She knew you would come for me, and that together we'd raise an army to reclaim Kinloch."

"Anyone could have predicted that. And are you forgetting that she *didn't* predict you'd be a father?"

The mention of his unborn child caused something inside him to shudder. "Maybe I won't be—because I'll be dead."

They stopped at the door to the powder magazine, and Angus dug into his sporran for the key. What he found was the letter he had written to Duncan.

He thought for a moment that he should just rip it up. He already had enough distractions. And what was the point in trying to rekindle an old friendship if he was not going to live long enough to even see Duncan again?

At the same time, he knew it would benefit his clan to have allies at Moncrieffe Castle, for Duncan was one of the most powerful and influential Scottish nobles, and his castle was a mere two-day ride from here. If Gwendolen delivered a son, the boy might be chief one day. He would require friends and allies. Perhaps Duncan, the great Earl of Moncrieffe, would watch over them . . .

He withdrew the letter and handed it to Lachlan. "See that this is delivered to Moncrieffe. Send a dispatch rider today and tell him to wait for a reply. If there is one."

Lachlan reached out to take it. "I thought you and the earl were not on speaking terms."

"We aren't, but it's time I remedied that." Angus unlocked the door to the powder magazine and entered. He lifted the lid on one of the wooden barrels. "Are all of these full?"

"To the brim. We have enough powder to blow the entire English army halfway across the Irish Sea."

Angus looked around. "What about the armory? Are all the muskets in working order? Do we have sufficient ammunition?"

"Aye."

"Good." He started for the door. "Assemble the men, Lachlan. I wish to speak to them in the bailey."

How was it possible that a person's emotions could shift from one extreme to the other in the space of a single heartbeat? Gwendolen wondered miserably as she passed through the castle corridors toward the South Tower. Earlier that morning, she had been drifting along on a happy cloud of bliss while supervising the weavers in the spinning room, and anticipating the moment when she would tell her husband about the child in her womb.

The next thing she knew, he was bursting through the door and announcing that the oracle—a woman who had shared his bed quite recently—had envisioned his death by hanging. And that Gwendolen would be the cause of it.

She arrived at the door to the oracle's guest chamber and fought a sickening ball of apprehension in her belly. She had never met this woman, but she despised her already, for planting false seeds of doubt and mistrust in her husband's mind.

At the same time, however, she knew she could not be too hasty with her anger. This woman had foreseen her husband's death, and perhaps knowledge of such an event could provide a defense against it. Despite how furious she felt, she did not want to lose Angus. She would therefore have to be calm and press Raonaid for more information about her visions, and ascertain if she was, in fact, correct—or simply here to cause mischief and lure Angus back to her bed.

Struggling to keep a firm grip on her emotions, Gwendolen knocked on the door. No one answered, so she knocked again, a second time.

At last, the door opened, and she swallowed uneasily at the disturbing image of the woman before her.

Raonaid, the famous oracle.

Mad as the devil. Crafty as a fox. And the most beautiful woman she had ever seen.

She was tall and buxom. Her hair was the color of a raging inferno, her complexion pure white, like polished ivory.

But it was her eyes that caused Gwendolen the most distress, for they were a spectacular shade of blue, and brilliantly, ruthlessly calculating.

Chapter Nineteen

"I knew you would come," the oracle said, appearing more than a little satisfied with herself, as she turned her back on Gwendolen, walked with a sensual swagger across the room, and left the door open behind her.

Gwendolen entered and looked around the quiet chamber. A hot fire was blazing in the hearth. The whisky decanter had been emptied almost entirely, and the bedclothes were torn off the mattress and thrown to the floor in a massive heap of silks and linens.

Gwendolen took in Raonaid's overall appearance—her tattered, homespun skirt and bodice, her tiny waist and ample bosom, and the strange cord of bones tied around her neck.

She hated to admit it, but there was a natural majesty about her husband's former lover, especially in the way she carried herself, with such pride and dignity.

Any fool could see that she embodied everything a man would find appealing in a woman, and exuded an air of sexuality as well. Gwendolen had to fight against the sudden twinge of jealousy that poked at her confidence.

"Are you enjoying yourself with the great Lion?" Raonaid asked, tossing back a sip of whisky. "Spending lots of time on your back, I expect. I'll bet he's taught you all kinds of interesting things you never imagined."

Gwendolen raised her chin. "How kind of you to ask. Indeed, I am enjoying him tremendously. He is an excellent lover and I feel drunk with lust most of the time, but of course, you would already know that. You would remember how it once felt."

Raonaid frowned and spoke with spite. "I know all kinds of things about him, lassie. Things you'll never know."

"I doubt that."

Gwendolen stood just inside the door, keeping to her spot on the braided rug, while the oracle paced back and forth in front of the fireplace. She looked as if she were about to pounce and rip Gwendolen's throat out.

"I didn't come all this way to see *you*," Raonaid said. "I came to see Angus."

"In case you haven't heard, I am mistress of Kinloch, therefore you are my guest as much as you are his."

Raonaid reached for the iron poker and stirred the fire. "What do you want from me, great mistress of Kinloch?"

"I thought you said you knew I would come," Gwendolen replied. "Do you not know why? Do you not see everything?"

The oracle ignored her question. She finished tending to the fire, then leaned the poker against the hearth.

"Fine," Gwendolen continued, "I'll tell you why. You saw my husband's death. I want to know how and why it happens."

As she swung around to face her, Raonaid's eyes burned with accusation. "You of all people should already know that, you manipulative slut. You're the one who leads him to the noose."

"That is ridiculous."

"Is it?"

Gwendolen's stomach turned over with dread. "You cannot possibly see the truth, Raonaid, because I would never betray my husband—which makes me question your so-called gift of sight. I do not want him dead. I love him. I want him to live."

Good God, she had just declared her love for her husband. She had never spoken those words aloud before, not to anyone, not even Angus. *Especially* not him. She wondered how he would react if he knew she was here in his former lover's bedchamber, pouring her heart out in this manner.

Would Raonaid tell him what she had said? If she did, he would probably take it as further evidence that his wife was a liar. Not long ago, they were enemies, and she'd wanted to shoot him through the heart.

She took a deep breath and fought to remain calm. "Angus told me that you saw his head in a noose. What else did you see?"

"What does it matter?" Raonaid replied. "He'll be hanged, right here at Kinloch. What else is there to know?"

"But *why* is he hanged?" Gwendolen asked. "It makes no sense. The English have already awarded him full custody of Kinloch. He has a powerful army here to protect him, and the members of my clan have accepted him. He has been a fair and generous chief."

"But there is someone else you are forgetting," Raonaid said with devilish taunting. "Your long-lost brother, who could return any day with an army of his own. Surely *he* hasn't accepted the loss of his birthright."

Gwendolen pushed a lock of hair behind her ear and noticed uneasily that her fingers were trembling. "That may be true, but I am pledged to my husband now. I have given him my solemn vow that I will not betray him. If Murdoch returns, he will not find an ally in me. Not if he means to unseat my husband."

It occurred to her suddenly that she had given very little thought lately to the possibility of Murdoch's return. She had become so immersed in the pleasures of married life, she had all but purged it from her mind.

Raonaid's clear blue eyes narrowed. She sat down in an upholstered chair and reclined comfortably. "The words you speak make you sound very sure of yourself, lassie, but your eyes tell another tale."

"You see only what you want to see."

"That may be true—but what is it, exactly, that you think I want to see? Enlighten me."

Gwendolen chose her words carefully. "You want me to be disloyal to my husband, so that he will come back to you."

The oracle threw her head back and laughed. "I couldn't care less if I ever saw that man again."

Gwendolen's annoyance was beginning to stew. "Then why did you come here, if you care so little about him?"

"Because I gave him my word. You can say and think what you like about me, and most of it will be true—but one thing you cannot call me is a liar. I speak my mind, and I keep my promises. That's why I told him the truth—the truth I see in your eyes now."

"And what truth is that?" Gwendolen asked incredulously.

Raonaid leaned forward. "When your brother returns, you will stand by him, not Angus, because he is your mother's son."

"That's a lie."

"Are you sure about that?" Her eyebrow lifted knowingly. "He's your brother, lass. Would you let your husband cut his throat?"

Gwendolen's pulse began to beat erratically. "Of course not. I would try to come between them."

"But you cannot come between them without choosing a side. You'll do what you must to save your brother's life."

Gwendolen began to pace back and forth. "You are guessing these things," she said, "the same as anyone else might do."

Raonaid gave no reply.

Gwendolen watched her from across the room. The woman was like some kind of animal. Everything about her was predatory.

"How is it that you experience these visions?" she asked, moving to a chair and sitting across from Raonaid. "Are you having one now? Is that why you ask me these things?"

"Nay, I'm not having one. I'm just reading you."

Gwendolen leaned back. "So you *are* just guessing."

The oracle shrugged. "I'm very good at it, and I base everything on the visions in the stones."

"But what, exactly, do you see in the stones? How does it happen?" Gwendolen thought of her own dreams that often foretold future events. There was nothing strange or mystical about them. They were just dreams.

"I see the events unfold through shadows and light," Raonaid explained, "and the meaning is always clear to me. I feel it."

"Do you hear people talking?" Gwendolen asked. "Or do you ever read words in the stones, as if they were written in a book?"

Raonaid shook her head. "Nay, I just see shadows and movement."

Gwendolen wanted very much to prove that Raonaid was mistaken about her morbid premonitions, for she could not bear to imagine that Angus would die, nor could she accept the possibility that she would be responsible . . .

"I think what you might have seen," she carefully suggested, "were images from a letter I wrote the day after Angus invaded Kinloch. I pleaded with Colonel Worthington at Fort William to come with an army of redcoats and drive him out by force. I wanted him to be hanged for treason as a Jacobite. I was very clear about it, and I did this after I promised Angus that I would not betray him."

It was a difficult thing to confess to this woman, of all people, but she wanted her to know the truth.

Raonaid tilted her head to the side. "Does he know of this?"

"Aye. Colonel Worthington came here and showed him the letter. Angus immediately confronted me about it, and I confessed my guilt, and he forgave me." She clasped her hands together on her lap. "So you see, I am not perfect. I was deceitful, I admit it, but things were different then. For that reason, I believe what you saw in the stones was a vision of those events as they were unfolding, and that Angus is no longer in danger—at least not because of me."

Raonaid's cheeks flushed with color. She stood up and walked to the window. "You confuse me."

Gwendolen stood up as well. "That's good! If you are not sure . . ."

Raonaid whirled around and pressed her lips together. "I see through you, Gwendolen MacEwen," she growled. "You are his enemy. You want to crush and destroy him because he conquered your clan. He disappears from the stones because of you. There is no escaping it. I saw what I saw. Even now, he is as good as dead." Tears of fury stained the oracle's eyes and choked her voice.

Gwendolen thought carefully about what Raonaid was describing, then moved closer and spoke in a gentler tone. "Maybe he just disappears from *your* life, Raonaid. Perhaps that's all it means."

The oracle darted forward and pushed Gwendolen out the door. "Get out!" she shrieked. *"Get out of here!"*

Gwendolen stumbled backward into the corridor, and the door slammed shut in her face.

It took a moment for her to recover her composure. She smoothed out her skirts and ran a shaky hand over her hair, then closed her eyes and took a deep, calming breath. She had never encountered anyone quite so volatile before. Clearly Raonaid did not respond well to separations.

"What are you doing here, Gwendolen?"

She jumped at the sound of her husband's voice at the end of the corridor. Her body tensed at the awesome sight of him. His thick, tawny mane of hair was tied back off his shoulders. A round shield was strapped to his back. In addition to his usual arsenal of weapons, he held an axe in his hand.

Heaven help her, even through the haze of her confusion and anger, she still believed him to be the most handsome and impressive Scotsman alive. He never failed to upset her equilibrium.

For that reason, she could not let him continue to doubt her. Nor could she tolerate any further attacks on her honor and dignity. She was carrying his child now, and had assured him that she would never betray him. If what Raonaid said was true—that Murdoch would come with an army to reclaim his birthright—it was important that they stand together and trust one another. There could be no dissension, because *that* was where the chink in Kinloch's armor would be found.

She faced him and spoke with a sharp note of accusation in her voice—for it was not lost on her that they were both standing outside Raonaid's bedchamber door.

"More importantly, what are *you* doing here?" she asked. She strode forward to meet him at the end of the corridor. "Are you looking for *me*? I certainly hope so, because we have much to discuss. But if you are here to see Raonaid—who just called me a manipulative slut—I might have something very different to say to you. So which is it, Angus? Are you here to see me? Or did you come to see her?"

Chapter Twenty

Angus decided at that moment that this marriage had indeed done something to him, because his passions were exploding inside of him like torched gunpowder. He was not the same man he had once been, and he was not happy about it. He had not taken a wife so that he could become a contrite, lovesick husband. He had not been seeking affection, or sentimentality, or attachment. To the contrary, he had wedded this woman to produce a son and provide an heir that would unite the clans of Kinloch, and one day become chief. It had been a political arrangement, nothing more.

Yet here he stood, looking at the stunningly beautiful woman who was carrying his child, and all he could think about was the fact that he might not live to see the day when she gave birth, and that his time with her was limited, and that she was angry with him.

He wanted more than anything to fix it, and apologize for his unforgivable behavior that morning. Even when he knew it was possible that she might betray him, he still desired her, and could not bear to think that she was cross with him.

Did he truly believe she would betray him?

His gut said no, it could not be so, but he simply

could not take the risk that he was wrong. He knew what love did to perfectly sensible men. It made them blind and foolish.

"I came to see Raonaid," he said vindictively, knowing it was not what she wanted to hear, but he said it nevertheless, in a passionate attempt to convince her—and himself—that he did not care how she felt.

But dammit, he did care. The sick feeling in his stomach proved it. He was done for. He should just send for a rope and a stool right now.

"Fine," she said, pushing past him. "I'll leave you two alone. I hope you enjoy yourselves."

She walked haughtily to the stairs and disappeared from sight, but as he listened to the light tapping of her footsteps down the curved staircase, his passion for her exploded tenfold, and he had to follow. *"Wait, damn you!"*

She stopped and looked up at him. He shoved the axe into his belt and descended to where she stood, took hold of her hand, and dragged her the rest of the way down.

"Where are we going?" she asked. "Let go of me!"

He led her through the stone passageway, found an arbitrary open door, and entered what turned out to be the steward's chamber. He shut the door behind them, locked it, then backed her up against the desk.

He said nothing. For the longest time, he just looked into her angry brown eyes, then cupped her face in his hands. She blinked up at him and seemed to recognize his urgent need for sex.

Yes, he wanted sex—and hell, he wanted it now. When she told him to go to Raonaid and enjoy himself, he couldn't let it pass, and he needed to make sure she understood that he could enjoy himself with no woman but her.

He needed also to prove that she belonged to him, and that he was still in control. She had not made him weak. He was strong. She was his wife, and if he wanted her, he would damn well have her. He intended to prove that now.

Keeping his eyes locked on hers, he lifted her onto the desk. Quickly, he wrenched her skirts up and thrust himself up against her, while taking careful note of her mounting desires: her breasts heaving lusciously, her wet lips parting. She let out a tiny moan of need that aroused him beyond comprehension.

Angus hooked the back of her knee with the crook of his arm, while he quickly swept his kilt out of the way.

"I want no woman but you," he told her.

She grabbed hold of his tartan. "Then prove it."

Feet still on the floor, he entered her in one swift rush of fire, and felt as if he were charging forward with his sword in the air, riding headlong down a steep hillside toward an enemy on the battlefield. The damp heat between her legs provoked his lust, and he pushed hard, needing to claim her without boundaries or conditions.

He worked smoothly inside her on top of the desk, and their bodies moved in a perfect rhythmic harmony. She clutched at his shoulders and cried out with pleasure, and simultaneously, he felt the throbbing compressions of her orgasm squeeze and pulse around the impetus of his desires.

His own orgasm grew in force and spread through him in a steamy blast of vitality, until he couldn't hold back another minute. He bucked wildly as he ejaculated into her and knocked a vase of flowers off the desktop. It landed with a smashing clatter.

Afterward, the whole world seemed to go quiet, while he held his wife tightly in his arms. It took some time for his breathing, and hers, to return to normal. Then slowly he withdrew from inside her. He let his kilt fall, and touched his forehead to hers.

So much for being in control.

Gwendolen took hold of his face and kissed him hard. "If you go to that woman now," she said, "I swear on my mother's life that I will run you through with your own sword. You'll be a bloody mess on this floor, and of no use to Raonaid or anyone else for that matter."

God help him, no woman had ever aroused him more.

"I don't want her," he said. "I give you my vow as a Scotsman that as long as I live, I will never want any woman but you. But if you betray me, lass . . ."

He didn't finish the threat, because he couldn't imagine what he would do.

"I will not betray you," she assured him. "How can I make you believe it?"

"I don't know."

She pulled him in for another deep, searing kiss, then pushed him away. "Your precious oracle said I would stand by my brother if he returned, and that I would choose him over you. But I am carrying your child now, Angus. That makes me yours. You must have faith in my loyalty and tell her so. Then, for God's sake, send her away. If you don't, she'll do nothing but wreak havoc here."

"But she sees the future," Angus said. "I must know her prophecies."

Gwendolen hopped off the desk and moved to the center of the room. "You cannot trust what she sees, for she has painted me with a false brush. She could be wrong about other things, too, and lead you down the wrong path."

"What other things?" he asked.

"Your death, for one." She approached him again. "I've had my own dreams, Angus. I have envisioned our future, and what I see is very different from what she has seen in the stones."

He felt an unexpected curiosity. Did every woman in the world wish to control him with mysticism? "What do you mean, you've had your own dreams?"

"Dreams," she repeated, with a noncommittal shrug. "Sometimes I dream about certain events, and later there is truth in them."

"What events?"

She shook her head as if she didn't want to speak of it, but continued nonetheless. "I dreamed of your assault on Kinloch the night before you stormed the gates. I saw our passion together. And before our wedding day, I dreamed of the swallow that was nesting in the Great Hall. I saw her fly away and leave us."

He shook his head in disbelief. "Why have you not told me this before?"

"Because it's probably just a lot of superstitious nonsense, and besides, when I have the dreams, I don't know if they will come true or not. I don't recognize the prophecy until it occurs, and then I look back and remember that I dreamed it. So you see, I am no oracle."

"But your dreams do come true."

"Sometimes."

He walked to the window and looked out at the surrounding meadows and forests, and wondered what he was supposed to do with this information. He had married a woman who was not only beautiful and spirited, not to mention sexually eager and gloriously fertile, but had prophetic dreams as well.

"What else have you seen in your sleep?" he asked. "Have you ever seen my death?"

She spoke with conviction. "Nay, but I have seen our life together, many years from now."

He faced her. "What did you see? Tell me every detail."

"I saw you pass your sword to our eldest son on his wedding day, and all was well."

All was well?

Angus found that difficult to believe, for there was always violence or death in some corner of his life, waiting to rear its ugly head. Even now, the dread of it was haunting him like a demon. Which left him only one choice.

"I am laird here," he said, looking out the window again, "and it is up to me, and only me, to decide who stays and who goes."

"And Raonaid stays, I suppose?"

"For the time being."

For a year, he had lived with Raonaid and listened to her prophecies. She had saved him in more ways than one. Helped build him up when he was broken. She made him strong when he was weak. He simply could not banish her now. He owed her his life, and he needed to know all there was to know about the future. Because of Gwendolen.

She regarded him with disappointment, and he was suddenly aware of the fact that his army was being assembled in the bailey, yet he was here in this room, talking to his wife about dreams and prophecies, when he should be out there, preparing his men to fight and defend.

"Do you still love her?" Gwendolen asked.

He scoffed bitterly. "Are you mad, lass? I never loved her. I've never loved anyone."

Color rushed to her cheeks, and she turned quickly for the door. "I beg your pardon, I forgot. I suppose I have nothing to worry about then." She walked out and slammed the door behind her.

Angus stood in the empty chamber and knew very well that she was upset with him—because he had just told her in no uncertain terms that he did not love her.

But how could he have said anything different?

He didn't even know what love was.

That night, Gwendolen waited hours for Angus to come to her bed, but he chose to stay away.

A part of her wondered if he had gone to Raonaid's bed instead, but she could not let herself imagine such a thing. She had to believe that he would not be unfaithful, not after what occurred in the steward's chamber that afternoon. He'd vowed that he wanted no woman but her, and he seemed to take her threat of running him through with his own sword seriously enough.

It was not love, he had said—but his sexual desire for her was something at least.

Alas, when she finally drifted into a deep but uneasy slumber, she tossed and turned in her bed, moaning softly into her pillow, as disturbing images of a distant land troubled her mind . . .

She woke with a start. Dawn was creeping across the sky, and the fire had gone out.

Sitting up, she gasped for air. She choked on a scream that would not escape her tight, burning throat.

She had dreamed of her brother, Murdoch, floating down a long, winding river that drained into the stormy waters of the English Channel. His body rested on a funeral pyre, and there was a noose around his neck. When he plunged beneath the surface, he called out her name.

But there was nothing she could do. She reached out, but could not save him, for he was gone—sinking alone into the cold, dark depths below.

At that moment she knew. She had lost her brother forever.

Chapter Twenty-one

Angus stood on the tower rooftop, watching the rising sun splash bright patterns of color across the horizon. The eyes of the world would soon flutter open, and he would begin another day with no idea how to navigate through the muddy terrain of his life and emotions. He was someone's husband now—he was Gwendolen's husband—and imagining the loss of her was like imagining the loss of his own soul.

Angus had never put much stock in the fate of his soul before, nor had he feared death. He had witnessed his own mother's tragic passing as a child, and not even that had made him anxious about his own. All his life he had charged fearlessly into battle without the slightest hesitation. If he died, so be it. It was enough to know that he would die with honor, for outside of that, he'd never had much to live for.

Everything was different now. Raonaid's prophecy forced him to look at his life and all that he had yet to experience and achieve. He and Gwendolen had created a child together, and for that reason he needed to live. He needed to protect his family and care for them, and prove that he could be something other than the ruthless brute that everyone believed him to be.

Perhaps he knew what love was after all. Or at the very least, he was discovering it, one day at a time.

The sound of footsteps up the tower stairs caused him to turn, and he found himself staring, speechless, at his wife. She wore a white shift and lace-trimmed dressing gown and looked like an angel in the breezy pink radiance of the morning.

His gaze fell to her bare toes peeking out from under the hem. "You ought to be wearing shoes, lass. The stones are cold."

"Why are you always concerned with my feet," she asked, "when you should be wondering what I'm doing here in the first place? Is it not worth noting that I am on a tower rooftop at dawn searching for you, when the last time we spoke, I stormed out of the room and slammed a door in your face?"

He approached her. "Aye, it's definitely worth noting, and I'm pleased to see you." He swallowed hard. "I'm sorry I didn't come to your bed last night."

There. See? He could be gentle when he tried. He could offer his wife an apology.

She pulled the wrapper more tightly closed to ward off the morning chill. "I wasn't surprised when you didn't come," she said. "We were angry with each other yesterday."

"Nay, lass—you were angry with *me,* and for good reason. I was wrong not to believe you about the child."

"And what about the other thing?" she asked, shivering slightly. "The fact that Raonaid said I would betray you? Do you still believe her about that?"

For a long moment, he considered it. "I don't know."

Her shoulders rose and fell with a resigned sigh. "Well, I can't force you to believe it, can I? All I can do is ask that you follow your heart, and hope that over time you'll learn to trust me."

He inclined his head at her. "There was a time you didn't believe I had a heart."

"There was also a time when I was a virgin and knew nothing about what went on between a man and a woman in the marriage bed. I am not the same person I once was, Angus. Everything is different now. I hope it is different for you, too."

He laid a hand on the small of her back and led her toward the tower battlements, where they could look out over the distant fields and forests of Kinloch.

"Why are you here, lass?" he asked, admiring her profile and her shiny black hair, blowing lightly in the breeze. "Why are you not sleeping, warm in your bed?"

She faced him. "Because I had a dream this morning, and I needed to tell you about it, in case it turns out to be a premonition. Though I sincerely hope it does not."

"If you tell me you saw my head in a noose . . ."

Gwendolen quickly shook her head. "Nay, it was not that. It was something else, though it was just as morbid. I couldn't breathe when I woke."

Angus laid a hand on her shoulder. "What did you see?"

"My brother," she answered. "I saw Murdoch floating on a funeral pyre out to sea. I fear he will never return to us now, and my mother will be forced to mourn the loss of her only son."

A funeral pyre?

Angus recalled his instructions to Lachlan on the day of the invasion. Lachlan was to send MacDonald warriors on a hunt for Murdoch, and do whatever it took to prevent another attack. *Whatever it took.*

Tears filled Gwendolen's eyes, and she stepped into Angus's arms.

"Perhaps it was just a dream," he said, "and he will return any day."

Or perhaps not.

He held her close and struggled with his bucking conscience, while he wondered who, at this moment, was the real traitor in this marriage.

The answer was simple, he supposed—for he had put his instincts as a warrior and chieftain before any thoughts of compassion for his wife. Her feelings had not even entered into his decision to crush his enemy, and he was quite certain that given the same circumstances, he would do the same thing again.

Perhaps he had not come so far after all. Perhaps he would always be the same ruthless warrior he had always been.

Angus entered the stables, where Lachlan was grooming his horse. "Has there been any word about Murdoch MacEwen?" he curtly asked. "Damn you, Lachlan. Have any of our clansmen returned with news of him?"

Tossing the brush into a wooden bucket, Lachlan wiped his hands on a cloth and approached. "No word yet. Don't you think I would've told you if there was?"

Angus pressed the heels of his hands to his forehead. The air inside the stable was heavy with the scent of hay, leather, and horse. It was stifling and suffocating, and made him want to hit something. "*Och,* I can barely manage my impatience. I need to know what's become of him, and I need to know very soon."

Lachlan eyed him with concern and moved out of the stall. "Any particular reason why? Are you worried because of what Raonaid predicted? Do you think he'll try to take Kinloch?"

"Until he's found, he will always be a threat."

Lachlan rested a hand on his shoulder. "We're doing everything possible to assure a strong defense, Angus. But if you want, I can send out more men to act as spies."

Angus considered it, then shook his head and walked to the door. "Nay. We need all our best men here. I'm sure we'll hear something soon."

He was still unsatisfied, however, as he strode out of the stables in search of Raonaid.

It was like an addiction—this need to know his future—and he could not help but fixate on the extraordinary fact that not one but *two* women inside the castle walls claimed to have the gift of sight, and he had bedded them both.

But which one was correct about his true destiny?

He found Raonaid in the kitchen, harassing the cook. He waved her over and led her into the stone passageway that led to the hall.

"What do you know of Gwendolen's brother?" he asked.

He had already decided not to reveal Gwendolen's dream to Raonaid, for it could be just that—a dream and nothing more. He didn't want to influence Raonaid's visions. He wanted to test her.

"I believe that she will choose him over her loyalty to you as her husband," she said.

He took hold of her arm. "In what circumstances? Why does she not honor her pledge to me?"

He had already considered the possibility that his

men had by now murdered her brother, and when Gwendolen learned of it, she would never forgive him for his treachery. She would despise him forever and wish terrible ills upon him.

He was no stranger to such outcomes, for he had once deceived his closest friend. This was all very familiar territory. Was he destined to always disappoint and drive away those who mattered most to him? He had lost the good opinion of his father—which he could never regain, for his father was dead. He had also lost Duncan—whom he had once believed to be the deceitful turncoat, but in the end, Duncan had been the one with greater wisdom and a higher sense of humanity.

"You're obsessed with your guilt," Raonaid said, reading him like a book. "You think you bring this on yourself, because of all the evils you've done."

"But do I succeed in bringing it on myself?" he asked. "What is next to happen?"

He was determined not to openly provide her with information, for he didn't need to hear what he already knew—that he was guilt-ridden. If she was a true oracle, she would tell him something more.

"You must let go of the past," she said, "or you will not be able to focus on what matters."

"And what is that?"

She spread her arms wide. "These walls of stone and mortar."

His gaze traveled up the side of one wall, across the vaulted ceiling, then down the other, and then he recalled the words Lachlan had spoken on the day of the invasion: *But what is Kinloch, if not for its people?*

Angus gazed into the cool blue depths of Raonaid's eyes. "What good am I as a leader if my people despise me? What is the point in having all this power if everyone wants me dead?"

"At least you will have achieved something," she replied. "You reclaimed this great Scottish stronghold that once belonged to your father, but was stolen from your clan. Your fighting skills are unmatched. You have been invincible in battle. Your father would be proud, Angus, and wasn't that what you always wanted? Wasn't that why you returned to Kinloch? To redeem yourself in his eyes?"

"But my father is dead, Raonaid, and he didn't banish me because I failed in battle. There was never any question that I was good with a sword." Angus looked away, toward the bailey. "My skill as a warrior meant nothing to him in the end. All he saw was my heartlessness, and that was why he sent me away. He was ashamed of me. I was his son, yet he could not even look at me."

He realized suddenly how his perspective on life and the people surrounding him had changed since those cold, lonely months in the Hebrides. All he'd cared about then was his bitterness.

It was all Raonaid had cared for as well. It was what had brought them together. It was the one thing they shared—a basic contempt for the world.

Now, since his return to Kinloch and the unexpected intimacy of his marriage, all he wanted was peace. Prosperity for those who had placed themselves in his care.

And to never again disappoint those who trusted him.

That night, nothing could keep Angus from Gwendolen's bed. He'd spent the entire day going over all the possible directions his life could take from this day forward—everything from his own death to the loss of his wife's affections because he had ordered the death of her brother.

He had always been very adept at disregarding his emotions. He had never been one for empathy or compassion. He did what was necessary to survive, without pause or regret. He killed men in battle. He lived for duty and patriotism alone.

But tonight, he felt uncertain. He had sent a basket of roses to Gwendolen's room when she was still dressing for dinner, and now, after the meal, he was escorting her back to her chamber, not entirely sure where they stood. Had she seen his treachery in her dreams? Did she know that he was not worthy of her goodness?

When they entered her bedchamber, he took the liberty of dismissing her maid, for he wanted to assist her himself. He removed each article of clothing, piece by piece, and all the while, his hands shook with both arousal and uneasiness.

A short time later they slid beneath the heavy covers, where he laid a trail of kisses down her soft, quivering belly and wondered how it was possible that he could feel such apprehension at a time like this, when his body was aroused and he was passionately in the mood for sex. He had come here to make love to his wife and lose himself in her sweet, honeyed depths, but perhaps what he really needed to do was distract himself from everything else. For their future together was uncertain at best.

Would she betray him? he wondered, as he kissed her soft shoulders and relished the sweet sounds of her breathless moans.

Or would he simply disappoint her and lose her affections forever because of the thoughtless command he had given to Lachlan a month ago?

After a generous session of foreplay, he entered her with great sensitivity, and watched her expressions in the dim, flickering candlelight. She thrust her hips forward to meet each of his deep penetrations, and their bodies moved together in a physical harmony he had never imagined possible. It was magic, and he wanted it. Needed it. He would die for it.

He drove into her vigorously, again and again, and grew quite certain that the irresistible joy he was feeling was nothing but a house of cards built on a shaky table, and soon that house would collapse.

He held his climax at bay for as long as possible, and when it came, it was cataclysmic; hers was savage and intense. He felt the power of their passion in the sharp sting of her fingernails digging into his back.

"I love you," she whispered, and he sucked in a breath of surprise.

"I love you, too."

God in heaven . . .

He had never spoken those words before, but they spilled out before he had a chance to stop and think.

Something inside him shifted. Should he have said it? Was it true? Did he even understand such an emotion? He felt as if he did, but he was still unsure.

Later, they fell asleep in each other's arms, quiet and restful, stretched out on the bed, basking in the warmth from the fire and the heavy scent of roses.

He had not expected to reach such a state of repose. Perhaps it was exhaustion. Or surrender. Or something else. Whatever it was, he accepted it. He did not rise to go to the chapel that night. He slept soundly for hours and hours, and dreamed of purple heather in the glen.

So it was with a jolt of shock that he woke to a noisy rapping at the door. He sat up and managed to slide out of bed without waking Gwendolen. He wrapped his tartan around him, and crossed the room to answer it.

"I'm sorry to disturb you so early," Lachlan whispered, "but there is news of Murdoch MacEwen, and I thought you'd want to know straightaway."

Angus stepped into the chilly, torchlit corridor and closed the door behind him. "What is it?"

"One of our spies has returned from Paris. You ought to come now and hear what he has to say."

Angus dropped his gaze to the floor, and wondered if he had made a terrible mistake in not visiting the chapel that night to light a candle and say a prayer, because the time seemed rather appropriate for God to come and collect for past sins.

Angus feared the worst would happen—that he was about to lose everything, as he always had before.

Chapter Twenty-two

The next morning, Angus waited impatiently in the solar for Gwendolen and her mother to arrive, and when they walked in, he rose from his chair.

"You sent for us?" Gwendolen glanced at Angus, then at Lachlan, and a third MacDonald clansman she could not have recognized, for he had left the castle the day after the invasion.

Angus gestured to two chairs brought in especially for their meeting. "Please take a seat."

Lachlan remained standing by the bank of leaded windows, and the clansman who went by the name of Gerard MacDonald stood beside Angus, waiting to speak.

Angus turned to Onora. "I have news of your son, madam."

He noticed that Gwendolen clasped her hands together on her lap, as if to brace herself. Onora, however, looked hopeful. She did not know of Gwendolen's dreams. Gwendolen had shared her secret prophecies with no one but him.

"There is news?" Onora smiled cautiously. "Please, Angus—I beseech you to disclose it without delay. Murdoch has been gone too long. Will he come home to us?"

Angus met Gwendolen's eyes. They began to fill with wetness; her knuckles turned white on her lap.

"I am deeply sorry, madam," he said to Onora. "Your son will not be returning. He died, weeks ago, in France."

Gwendolen bowed her head.

Angus glanced over his shoulder at Lachlan, who moved to kneel before Onora. He took her hands in his.

Her voice shook. "It cannot be true! How do you know this?"

Lachlan began to explain. "After we invaded Kinloch and realized that we had not fought your son, we needed to establish his whereabouts and ensure that he would not return to seek vengeance. I sent men to search for him, and this man . . ." He gestured toward Gerard who stood behind him. "This man found Murdoch in Paris and arranged to speak with him."

Onora stood and approached Gerard. "You saw my son? You spoke with him?"

"Aye, madam, but he was not well. I was permitted to visit his sickbed, and he asked me to tell you that he was sorry for deserting you, and that if he could turn back the hands of time, he would never have left his beloved Scotland. He would've stayed to defend you against your invaders, and he wished he could've died here, rather than be buried so far from home."

Tears filled Onora's eyes. "Did he know who you were? Did he know what happened here?"

"Aye. I explained everything to him."

She gestured with desperation to Gwendolen. "Did you tell my son that his sister was forced to marry the conquering chief?"

Gerard fumbled with his tartan, growing uncomfortable with the emotional nature of Onora's questioning. "Aye, I told him that, too. And I'll not lie to you, madam. He was concerned for her safety."

Gwendolen quickly stood. "Of course he would be concerned. He was my brother, and he knew how I valued my virtue. He would not have wanted to leave this world believing that I'd been forced into wedlock, or beaten or subjugated. He cared for me very much." She addressed Gerard directly. "Did you tell him that I was agreeable to the match? Because I cannot bear to think that he died believing I was unhappy. If I could have been there, I would have told him that all was well. That the MacEwens are in good hands."

There it was again, Angus thought. That expression she tossed around so freely—that "all was well."

Was it? Now that her brother was dead, and Angus was not responsible for his passing, would everything be well? Would this mean she would never betray him as Raonaid predicted? And would Angus finally be able to stop looking over his shoulder at every turn?

He despised himself suddenly for such selfish thoughts, when he should be thinking only of his wife's grief. She had just been told that her brother was dead.

Angus went to her. He wanted to take her into his arms—it seemed the right thing to do—but she held up a hand, indicating that she had no intention of weeping or collapsing, at least not here.

Onora, on the other hand, dropped to her knees, let out a gut-wrenching sob, and wept into her hands.

Lachlan knelt down and held her close, while Gwendolen stared into Angus's eyes.

"Take me out of here," she said. "Take me beyond the gates of Kinloch."

Somehow, he understood exactly what she needed, so he reached for her hand and led her out.

A light rain began to fall shortly after they crossed the drawbridge and galloped toward the forest, but Gwendolen did not wish to turn around. "Don't stop," she said as she raised the hood of her cloak. "Keep riding."

Her arms tightened around his waist, and he urged his mount forward, but slowed to a trot when they entered the woods, where they were sheltered from the rain.

When they emerged a short time later, out of the brush at the edge of the river, he felt the cold drops pelt his cheeks and wondered if this particular destination had been the wisest choice.

He walked the horse upriver to the waterfall. Angus looked up at it and realized why he had come here so often in the past, in particular, as a lad, in the years after the death of his mother. He had come to drown out the sound of his own thoughts. The noise of the water rushing headlong over the rocks and plunging into the eddying pool below was deafening in his ears, and the chilly mist that rose up from the raging waters had a numbing effect on his body.

Gwendolen swung off the horse and strode to a rocky perch that overlooked the foaming pool below. Angus tethered his horse to a tree branch and joined her on the outcropping. The violence of the cascading water churned up a breeze that blew the damp, ebony locks of her hair. She pushed her hood away from her face and breathed in the fresh scent of the water and the pines surrounding them.

"I've been here before," she said, shouting over the din of the falls. "Murdoch showed me this place not long after Father claimed this territory as his own. Did you know that? Is that why you chose it?"

"Nay. I chose it because I used to come here as a lad after my mother died. I've not been here for many years, but I always suspected something would bring me back one day."

Gwendolen looked up at the ashen sky, which mingled with the rising mist. Her face was wet from the weather, and her full lips glistened with moisture. "And here we are, mourning the loss of another loved one. Perhaps you have some gifts of sight as well, Angus, but you are not aware of them. Perhaps we all do."

"I have no such gifts." He touched her cheek with the backs of his fingers. "Otherwise I would have seen you entering into my life. I would have had more hope earlier for some kind of a future."

She gazed at him wistfully. "I saw you coming into *my* life. The night before you invaded, I dreamed of a lion breaking down my bedchamber door and growling at me. Then he tore my room apart before my very eyes."

Angus felt his brow pucker. "You did not tell me this before. Is that why you hated me with such passion, and feared my touch?"

"No, I hated you because you were my enemy and you killed my clansmen. In my dream, I spoke softly to that lion, and soon grew to love him. Perhaps that's why I resisted you so desperately. I didn't *want* to love you."

Angus studied the flecks of silver in her brown eyes. "So you tamed the lion in your dream."

"Aye, and he was gentle after that, but I continued to fear him. I still do. He is a lion after all."

More than anything, Angus wanted to protect Gwendolen from harm or discomfort, and for that reason he felt compelled to warn her against loving him—for he was not sure he could ever be the man she wanted him to be. He was trying, but he was certain that the violence in his nature would always persist.

"You should continue to fear that beast," he said. "A lion has sharp teeth."

"And a mighty roar." Abruptly, she turned and stepped into his arms, knocking him off balance. "Angus, my brother is dead, and I am ashamed."

His eyebrows lifted. "Ashamed? Why?"

She was not the one who had ordered his death, and if Murdoch had not been lying on his deathbed when Gerard arrived in Paris, he might be just as dead today from a knife in the belly.

"I cursed my brother for not returning to us sooner," she explained. "I cursed him before God. What kind of a sister am I? What if this is my punishment for such wicked thoughts?"

Angus could not fathom such a thing—that God would choose to punish Gwendolen. If anyone deserved to be punished, it was not she.

"I was so angry with him," she continued, "for not coming home when Father died. I blamed him for the defeat of the MacEwens after you broke through the gates. I prayed that he would somehow see what had occurred on that day and suffer a lifetime of remorse for his selfish desires to better himself with education and culture, while we were here, fighting to defend his birthright."

Angus kissed her on the forehead and held her close. "Do not blame yourself, lass. You had good reason to be angry with him. You felt abandoned."

"But it was not his fault," she said. "He was ill, and he was not able to return home, even if he wanted to."

"But you knew nothing of that. His death is not your fault. You did nothing wrong."

"Then why do I feel so wretched?"

"Because your brother is dead," he replied. "There is no escaping the grief."

She stepped back and looked into his eyes. "You said you came here after your mother died. You have never spoken of her to me, except that one time in the chapel, when you said she was a saint."

"Aye. At least, that's how I remember her."

"How old were you when she died?"

"Four."

She watched him closely, waiting for him to offer something more, but he did not like to speak of his mother.

"What happened to her?" she asked.

He looked at the waterfall. The sound of it filled his head with noise, made him feel as if he did not exist. But he *did*. There was blood running through his veins, and sensation in his heart. There was no escaping either of those things, but he found he did not want to escape them. He had wanted to for most of his life, but not now.

"I know what guilt is," he said, looking down at her again, "because my mother was killed at Glencoe."

Glencoe . . . where dozens of MacDonalds had been massacred because their chief failed to sign an oath of allegiance to the English Crown. Glencoe was not Angus's home, but it had been his mother's, before she married his father.

"She threw me into a trunk to hide me from the enemy," he explained, "then she was marched out into the snow and shot dead."

"You were at the Glencoe massacre?" she said with concern. "I had no idea."

He shrugged. "It was a long time ago." Though he still remembered with astounding clarity how he had climbed out of the trunk and seen his mother's dead body, and her blood staining the snow. He would never forget it.

"I am so sorry," she said.

Neither of them spoke for a moment. They simply stood on the rocks and watched the water in the basin below as it rushed and swirled.

"Is that why you have always been so fearless," she asked, "and ready to sacrifice yourself in battle? Because of what happened to your mother?"

"I suppose. For a long time I lived only for the kill, and most who knew me would probably say there was revenge in it. Especially against the English."

She nodded with understanding, then tilted her head to the side. "Did you tell Raonaid about your mother?"

"Why do you ask that?"

"Because she told me that I didn't really know you. She suggested that she knew you better." She dropped her gaze. "It bothered me."

Angus sat down on the cold ground. "I did not tell her, lass. She saw it in her visions. That's what convinced me that she was a true mystic and not just a mad witch. But it didn't mean anything. I didn't *choose* to confide in her."

"But you did trust her with private information

about yourself," Gwendolen said. "I wish you could talk to me like that."

"I just did."

A hint of melancholy colored her expression, and she sat down beside him. "Perhaps all we need is time to get to know each other better. There are so many things I want to know about you, Angus."

But would they ever have enough time to learn all there was to know? he wondered. Did anyone ever have enough time? Life was fragile and unpredictable, and he could not seem to push Raonaid's prophecy from his mind.

Gwendolen laid a hand on his arm. "I don't want there to be any secrets between us."

He covered her hand with his own and pondered the unexpected feelings he had for her, as well as the nature of this place. He had come here as a lad, always alone, never finding the peace and contentment he longed for, but always searching for it.

He felt it now, with Gwendolen expressing her grief and regrets—and her foolish petty jealousies.

On top of that, she was carrying his child. There was something very profound about that. It changed everything. It changed how he felt about the world and his purpose in it, as both a warrior and a common man.

All his life, he had believed himself to be disposable. Unessential. All he ever did was chase the sort of death that would bestow honor upon him—and perhaps drag a few vile redcoats down into the hot, fiery flames of hell. But everything was different now.

"I must confess something to you," he said, wrapping his fingers around Gwendolen's tiny hand.

"I'm listening."

He paused. "You should not feel guilty about your brother. Thoughts are one thing, but actions are another. Give all your guilt to me. I will shoulder it for you."

"Why?"

His blue eyes clung to hers as he braced himself for her reaction to his next confession. "Because I sent men with orders to kill your brother if he did not accept me as Laird of Kinloch." He bowed his head. "I am not proud of it, because I would never want to see you hurt, but Kinloch is my home. I couldn't risk losing it again." He swallowed hard. "So you see, I am no better than the English officers who ordered the massacre at Glencoe. I am a brutal and heartless man. I am like that lion in your dream, and you should be wary of me. Always."

She pulled her hand away. "When did you order this?"

"The night of the invasion," he replied. "At the triumphal feast."

She swallowed uneasily. "Why didn't you tell me? You let me hope that my brother would return."

"I had hoped he would return as well. If he had agreed to accept me as laird, I would have treated him like a brother. But if not . . ."

"You would have had him executed."

"Aye."

She rose and walked to the edge of the rocks, where she stood for quite some time with her back to him.

He deserved her loathing, he knew it, and he wondered what had ever compelled him to confess his actions when he had just escaped the responsibility for her brother's death. It had been God's will in the end, and yet he had put himself forward to undertake the blame and the heat of her censure.

Gwendolen faced him. "I do not believe he would have pledged loyalty to you. I know my brother. He is ambitious, and he would not have accepted your offer of land and position. He would have come with an army, and he would have killed you if you did not kill him first."

Angus did not speak. He merely waited for her to express all her thoughts and feelings on the matter.

She strode closer and sat down again. "Raonaid suggested that if Murdoch came here, I would choose him over you, and that you would die because of my betrayal." She looked down at her hands in her lap. "I told her that I would never be disloyal to you, but I must now confess something as well." She met his gaze directly. "I was not absolutely certain of that commitment. I had doubts. Terrible doubts. I was afraid that if I was forced to choose, I would do whatever I must to save his life, for he was my own flesh and blood. So I must forgive you for the order you gave on the day you claimed me as your bride-to-be. You did what any chief would do to protect his clan and castle. By the same token, I will ask that you forgive me also for any hint of disloyalty that may have existed in my heart before today, even after I promised my fidelity on our wedding day." She took hold of his hand. "I cannot condemn you or hate you, Angus, and I believe that God has intervened to prevent such a dispute between us. My brother is dead through no action of yours. Neither you, nor I, were forced to choose one over the other and betray our marriage vows. I believe that we have just been liberated from any treachery that might have occurred, had my brother lived. It was God's will. Just as it was God's will to provide Kinloch with an heir with the blood of both the MacDonalds and MacEwens running in his veins."

Angus's heart lurched with something remote and forceful and mystifying. He reached out and pulled Gwendolen into his arms. All he wanted to do was hold her, protect her, care for her—and celebrate the fact that their quarrels were behind them now. There were no more secrets. She knew all his sins, and still, she was willing to forgive.

As was he.

He took her face in his hands and pushed her hair out of her eyes. "I am sorry for the loss of your brother. I know you cared for him and imagined that he would be your protector. I would have preferred to give him land and welcome him as a brother, if he had been willing to accept me. This is not what I wanted."

She nodded and sat back, wiping a tear from her eye. "Thank you. But there is one last thing I must ask of you, Angus. A favor." She swallowed hard and spoke decisively. "Please send Raonaid away."

He lowered his hand to his side and sat back.

"I realize that you value her gifts as an oracle, but clearly she was wrong about the future, because I will no longer have any cause to betray you. We do not need her, and I don't want her here. She was your lover. You must understand. She will only tear us apart. I believe she wants you for herself and means to sabotage our marriage."

"She wants no such thing," he told her. "Raonaid is not sentimental. She cares for no one. You are imagining things."

It was the wrong thing to say. He knew it when he saw the color rush to her cheeks.

"If you think that, then you are blind," she said defiantly.

He was reminded suddenly of that first day, when she challenged his authority in the Great Hall, and he dragged her to his private chamber to teach her a lesson about defiance and disobedience. But was he willing to treat her that way now? After all they had been through together?

No, he was not. But was she correct about Raonaid? Did his former lover want him back?

Did it even matter in the end?

"I will speak to her," he said, "and I will send her away, if it will make you happy."

Gwendolen looked toward the waterfall. "Yes, it will. Can we go home now?"

He rose to his feet and offered his hand, but she kept her gaze lowered as he assisted her onto the horse.

Chapter
Twenty-three

Angus found Raonaid in the village alehouse, seated like a proper hostess at a dinner table, at the far end of one of the long planked tables. Laughter and the clatter of plates and pewter tankards filled the air. A few clansmen were crowded around her, singing and clacking their mugs together in a chorus of cheer.

Angus strode the length of the long table and rested his hand on one man's shoulder. "If you'll pardon the interruption, I need to borrow this lassie for a minute or two."

"If you're looking to have your fortunes read, chief, you best have coins in your sporran! She drives a hard bargain, this one does!"

The others laughed merrily.

"I already know my fortune," Angus replied, as he held out a hand to Raonaid.

She glanced at it with cool suspicion, then finally let him escort her to the door.

Outside, the rain had stopped, the clouds had moved on, and the sun was shining. Raonaid lifted a hand to shade her eyes. "What time is it?" she asked.

The smell of whisky on her breath wafted to Angus's nostrils, and yet she showed no signs of drunkenness, for she could hold her liquor as well as any sword-swinging Highlander.

"Have you been in there all day, Raonaid?"

Her piercing blue eyes turned to him, and when she spoke, her voice was melancholy. "Does it really matter to you?"

He regarded her for a prolonged moment in the hazy afternoon light, and recalled a time when they had found pleasure and solace in each other's arms. She had helped him through a difficult chapter in his life, and he, in turn, had been a friend to her when she had none.

But just as often, they had clashed passionately and fought for days on end. Most arguments ended with Raonaid smashing something.

"Let me help you into the saddle," he said, crossing to his horse and gathering up the reins.

"I don't need your help."

Angus was in no mood to argue, so he waited for her to mount on her own, then swung up behind her. Together, they trotted toward the creek.

The distance was not great, so Angus was surprised when she tilted her head back and fell asleep on his shoulder.

He was careful to walk the horse most of the way over easy terrain. Thankfully they were the only travelers on the bridal path that led him into the forest, where he drank in the fresh scent of the pines and contemplated what he was going to say to Raonaid and how he was going to say it.

When they reached the creek, which flowed deep

and still through a quiet green glade, he urged his horse out of the shady forest and shook her awake.

Disoriented and confused, she turned slightly in the saddle. "How long was I asleep?"

"Not long." Angus dismounted and tethered his horse to a branch, then held his arms out to her.

This time she accepted his assistance and rested her hands on the tops of his shoulders. With a sleepy sigh, she slid gracefully down from the saddle.

"Always so gallant and strong," she murmured with an appreciative grin as she ran her hands over the width of his chest.

Angus immediately clamped her wrists and held them away.

She regarded him with questioning eyes, as if gauging his true desires and the strength of his devotion to his wife. Then at last, she stepped back and turned toward the water.

"What am I doing here?" she asked.

"You're an oracle," he replied. "Did you not see this coming?"

"See what?" she asked over her shoulder. "That you wish for me to leave? Why? Because your pretty Mac-Ewen wife does not approve of my presence here? Is she afraid that I'll lure you back to my bed?"

He frowned. "Is that your plan, Raonaid?"

She knelt down, picked up a stone, and tossed it into the water. "I haven't decided yet."

Angus watched her as she searched for another stone, found one and picked it up. She turned it over in her palm, dropped it onto the ground, then went looking for another.

Moving forward, he too began searching for a certain kind of stone, picked one up and handed it to her. She inspected it carefully, then hauled back and pitched it upstream.

Angus watched her resume her searching and decided it was time to say what must be said. "You cannot stay here, Raonaid. Surely you know that."

She swung around and exhaled with agitation. "After I came all this way to keep my promise to you? That is all you can say to me?"

She glared at him like a hissing cat, turned around and waded into the creek. He took an anxious step forward to follow—for he never knew what to expect from Raonaid. She was quick-tempered and volatile. It wouldn't surprise him if she tried to drown herself right then and there.

But she only splashed water on her face and waded out again.

Sitting down on the grassy shore, she tipped her head back and looked up at the sky, basking in the sun. "Why don't you come over here," she said, patting the ground beside her, "and lie down with me. There's no one around to see. You can slide up under my skirts if you like, or I could do that swirling thing with my tongue that you like so much." When he did not respond, she added, "A few minutes with me might help you see things more clearly."

He stood behind her, staring at the back of her head. "How so?"

"If you remember what it was like between us in the Hebrides, you might let go of the foolish notion that your wife is your one and only true love. That's what you think, isn't it? When you take her to bed, you believe that you are her true love as well, and always will be."

His gut clenched with annoyance, and he spoke in a low growl. "She is my wife, Raonaid. Mind what comes out of your mouth."

She smiled up at him deviously. "But I have so many interesting things to say. I still maintain that she will betray you. When her brother returns, she will choose him over you, and you will be dead because of it. The MacEwens will rule here once again, and when you are burning in hell with that rope around your neck, you will wish you had listened to me."

Angus rested his hand on the hilt of his sword, and watched the shiny water in the creek churn and flow slowly downstream. After a moment of quiet reflection, he sat down in the grass beside her.

"You truly believe that her brother will return, and that she will take steps to make him chief?"

"I know she will," she replied confidently. "Which is why you should not send me away. If anyone should be banished, it is the wife you claimed by force, who never wanted you in the first place. You were her enemy, Angus. She wanted you dead the very moment you stormed the castle gates."

He sat forward and looked at her intently. The loose tendrils of her hair hung in graceful curls around her face, but nothing could soften the shrewd, determined vengefulness in her eyes.

"Why did you not tell me about Gwendolen when you first saw my triumph in the stones?" he asked. "You saw everything else—my father's death, Lachlan's arrival, and the faithful army he would help me to raise. You described the battle in great detail, as well as the feast that would celebrate my return. But you said nothing of Gwendolen."

Raonaid shook her head, as if she did not quite understand it herself. "She was never there. It was as if she did not exist."

A blackbird fluttered suddenly out of a treetop, and they both looked up in surprise. Then Raonaid inched closer. She reached under his kilt and slid a hand up his thigh, and was just about to enter forbidden territory when he grabbed hold of her wrist. "That's off limits now, Raonaid. Only one woman is allowed under there."

Her eyes narrowed with frustration. "You're a fool if you think you'll be happier with her than you were with me. You should never have come back here. You should have left this place to rot."

"And stayed with you instead?"

"Aye."

He saw the unhappiness in her expression, the malevolence and loneliness, and could not bring himself to be harsh, even though he knew she was not what he once believed her to be. She did not know him as well as she thought she did. And she did not see everything.

"Murdoch is dead," he told her. "He'll not be returning to reclaim Kinloch."

Raonaid sat back and stared at him with a wrinkled brow. "Who told you this? Your wife? She's just trying to divert your attentions, so that you will send me away. She's afraid you will make me your mistress."

"Nay, she was not the one who informed me. I was the one who delivered the news to her."

Raonaid grimaced. "And you believe this is true?"

"Of course I believe it. It was my own man—a trusted and dependable MacDonald—who found Murdoch on his deathbed in France."

Raonaid stood up and stalked to the river's edge. "Your wife throws rocks at my visions!" she said. "She makes me doubt what I see!"

Angus rose to his feet and spoke firmly. "That's because the future is always changing. Everything we do makes a difference from one minute to the next. What existed in the stones when I left Calanais no longer exists now. Gwendolen despised me when I invaded, but her feelings have changed. Her actions would no longer coincide with what you saw in the stones all those weeks ago."

He realized suddenly that everything had come spilling out of his mouth before he'd truly pondered the truth of it. But there it was.

Raonaid regarded him with a hellish fire in her eyes. She was shocked, and in some ways, affronted, for he had found fault with her special gift—the one thing that set her above the rest of the world. It was what separated her from the common man, and removed the necessity of interaction. It provided her with a reason to live alone.

He moved closer. "You can change your own future, too," he said.

She was not willing to listen, however. Her mouth twisted wryly. "You're only sending me away because *she* told you to do it. She's jealous of me. She fears me."

"Most people do," he replied, "and I can hardly blame

them." He turned away. "I'll take you back to the castle now and provide you with supplies and enough coin to get you anywhere you wish to go. But you must leave in the morning, Raonaid, and never return."

"You'll regret this," she snarled. "One day soon, you'll wish you had kept me."

Angus reached for the reins to untie his horse. "It's time to go."

"Wait!" Raonaid stalked after him, and the harshness in her voice softened. "Please don't send me away. At least let me stay in the village. You can come to me secretly whenever you wish. I'll use the bones and potions in my basket to read your future, and you can use me in bed, however you like."

"I don't want to *use* you!" he replied. "You deserve better than that."

Her eyes clouded over with dismay, and she backed away from him. "Mark my words, that bony wife of yours is going to dirk you in your sleep."

He untied the horse's reins. "You're wrong, and that's why I want you gone from here. I will not let you poison my head with evil and falsehoods." He faced her. "Now get on the horse, Raonaid. We're going back. You'll leave in the morning."

She glared up at him with malice. "You may pretend to be sure of yourself and your wife's affections, but I see the fear in your eyes."

"You see nothing." Anger pulsed through him as he helped her into the saddle.

A moment later they were cantering through the woods toward Kinloch, while Angus strove hard to banish her poisonous premonitions from his mind.

* * *

The following morning, when it was time for Raonaid to leave the castle, Lachlan stood just inside the open gate. He was there to ensure she left without incident.

"That dirty MacEwen wife will betray him," Raonaid said, slinging her basket of bones and potions over her shoulder as she mounted the horse she had been given. "And when she does, you'll wish you had kept me here."

Lachlan escorted her across the bridge. "I don't reckon I'll ever wish that."

"You could have had me for yourself, you know, if you were clever. Instead, you turned him against me. I blame *you* for this, Lachlan MacDonald. You're the one who took him away from me, and it's your fault I am being sent away. I know what you said about me. You called me a lunatic."

He led her off the bridge and tapped the rear flank of the horse, sending her galloping across the meadow. "Safe journey, now, and try not to ride off any steep cliffs."

She reined in her mount and watched him enter the bailey. He gave the final signal for the gate to be closed.

"He'll soon be dead!" she shouted. "And when that happens, it will be all your doing! I will curse you for this! I will hunt you down and make you regret the day you set foot on my island!" She wheeled the horse around and galloped toward the forest.

Lachlan watched her until the gates closed in front of him.

"I'm not sorry to see that one go," the young sentry said, as he barred the doors shut. "She was fetching, no doubt about it. I've never seen such a chest on a woman, but there was something wicked about her. The lass gave me chills."

"Can't say I disagree with you," Lachlan casually replied. "I haven't slept a wink since she arrived. But she's gone now, and that's all that matters."

He turned and headed back toward the hall, his expression laden with concern.

Chapter
Twenty-four

That night, Angus knocked gently on Gwendolen's door and entered. A warm fire was blazing in the hearth, and the bedclothes were tousled and strewn, as if she had just awakened from a nap. Her eyes were red and puffy.

"You are mourning the death of your brother," he said.

"Aye." She moved to the table by the fire and offered him some grapes. He reached out and tore off a bunch, then strolled about the room eating them, while she poured him a goblet of wine and held it out.

He accepted the glass, swirled it around, and raised it to his lips. It was a superb wine—full-bodied with a spicy mix of flavors. He tasted cinnamon and cherry. "This is very good. You're not having any?"

She blew her nose into a handkerchief and shook her head. "I'm drinking ginger tea now. Mother said wine makes the morning sickness worse. Besides, that bottle is for you, especially."

He looked down at it again. "Why?"

"Because it was your father's. According to one of his servants, he said it was the best wine he ever tasted, and I thought this was a special occasion. We haven't yet celebrated the fact that I am with child."

Angus was pleased to commemorate such a happy event, even though he hated that he knew nothing of this wine his father had cherished. He believed his heart would always ache for the rift that had existed between them, for it would never be closed.

Gwendolen strolled to the window and looked out at the sunset. "When my father took Kinloch from yours," she said, "he kept that bottle for a long time as a trophy. He intended to drink it when Murdoch returned, but in light of recent events . . ." She paused, then faced him. "You should have it and enjoy it. Kinloch is yours. There is no longer anyone who would dare to dispute your rule here. And now the trophy is our first child together."

A tear rolled down her cheek, so he approached and wiped it away. "It's never an easy thing to bury a brother," he said.

"Perhaps that's the worst part," she replied. "I didn't get to bury him. I never even had the opportunity to say good-bye."

Angus held her face in his hands. "I understand your grief. I lost my father in much the same way." He gave her a moment, then laid a hand on her shoulder. "No one can ever replace Murdoch or your father," he whispered, "but I'll do whatever it takes to protect you and our future children. I'll be a good husband. I promise. You won't ever be alone."

Splashes of coral light from the horizon illuminated her face in the window. "All I want to do now is live here in peace," she said. "I want to put all this death and conflict behind us. Raonaid is gone, and I am glad.

And though I grieve for my brother's death, I still feel joy in my heart, for I cling to the hope that we will be happy together. There is much to look forward to." She laid a hand on her belly. "I am going to give birth to your child."

Angus could barely think through the shifting fog of his emotions. *God,* but she was exquisite, and she was *his.* Never in his life had he felt such desire and affection for another human being. He would do anything for her. He would walk through the fires of hell. He would sacrifice everything he owned, everything that he was.

He was not sorry for expelling Raonaid from Kinloch. It was the right thing to do.

"To your brother and your father," he said, raising the goblet of wine and taking a deep, hearty swig. "Both brave and worthy Scotsmen."

After setting the goblet down, he softly touched his lips to hers. She curled into his embrace and clung to him with sweet, overflowing fondness.

"Come to bed," she pleaded. "Make love to me. I want to feel you inside of me."

He drew back slightly. "Are you sure, lass? You lost your brother today. If you would prefer that I just lie with you and hold you . . ."

He would do anything.

She shook her head and proceeded to remove his weapons. "No, I want to make love. I want to feel alive and grateful for all the wonderful gifts that are still mine." She pulled his pistol out of his belt and set it on the window seat, then slowly unbuckled his sword belt and laid the heavy weaponry there as well. Next, she slid his tartan off his shoulder, unraveled his kilt and tossed it aside. He pulled his shirt off over his head.

As he stood naked before her in the golden twilight, his heart pounded in his ears and his body quickened with a desire that was both tender and demanding. All he wanted to do was ease her woes, assure her that she was loved and adored, and that as long as he lived, he would stand between her and harm's way. He would make her happy somehow. He would comfort her and satisfy her.

Yes. She was loved.

He loved her.

He inhaled sharply at the realization as she stepped forward into his arms. He buried his face in her neck, unable to get close enough. All he wanted to do was hold her like this forever. And when forever drew to a close, because of her, heaven might just be possible.

She led him to the bed and removed all her clothes while he stood and watched, assisting her when assistance was required. Together, they slid beneath the covers.

Her nipples hardened instantly under his touch, and she moaned softly as he took her breast into his mouth and pleasured her with careful, hungry caresses. She wrapped her legs around his hips and writhed beneath him, and their bodies moved together in perfect sensual accord.

When at last he entered her, his steely defenses began to slip away, and nothing could have kept him from opening his heart to her. He made love to her with agonizing, soul-drenching passion, and welcomed the flood of emotion that came when he climaxed. And when

Gwendolen clutched his shoulders and cried out with a rush of orgasmic rapture, he couldn't fight it any longer, nor did he wish to. There was nothing to be gained from resisting what he felt. He had not truly lived until now. Finally, he knew what love was, and now that he'd found it, he was never going to let it go.

Onora backed out of the Great Hall and crooked her finger at Lachlan. "Come hither," she purred, as she watched him set down his tankard of ale and follow with tantalizing amusement. "I don't feel like dancing," she said. "I want to go for a walk, and I'm craving one of those raspberry tarts from the kitchen."

"How remarkable," he said with a smile. "I am craving the same thing. You do realize it is a MacDonald who is in charge of the kitchen, and not a MacEwen?"

"And what is your point, sir?"

"My point is that you must bow to our superiority in all things connected to pastry."

Onora chuckled and scampered down the dimly lit passageway. "Fine. I will get down on my knees if it will please you, and I will be forever indebted to you for accompanying me."

"Why?"

She twirled around to face him. "Because I hate the castle corridors at night. Everyone knows it. I am afraid of the dark."

"You could always take a candle."

She playfully poked him in the ribs. "I'll have none of that insolence from you, sir. Not when I want something delicious in my mouth. Listen . . ." She halted and put a hand to her ear. "Those tarts are calling my name, and I think they are calling yours, too."

Lachlan laughed, and her cheeks flushed with excitement. He was the most beautiful man she had ever known, and a flash of wild grief ripped through her.

"All right," he said, "I'll come with you, but then you must promise to release me. I'm weary from all this dancing and singing, and I have many responsibilities. I need my rest."

She ran ahead, scampering down the corridor like a child. "Aye, I understand. I promise I will let you sleep when we are done. Now hurry up. My belly is aching with desire."

"I'm right behind you." His words were cut short, however, as he was struck in the back of the head by a wooden club. He crumpled to the floor, and Onora stopped short. All joy left her.

She whirled around to witness the second blow, then rushed closer and held up a hand. "No! You promised to let him live!"

Slevyn MacEwen lowered the club to his side and wiped a thick forearm over his shaved head. He was a large man—as big as an ox—and just as dim-witted. His two front teeth had been missing all his life, which was the result of a childhood scuffle, and a jagged scar stretched from his left ear to the corner of his mouth. *That* he had done to himself while shaving his head; he had used the blade to point up at a cloud that looked like a boat. He had pointed the blade too quickly.

"I don't know what difference it makes now, Mrs. MacEwen," he said densely. "He won't like you much after this."

"I just don't want him to die."

Slevyn shrugged, then gazed down at Lachlan,

unconscious in the flickering torchlight. He tilted his big heavy head to the side.

"He is quite fetchin', ain't he?"

Onora grimaced up at him. "You are not fit to even *look* at him." Then she covered her nose with a hand. "And you stink! Where have you been, Slevyn?"

"I crawled up the sewer to get past the sentries." He chortled, then bent down and lifted Lachlan up off the floor. He tossed him over his shoulder like a pliable sack of wheat. "Let's go, Mrs. MacEwen, before someone else comes along and I have to club them, too."

Onora followed him to the staircase. "You are a revolting beast."

"Aye, but it's served me well. It's why your son keeps me so close. Come along now. Slevyn is hungry. I heard you talking about raspberry tarts. Were you lying about that?"

"Nay," she replied. "I was being quite truthful. About that, at least."

She followed him down the stairs and laid a hand over the sickening knot of regret in her belly.

Gwendolen woke to a light knock at her door, sat up and laid a hand on her stomach. So much for the benefits of ginger tea. The morning sickness had already begun, and the sun was not even visible on the horizon.

She glanced at Angus asleep on his side. She didn't want to be sick, but wasn't sure how much choice she would have in the matter. She leaned over the side of the bed to see if the chamber pot was handy . . .

The knock sounded again, and she heard her mother's voice. "Gwendolen, are you there? Are you awake?"

Groaning with queasiness, she rose from bed, pulled

on her shift, and answered the door. "What do you want, Mother? It's the middle of the night."

"I know that, and I am sorry to disturb you." Onora rose up on her toes to peer over Gwendolen's shoulder. "Is Angus with you? Is he asleep?"

"Aye," she replied. "What is it?"

Nervously, Onora glanced up and down the corridor. "Something has happened," she whispered. "It concerns Murdoch. There is news of him."

"What sort of news?" Gwendolen asked.

Onora hesitated, then squared her shoulders and spoke directly. "I don't know how to tell you this, but he is alive. Your husband lied to us."

A jolt of shock distracted Gwendolen from her queasiness. Her voice faded to a disbelieving hush. "What do you mean, he lied? Why would he do that?"

"*Shh,* you'll wake him. Just come with me now, and I will explain everything."

She made a move to leave, but Gwendolen resisted. "No, Mother. I don't want to go with you. I want to ask my husband what this is about." She turned to go back inside.

Onora grabbed hold of her sleeve. "Wait! Please let me explain first. We don't know who we can trust."

"We can trust my husband," Gwendolen firmly assured her.

Her mother shook her head. "No, we cannot."

Chapter Twenty-five

Onora led Gwendolen into the solar. She stopped just inside the door and felt as if she were staring at a ghost.

Her brother.

Back from the dead.

"Murdoch . . . !"

She dashed across the room, straight into his arms. Here he was—the brother who had taught her how to ride a horse, how to shoot a musket, and how to play shinty with the boys. He was not dead. He was here!

"You're alive." She buried her face in his shoulder, while her body shuddered with a weeping flood of wonder and relief. How she had longed for his return, for so many, many months.

"Aye, my darlin' lassie." He held her close. "I'm so sorry I didn't come home when you needed me. I heard it was difficult."

She stepped back and laid a hand on his cheek, while she looked into his eyes and noted the changes in his appearance. His straight brown hair was cropped short, and his skin was deeply bronzed from the sun. It had been almost a year since she had seen him last. There were tiny lines at the outer corners of his warm brown eyes, where there had been none before—but he was still as handsome as ever, if not more so.

"It was difficult at first," she replied. "But it's better now."

Murdoch glanced with some concern at Onora, who raised her eyebrows as if to say, *I told you so*. He then crossed to the other side of the room, where he stood for a moment with his back to them.

Gwendolen knew immediately that something was afoot—something suspect and perhaps unsavory. The MacEwens and MacDonalds were enemies, and Murdoch had not been present for all the little alliances that had formed over the past month. He knew nothing of Angus's character and strength as a leader. He did not understand the history of her husband's claim over Kinloch, nor did he know that Gwendolen was happy and in love. As far as Murdoch was concerned, Angus was their enemy, and their clan had been conquered and subjugated. His sister had been forced into an unwanted marriage.

"I am expecting a child," she blurted out, hoping desperately that her brother would recognize her happiness and listen to her account of what had occurred at Kinloch since he had been gone. It was not as bad as he thought.

"Is that a fact?" Murdoch coolly replied.

"Aye." She thought carefully about how she should explain things. "When Angus arrived and claimed the castle, it was his intention to unite our clans, and he has done so with great success." Her brother did not turn around, so she continued to describe the situation as best she could. "He always said that if you returned, he would honor you with land and status. You must meet him, Murdoch. He is a good man, and there can be peace between the two of you, as there has been between our clans."

At last, her brother faced her. His eyes were clouded with disdain, and his lips hardened into a thin line. "You think there is peace here?"

"Aye, I do."

Oh God, what was happening? Had Angus indeed lied to them about her brother's death? Or was this some other secret treachery against her husband?

Her stomach churned with a rapid infusion of frustration and anger. She did not like being kept in the dark. "Tell me what is happening here," she demanded to know. "What are your intentions?"

Onora strode forward and took hold of her hand. "Come and sit down, Gwendolen. Listen to what your brother has to say."

"I don't want to sit," she tersely replied. "I want to stand."

Onora and Murdoch exchanged another concerned look, and Gwendolen's anger swelled like a blazing inferno in her belly. "You told me that we could not trust Angus," she said to her mother. "Why did you say that? Did he truly lie to us? Or was that *your* lie?"

Onora paused. "It's complicated."

"Mother, what have you done?"

"You may as well lay it all out in the open," Murdoch helpfully offered, "and let her choose for herself."

"Lay *what* out in the open?" Gwendolen asked. "Tell me what is happening here."

Onora sat down on a wooden chair and sighed with defeat. "The man who allegedly witnessed Murdoch's death," she said, "was paid handsomely to . . ." She paused. "To *manipulate* the truth for us. Murdoch was never ill. He has been in France for quite some time, and more recently in Spain. But he's been home for almost a month now," she added. "He returned not long after your wedding."

Gwendolen regarded her brother with surprise. "You've been here all this time? Why did you not show yourself? I was worried about you."

"Because I had to determine the lay of the land, so to speak. I needed to know what sort of enemy I was facing. Angus is . . ." He hesitated.

"He is *what*?" Gwendolen demanded.

"You know it yourself, Gwen. They say he is invincible. I could hardly come marching in here on my own and go to battle with him. He can't be beaten. He cannot be killed."

"He's a man, just like you," she argued, though it was not entirely true. Angus was like no other man.

But he was not invincible. He was human in every way.

"Were you responsible for the attempt on his life?" she asked, recalling that horrific night in her bedchamber. "Did you send that clansman to kill him in his sleep?"

"Aye, but that was no ordinary clansman. I sent a skilled Spanish assassin, and even *he* could not do what needed to be done."

She turned to her mother. "Did you assist him in this? Were you the one who provided the key?" Her blood was racing through her veins like shooting flames of hatred.

Onora lowered her eyes. "I'm sorry, Gwendolen, but Murdoch is my son. I had to choose."

Gwendolen regarded her brother and spoke with a dark and bitter loathing. "So what is your plan now?"

"There can only be one way for the great Lion to die," he explained. "By the noose—so that is exactly how it will occur."

"Where did you hear this?"

"From the oracle."

Gwendolen backed away in horror. "No, this is all wrong. You are misguided. Tell him, Mother. Tell him that Raonaid is mad."

Onora rose to her feet. "Murdoch, stop this, please. You are making it worse. Tell her about James Edward and the uprising. Tell her what you have been doing in France and Spain."

"James Edward?" Gwendolen repeated. "The Pretender to the throne of England? Are you involved in another Jacobite uprising?" Their silence confirmed her suspicions. "But we are not Jacobites," she argued. "This castle was awarded to Father because he was a Hanoverian. He supported the Union of Great Britain."

Her brother paced about the room. "That was Father, not me, and the Union has never been less popular, Gwen. Even those Scots who once supported King George are bitter toward the London government. We need our own parliament here in Scotland and our own Scottish King to lead us—and now is the time to strike. It is almost certain that England will go to war with Spain before the year is out. If that occurs, the Spanish King will send ships and support us in a full attack."

Onora broke in. "King James has promised your brother a dukedom if he succeeds in leading a Scottish rebellion. Imagine that, Gwendolen. Your brother—*a duke*."

"But we are not Jacobites," she repeated in disbelief, "and James Edward is not our king."

"Not yet, but he will be," Murdoch said.

She frowned at him and spoke with venom. "Is *that* why you left us a year ago? Is *that* why you and Father became estranged? I thought it was because of a woman."

He glared at her in silence, and she knew she had her answer.

"Angus wants peace," Gwendolen tried to explain, "as do I, and most members of our clan. It's too great a risk to go to war with England. Too many will die. I am begging you, Murdoch. Let this go."

Color rose to his cheeks. "I'll never accept their tyranny. We must have our own parliament."

"Then petition for it!" she shouted. "But do not drag us all into another violent and bloody battle that cannot be won!"

Heavy footsteps sounded in the doorway, and she was seized by the arms. *"Get your bluidy hands off me!"* she barked.

Onora stood up. "No, Slevyn! This is completely unnecessary. Murdoch, tell him to release her!"

Murdoch glanced uncertainly at Gwendolen, then at Onora. "I cannot," he said. "I don't want to hurt you, Gwen, but I need Kinloch. I already have an army assembled. They're just waiting for me to open the gates." He pointed at Slevyn, the foul-smelling brute who was dragging her to the door. "Take her to my father's chamber and lock her in. Keep her quiet until this is over."

"Until *what* is over? Murdoch, what are you going to do?"

Slevyn grumbled and squeezed her around the waist.

"We're going to hang the great Lion, lassie, so that your brother can be laird."

"But he'll fight you to the death!" she cried. "He'll *kill* you!"

"Nay, he will not," Murdoch replied, "because he's already been poisoned. All Slevyn has to do is haul him up to the rooftop and finish him off."

"You poisoned him?" Her whole world seemed to be disintegrating in front of her eyes.

"Nay, lass, *you* did."

She fell weak in Slevyn's grip, as a terrible realization flooded through her.

Her mother gave her an apologetic look. "It was in the wine, Gwendolen. Some kind of sleeping potion. We got it from Raonaid."

Gwendolen pleaded with her brother. "Murdoch, *please* . . ." But Slevyn was already dragging her through the door. "He is my husband, and I love him."

Her brother turned his back on her and spoke without feeling. "I am aware of that, Gwendolen, but I'm sure you'll get over it."

Angus woke to a pounding sensation inside his skull, like a hammer ringing on an anvil, and the foggy awareness that his arms were stretched over his head, and he was being dragged across a cold, hard floor. His wrists were bound—not that it mattered, for his body was unresponsive. He barely felt the scraping of his back across the stones, and he wasn't quite sure if his heart or lungs were even working.

"Here is good." It was a man's voice.

The dragging stopped. Angus's arms fell to the

ground. Slowly becoming conscious of the fact that he had been taken prisoner, his eyes opened instantly.

Gwendolen.

Christ. Where was he?

He was outside. Looking up at the stars.

How long had he been unconscious? He turned his head slightly and discovered he was lying next to a stone wall.

He turned his head the other way. Feet . . . A man's legs walking by his head . . .

The feet stopped moving. "Shite! He's awake!"

"Relax, Slevyn. His hands are tied, and remember, you're bigger than he is. Just put the rope around his neck."

A noose was slipped over his head and pulled tight.

Angus found the strength to jerk his body once, but that was all he could manage. He couldn't seem to move his legs. Then suddenly the rope was chafing his neck as he was being dragged again across the stone floor, this time by the throat.

He couldn't breathe!

The rope was strangling him, and he could do nothing about it, for his wrists were bound.

He was on the roof. That much he knew.

The smaller man, who had spoken first, grabbed him by the shirt collar and pulled him to a sitting position. Angus stared groggily into a pair of intense brown eyes.

"You're going to be hanged," the man told him. "We're going to toss you over the battlements and leave your corpse dangling there for the MacEwens to gawk at for a few days. I'm Murdoch MacEwen, by the way, and this is my castle, not yours."

"Gwendolen . . ." It was all he could manage to say in a rough, raspy voice.

Murdoch's eyes darkened with spite. "Aye, that would be my sister. The one you took by force, just like you took Kinloch. I didn't take kindly to that when I learned of it. Nor could I have done this without her. She's the one who poisoned you, Angus. I thought you ought to know."

Angus shook his head, and the next thing he knew, he was being slung onto the other man's wide shoulders. He was vaguely aware of a terrible smell, and the world spinning in circles, as Murdoch tied the other end of the rope around the stonework.

Angus wanted to fight. His fury screamed inside his head. Where was his sword? He needed to cut this man in half!

He remembered Gwendolen removing his weapons and setting them on the bench by the window. He was naked with her . . . in bed, in her arms . . . but he was wearing his kilt now. Someone had dressed him.

Where was his sword?

Oh yes . . .

A moment later, he was pushed from the battlements. He rolled limply over the side. Falling, falling . . . The rope would soon tighten around his neck, perhaps snap his spine. His heart exploded with fear, and then his mind finally jolted awake.

Chapter Twenty-six

The rope went taut, the falling stopped abruptly, and Angus bounced rigidly in the noose. He swung back and forth against the exterior stone wall, kicking and fighting, while all air was cut off.

He could hear the sound of the rope creaking while he writhed against the force that was pulling him down. Veins bulged in his forehead. He felt as if his eyes were going to blow out of his head. The rope chafed and burned his skin as it strangled his neck, but he never stopped kicking and bucking, until suddenly, there was a loud *snap*!

The pressure let go, and he sucked in a breath as he splashed into the darkness below.

Water filled his nose and ears, frigid and deafening. He kicked his legs, while fiery adrenaline coursed through his body, obliterating the effects of the poison. His awareness of life and reality returned, and the will to live infused him with strength. He tugged and pulled against the rope binding his wrists, and shredded his skin in order to slide his hands free. Then he broke the surface and sucked in a vital gulp of air. He bobbed below again, still weak and disoriented, while the sound of bubbles engulfed his ears.

* * *

"What the devil just happened?"

Murdoch leaned out over the battlements and looked down at the inky water below. He could hear the sounds of splashing, but could see nothing through the darkness.

"The rope broke!" Slevyn explained.

"Ropes don't break, you bluidy fool!"

"There was a knot in it. I had to tie two lengths together."

Murdoch regarded him furiously. "What are you standing here for? Get down there, pull him out, and kill him."

Slevyn ran to the stairs and descended to the bailey. He hurried to the gate, lifted the iron bar, then pushed the heavy oak doors open.

He turned around, deciding it would be best if he was mounted, for he might have to chase the invincible Lion down. Murdoch's horse was saddled and tethered a few feet away, so he climbed onto his back and rode hell-bent across the bridge, drawing his sword, but wondering uneasily how he was going to kill a man who could only die by the noose.

Angus crawled out of the moat and coughed up muck and slime. Shivering uncontrollably, he glanced up to see a horse and rider thundering toward him like a phantom through the mist.

He thought of Gwendolen suddenly and wondered if this was to be the end of his life. If it was, he could at least say that he had discovered joy—and yet, at the same time, he was filled with bitter, raging anger.

Had she truly poisoned him? Had it all been a corrupt affair? A false dream?

He knelt breathless on the muddy bank, his mouth hanging open, watching the rider grow closer and closer. His enemy drew his sword and held it high. Angus felt a chill in his guts, then scrambled out of the moat. He roared like a vicious animal, waved his arms about, and dashed toward the oncoming beast.

The horse spooked and reared up. The rider fell to the ground in a pounding heap of flesh that thumped hard on the ground.

The instinct to survive bashed about in Angus's muddled brain. Mad with shock, he bolted forward before the bald-headed warrior had a chance to recover. He kicked him in the chest, grabbed the sword from his hands, and leaped onto the horse.

"Yah! Yah!"

Wildly and recklessly, Angus galloped across the dark field toward the forest. Leaning low into the wind, he heard the warrior cry out in fury and knew that his pursuers would not be far behind.

Angus crashed through the underbrush while sharp stinging branches whipped at his cheeks and arms. He knew these woods like the back of his hand. He knew where the footpaths and cart roads were, and which ones to avoid. He galloped insanely until the horse grew winded, then he wheeled him into a thick sheltering copse to rest for a moment.

Tilting his head back, he looked up at the canopy of leaves above. It seemed as if all the birds and creatures of the wood knew he was here and had gone silent.

Suddenly the poison in his system stirred anew. He dismounted and staggered toward a tree trunk, where he retched into a patch of ferns.

Dizzy and sick, he leaned his forehead against the tree and shut his eyes. He didn't want to believe it— that Gwendolen had given him the poisoned wine—but he had watched her pour it, hand it to him, and drink tea instead.

Part of him clung to the possibility that she had not known of its foul component, but then he thought of Raonaid's predictions and how she had tried to warn him.

But she had not been right about everything, he told himself. He was not dead this morning. He had swung by the neck in a noose, but had somehow survived. Raonaid had been wrong about that, unless Murdoch caught up with him in the next few minutes and affected the future.

He had to keep moving.

Pushing away from the tree, Angus returned to the horse—*but God, oh God* . . . Gwendolen was still back there. He had left her and all the members of his clan behind.

And what about Lachlan? In all likelihood, he was dead. Murdoch wouldn't allow Angus's cousin and Laird of War to survive, only to later rise up and plot against him . . .

He rested his head against the horse's neck, while every desperate quaking impulse in his body compelled him to go back. He needed to know that Gwendolen was safe. He couldn't just leave her there.

Nausea poured through him, and he surrendered to the fact that he was in no condition to fight for his clan or rescue his wife—if in fact, she even *needed* rescuing, which he was not entirely sure she did. He didn't know what to believe. Part of him hated her, and he hated himself, too, for becoming so entranced, so trusting and vulnerable, that he did not realize he was drinking poisoned wine.

The other part of him wanted to fall to his knees and weep for the loss of her, whatever the cause.

Only one thing he knew for sure: Kinloch did not belong to the MacEwens. It belonged to the MacDonalds, and this was not over. He just had to get his strength back.

A crack of light pierced through the treetops. Feeling more determined than ever to stay alive and see this through to the end, he mounted the horse and melted deeper into the forest. There was only one place left for him to go now. It was time to revisit an old friend—and say a prayer that this particular friend wouldn't also be inclined to tie a rope around his neck and toss him off a roof.

Because he certainly had good reason to.

It was a fate worse than death.

Gwendolen pounded with both fists on the locked door, shouting and screaming—first at her brother who had given the order to lock her away in Angus's chamber, and then at anyone who might hear her and come to her aid.

When no one came and she confronted the possibility that Angus was, at that moment, being executed, she resorted to smashing furniture against the door and breaking the window. She was too high up in the tower to jump out, but she screamed her lungs out, hoping someone, *anyone*, would hear her. But minute after agonizing minute passed, and she was left alone, powerless to save her husband, and blaming herself for his untimely doom.

She had been the one to poison him.

Because he had trusted her not to betray him.

Gwendolen collapsed to her knees on the braided rug. What if he was dying now, at this very moment? What if Murdoch and his army of Jacobite rebels were cheering and applauding, while the life was draining out of her husband's body?

She had never hated her brother more. She was seething inside with a hellish rage she had not known she was capable of. She now understood Angus's hatred toward the English after the violent deaths of his mother and sister. She felt that same darkening of her own soul, and a powerful need to fight and protect. She remembered the feel of his claymore in her hands and wished she had it now, so she could use it against her husband's executioners.

Indeed, Murdoch was going to have to kill her if he expected to succeed as Laird of Kinloch, because when she was released from this room, she would have her vengeance. By God, she would have it. She would never forgive him for this—for the complete and utter obliteration of her happiness.

And all for the unlikely dream of a dukedom.

A key slipped into the lock just then, and Gwendolen rose to her feet. Her mother swept into the room and locked the door behind her. She barely had a chance to turn around before Gwendolen was upon her, wrestling with her for the key.

"Give it to me!" she demanded. "I need to save him!"

She had to do something. She did not know what. All she knew and felt was a wild desperation that plagued her like a demon. She could not lose him. He could not die.

"Wait!" Onora cried. "Listen to me, Gwendolen. He escaped. He got away."

Every nerve in her body went still, then sparked anew with hope. Yet she was afraid to believe it. What if it was a lie?

"Are you certain?"

"Aye. They tried to hang him from the battlements, but Slevyn tied two ropes together and the knot didn't hold. Angus fell into the moat and escaped on horseback. They've gone after him of course, but I thought you should know."

Gwendolen turned away from her mother and covered her face with her hands. "Thank God."

Onora waited quietly, while Gwendolen strove to calm herself and think clearly. She needed to decide how to proceed from here, and there was no point in smashing furniture. She must be levelheaded from this point on.

Swallowing hard, she faced her mother. "Where is Lachlan?"

The color drained from Onora's face. She rested one hand on her hip and cupped her forehead with the other. "He's in the dungeon and they have released Gordon. Lachlan is alive, but just barely."

"Why? What did they do to him?"

"Slevyn clubbed him in the head, which is my fault entirely. I led him to that slaughter, and I will never forgive myself. Just now the gates were opened and Murdoch's army has seized control. I am sorry, Gwendolen. I thought this was what I wanted before, but now I am filled with such remorse, I cannot bear it."

Gwendolen eyed her with derision. "You deserve your pain, Mother, and do not bother to come to me for sympathy or absolution, because you will find none. You alone will have to live with what you did." She laid a hand on her belly and fought back the tears she had not been able to shed through the wall of her anger, but now everything inside her seemed to be a tumbling avalanche of emotion. "He is the father of my child. Your own grandchild. How *could* you?"

Onora sank into a chair. "I agreed to this plan before all of that. You, yourself, resisted Angus at first. You despised him. I was only trying to help and protect you. I told Murdoch I would assist him in any way I could, but I didn't expect that we would both grow to love our enemies."

"You are referring to Lachlan? You think you *love* him? You don't know what love is." Gwendolen walked to the window and looked through the broken glass. "Why didn't you at least tell me what was happening? You let me believe my brother was dead. You kept me in the dark the entire time."

"I knew you would never be able to keep the secret. You're not like me, Gwendolen. You're not capable of lying and manipulating. The truth always shines out of your eyes, and Angus would have recognized your treachery. He is very careful of such things. Murdoch suggested that we both distract Angus and Lachlan from the defense of Kinloch while he gathered his forces. I knew I could accomplish that quite easily, but you had to do it . . . *genuinely*."

Gwendolen whirled around. "And I most certainly did that." She hated herself for being so naïve and gullible, that she could be used as a pawn by those she trusted most. "I am such a fool."

Her mother stood. "No, you are not. Your heart is pure, and you trust those you love. You see goodness in people."

"But you used that against me."

"Aye, which makes *me* the fool, not you, because I have lost my only chance at happiness. Lachlan has witnessed my deceit with his own eyes. He will never look at me after this. He will despise me."

Gwendolen considered all of this. "As Angus will despise me." She returned to the broken window and looked out at the hazy morning light. "I was the one who poisoned him. He will never believe it was not deliberate. Not after everything that has happened. Raonaid's predictions have come true, and I was the one who pushed him to ignore them and send her away."

Onora crossed to her. "Aye, but she's the one who made it come true. She was the one who told Murdoch how Angus would die, and Murdoch believed her. He acted in a way that would be true to her prophecy, while she encouraged him and manipulated him in order to exact her own revenge and prove herself right."

"But it did not work," Gwendolen said. "Angus still lives."

She sat down on the bed and said a silent prayer of gratitude.

"We all choose our own destinies," Onora said, moving forward. "I realize that now. We all have the power to affect the future. We make it what we want. Angus did not want to die. He fought against Slevyn and he escaped."

Gwendolen faced her. "What do *you* want from the future, Mother?"

She pondered that question. "I want you to be happy. I want my grandchild to have a father, and I want Lachlan and the rest of the MacDonalds to forgive me." She lowered her gaze. "But it's not that simple. I don't want my son to die or suffer."

"Sometimes we all have to make difficult choices."

"But how do we choose?" Her eyes filled with anguish.

Gwendolen strode forward. "It's very simple, Mother. Sometimes we must put aside what we want, and do the right thing instead."

Chapter
Twenty-seven

It had been a long day in the saddle, and another long night traveling through dark glens and silent forests, stopping only briefly to rest and sleep for no more than an hour at a time. Under normal circumstances, it was a two-day ride to Moncrieffe Castle, but Angus had done it in twenty-four hours. A new day was dawning, but with the gray morning light came a chilly wind and heavy rain. By the time he arrived at the gate tower, he was drenched to the bone, shivering and numb, weak from hunger and the lingering effects of the poison still moving through his body.

Teeth chattering, his tartan draped over his head like a hood, he walked his tired horse across the bridge where he was met by a broad-shouldered, ruddy-faced MacLean.

The clansman drew his sword and stepped into his path. "What business do ye have with the earl on this wet mornin', stranger? He's not expecting visitors."

Angus pulled the hood off his head and raised his arms to indicate that he was unarmed. "I am Angus MacDonald, chief of the MacDonalds of Kinloch."

The guard's bushy eyebrows pulled together with concern as he looked Angus up and down and observed his battered appearance.

"Come this way." The guard stalked quickly through the arched gateway, then waved to two other guards who came running across the bailey. "The Laird of Kinloch Castle is here. Get him inside and see to his horse. Quickly now. And inform the earl straightaway."

The two clansmen looked up at Angus in horror.

He was not surprised. He suspected he looked like a corpse.

Angus woke many hours later in a warm, fresh-scented bedchamber, under silk sheets and heavy covers. His eyes fluttered open, but he was too weak to move much else.

A damp cool cloth touched his forehead, and he found himself gazing up at a flame-haired beauty with striking green eyes, leaning over him curiously.

"Lady Moncrieffe . . ." He could barely speak. His voice was raspy and low.

"My word. A miracle, to be sure. Welcome back to the world of the living." She gazed down at him with kindness in her eyes, which made no sense to him. He had once threatened to kill this woman. He had terrorized her with malice and violence, and gone on to betray her husband, the famous Butcher of the Highlands. Was he hallucinating?

"How long have I been here?"

"Since early this morning," she replied. "You slept all day after collapsing in the bridge corridor, but you're all right now. You just need to rest."

"I was poisoned," he tried to explain, wetting his dry, cracked lips.

"Yes, you told us that. The surgeon has already been here. He said you will survive." She leaned back and regarded him with some concern. "You also said that your brother-in-law tried to murder you—that you were hanged by the neck from the battlements at Kinloch. Is that true?"

"Aye." He closed his eyes. "I can't seem to stay out of trouble, can I?"

"No, you were always very good at riding straight into it, just like Duncan."

Angus lay very still and quiet, contemplating the strangeness of this situation. "God was watching over me for some odd reason this morning," he said. "I'll never know why. I hardly deserve His mercy."

Gwendolen entered his thoughts suddenly, and the loss of her made his chest ache. He took a deep breath and felt a heated rush of urgency rise up inside him.

He tried to sit up. "Where is Duncan? Will he see me? I must speak to him."

"Please be patient." Gently, the countess pushed him back down. "He'll be here soon." She turned from the bed and rinsed the cloth in a porcelain bowl.

Angus noticed immediately that her belly was round. "You're expecting a child."

"Yes, our second."

"And your first . . . ?"

"A healthy son." There was a gleam of happiness in her eyes as she answered the question.

"The boy's name?"

"Charles," she replied, "after my father." Lady

Moncrieffe returned to the bedside and dabbed at Angus's forehead with the cloth again.

"Aye, the great English colonel," he said. "A good friend to the Scots. Duncan always thought well of your father."

"Yes, he did, and the feeling was mutual."

But Angus knew that her father was dead now. It was a significant loss for the Union of Great Britain.

"Can I get you anything?" she asked, heading for the door with the basin in her hands. Angus tried again to sit up, but she set the bowl down on a table and hurried back to his side. "Please rest, Angus. I will go and fetch Duncan right away. I promise."

He studied the softness of her face, the compassion in her eyes, and said with bewilderment, "Why are you treating me with such kindness? Two years ago, I did everything I could to destroy you, and then I tried to destroy Duncan."

"Things were complicated back then," she replied.

"And they are less complicated now?" He did not think they were.

"You are my husband's oldest friend," she explained, then proceeded to straighten the bedcoverings. Almost as an afterthought, she added, "And I read your letter."

He relaxed back down onto the pillows. "So you received it. I was not sure. There was no return message."

"Duncan was going to come and see you in person," she explained, "but he couldn't leave yet. He wished to wait until after our child was born."

Angus regarded her steadily in the iridescent firelight. "I understand."

As it happened, he understood it all too well, and his s were churning at the thought of his own unborn child back at Kinloch Castle, without his protection, in the care of his enemies.

And Gwendolen. His wife. His love—who had fed him the poisoned wine . . .

His heart throbbed painfully in his chest. His emotions confused him. He didn't know what to think, how to feel, what to do. Not that he was capable of doing much of anything. He was still very weak. He had to get his strength back. And he needed to see Duncan. There was much to be said.

With no idea how much time had passed, Angus woke with a start. He sat up and clutched at his neck, gasping for air while battling a violent urge to fight and kick.

The bedchamber was quiet, except for the snapping of the fire in the grate. A log shifted and dropped, and he stared into the hellish dancing flames, willing his heart to slow its harried pace. He took a few slow, deep breaths.

"I reckon you will be dreaming about it for a while," a voice said.

Angus squinted through the blur of the night and saw Duncan lean forward into view. He was seated in a wing chair in front of the fire, rolling a glass of whisky back and forth between his palms.

Angus had not seen his friend in two years, and his first response was joy—incredible joy—but that emotion was immediately smothered by his own sense of guilt and the certain expectation of Duncan's loathing. Perhaps even some kind of aggressive retribution. God knew he deserved it.

Angus tried to relax onto the thick feather pillows, while he braced himself for whatever was about to come his way. "I thought I was dying," he explained, while keeping his eyes fixed on Duncan's.

"Well, you're not dead. You were just dreaming."

"And you weren't inclined to wake me?"

"Nay." Duncan rose from the chair and walked to a window seat adjacent to the bed. He sat down again and watched Angus intently.

Duncan MacLean. Earl of Moncrieffe. Known to a select few as the Butcher of the Highlands. He deserved every bit of fame and notoriety that had turned him into a Scottish legend, for he was an imposing figure at all times—a fierce and brave warrior with more honor and integrity in his little finger than most men could ever dream of achieving in their lifetimes.

Tonight he was dressed in the MacLean tartan with a loose linen shirt. His jet-black hair was tied back in a queue. Other times he wore a different style of dress— silk jackets, shirts with lace collars and cuffs, brocade waistcoats with brass buttons, and often a curly black wig on his head. It was part of his dual identity. Part of his disguise.

Sometimes, in the eyes of the English, he was a gentleman.

Other times, a savage.

What was he tonight? Angus wondered uneasily. A little of both, he supposed.

"I'm surprised you let me pass through the gates after what I did to you two years ago," Angus said, sitting up to meet Duncan's blue-eyed gaze. "You have every right to hate me. I know that. I should burn in hell for what I did to you."

He had told the English soldiers exactly where to find Butcher, and as a result, Duncan had been captured, beaten, imprisoned, and sentenced to death. He would not be alive today if not for the courage of his English wife who risked everything to save him.

And today, that same flame-haired woman had nursed Angus gently and tenderly. Sometimes he was astounded by the charity and forgiveness of the human heart. His own especially—for he had never imagined he had much of one to begin with. Yet he was feeling a deep, profound pain in that area tonight. He regretted his past actions, his disloyalty and treachery, and he longed for the woman he loved, even when he doubted her integrity.

"Aye," Duncan said. "You were a bastard and a tyrant two years ago. I ought to shoot you through the heart right now."

"Most men would do that very thing, in your position."

A moment of tense silence ensued while Angus wondered anxiously if Duncan was hiding a pistol in the room. How he must have dreamed of this moment, when he was lying in that prison cell, knowing he had been betrayed by his most trusted friend . . .

Duncan tipped back his glass of whisky and finished it. "I have a bottle of my finest over there," he said, tossing his head toward the table by the fire. "You ought to take some. It might ease the furor in your gut."

Angus scoffed. "I don't think there's any drink in existence that can accomplish that."

"But it's the finest whisky around." Duncan leaned back. "You need to relax, Angus. I read your letter. I remember the pressures we were both under two years ago. They were hard times."

Duncan rose to his feet, poured a drink, and carried it across the room. Angus sat up in bed to accept it.

"All I wanted was to see Richard Bennett's head on a spike."

Bennett was the English officer who had raped and murdered his sister, and Angus understood now that he had been so consumed by grief and rage, he had become obsessed to the point of madness. When Duncan had decided to let Bennett live, Angus had lost his mind.

"But I was wrong to do what I did," Angus said, "and I wouldn't blame you for wanting to do the same thing to me now."

Duncan's broad shoulders rose and fell with a deep breath. "I might not have let you in here two years ago, but time has a way of tempering one's rage and healing old wounds. And when you find a way to live that makes you happy, it gets easier to let go of the things that once tormented you."

Angus nodded. "I have begun to see that for myself. Ever since I returned to Kinloch, I've thought of other things besides the past. I took a wife, and for a short time, I thought God might be giving me a second chance."

"But let me guess. You don't think so now," Duncan put forward, "because of what just happened to you. When you collapsed this morning, you told us that your wife poisoned you. That's hard to swallow."

Angus finished his drink and set it on the table, then tossed the covers aside and swung his legs to the floor. "Aye."

"Do you truly believe she wanted you dead?"

Needing to test his strength, he stood up and went to refill his glass from the decanter by the fire. "I don't know. It kills me to think it, but it also kills me to think that if she is innocent, I've left her behind."

Duncan watched Angus return to the bed. "I cannot tell you one way or another if your wife is innocent. I don't know what's in her mind, but I can tell you what I know of the MacEwens—for I've had spies at Kinloch ever since they invaded and killed your father two years ago."

Angus nearly fell over. "Are you jesting?"

"Nay, I'm completely serious."

"Do you have spies there now? And how did I not know this? Who are these watchers?"

Duncan shook his head. "I can't reveal that, but don't worry, they're on your side. It's the MacEwens I like to keep an eye on. After your father's death, I needed to know what to expect from my new neighbors. And I learned a few things you ought to know."

"Such as?"

"Sit down, and I'll tell you about your late father-in-law's politics."

They both moved to the two wing chairs in front of the fire.

"Was he a Jacobite?" Angus asked as he seated himself on the thick, upholstered cushion.

Duncan rested his elbows on his knees. "Nay, but his son was. It's why he left Kinloch a year ago—to reorganize the Jacobite forces and plan another uprising. He and his father quarreled about it, but his father chose to keep his son's politics a secret."

"Which makes sense," Angus replied. "Kinloch was awarded to him for being a Whig and a Hanoverian." He gazed into the fire. "So I have lost Kinloch to a Jacobite. How ironic."

His own father had been a staunch Jacobite, and Angus had fought for the cause in countless battles during the rebellion, both large and small. Since his banishment, however, he had desired only peace. Though he could not call himself a Hanoverian—he still resented the English too much—he had hoped to remain neutral. But it seemed there was no right side to choose, no guarantee of peace either way. There would always be warmongers. He used to be one himself. All he'd ever wanted was to fight. He knew no other purpose, no other way to satisfy his voracious hunger for revenge upon the whole goddamned world.

"What about Gwendolen?" he asked, looking down at the whisky in his glass. "Did you ever learn anything about her politics? She always claimed to be in support of the Union, but now I don't know what to believe. It may have all been lies. Every last bit of everything."

Angus took a drink to drown out the noise inside his head, but realized it wasn't helping, so he set it aside. Nothing but the truth could help him now.

Duncan shook his head. "As far as I have been able to tell, she has supported the Hanovers. There was never any evidence to suggest she even knew about her brother's politics. But she could simply be a good liar. Her mother, evidently, can seduce a grown man back into the cradle."

"Aye, she's been attempting that very thing with my cousin."

"Lachlan MacDonald?" Duncan said with surprise. He took another drink. "He's a solid warrior, from what I know of him. Not the type to be ensnared by a seductive woman. It's usually the other way around, isn't it?"

Angus nodded. "Aye, he's a notorious heartbreaker. And I don't know if he's dead or alive."

They both sat in silence for a moment.

Duncan reached for the iron poker and stirred up the flames in the grate.

Angus tipped his head back against the chair and closed his eyes. "What if my wife is guilty of this deceit?" he asked. "She's carrying my child."

Duncan hung the poker on the peg. "If she tried to poison you and was truly behind this plot to see you hanged, then the choice is simple. Arrest her, divorce her, and take custody of your child."

Angus lifted his head. "And if she is innocent?"

Duncan reclined back in the chair, and considered the dilemma carefully. "If you believe there is a chance she was a pawn to her brother's treachery, then you ought to drag your sorry arse back there straightaway and get your wife and castle back."

Angus considered his friend's forthright advice. "But how do I know the truth? Raonaid always said that Gwendolen would choose her family over me."

"The oracle?" Duncan scoffed. "*Och,* she may be a fine thing to look at, but she's a conniving witch, that one. Do not listen to her. Listen to your own heart, nothing else."

Angus stared into the flames. "That's the problem. I don't know much about my heart. It's been numb for too long. And even if Gwendolen is innocent in all this, I'm not sure I'll ever be able to care for her again, for she has done the one thing I did not want her to do."

"What is that?"

"She has made me weak."

Duncan frowned. "How so?"

He wasn't sure how to articulate it exactly, because it

was all so new. "I never felt fear before this," he said. "Now I know exactly what it is, and I hesitate to do what must be done quickly and instinctively. I'm distracted all the time. Part of me hates her for that, and wants very much to go on hating her for the rest of my days. Life would be so much simpler, I think, without love to complicate it."

"Simpler perhaps," Duncan replied, "but far less meaningful. And did I actually hear you speak of 'love'?"

Ignoring the last part of the question, Angus stood up and crossed to the window, where he looked out at the moon on the water. "Like I said, this wretched heart of mine has been numb for a long time. It might not want to be revived."

"Be that as it may, you have a castle to reclaim, and a clan that needs you."

"Aye, and I have every intention of fulfilling my responsibilities in that area, but I have no army at present."

Duncan stood up. "You don't need an army, Angus. There's another way to do this."

"Is there?" Angus was not so sure.

"Aye, but you'd have to lay your old vendettas to rest, once and for all. Bury them deep, and say good-bye to them forever."

Angus frowned uneasily. "What is it you'd have me do, Duncan?"

His friend regarded him with shrewd eyes. "I'd have you form an alliance with the English. Go to Fort William and tell Colonel Worthington of Murdoch's plans to raise another rebellion. They'll come down on him like a hammer."

Angus sat down and stared into the flames in the hearth. "Betray another Scot to the English army?" He shook his head. "I couldn't do it, Duncan. You know how I feel about the English."

His sister had been murdered by a redcoat. His mother's death at Glencoe was the result of an English order.

Angus shook his head again and sat forward. "Nay, I cannot do it. I must handle this myself."

"How?" Duncan asked. "As you said, you have no army. Any warriors who are loyal to you are either dead or imprisoned inside Kinloch. How do you suppose you'll be able to conquer your brother-in-law, who has already brought in his own forces?"

Angus rested his elbows on his knees and clasped his hands together. "By asking a favor of you. I know I have no right to expect any generosity after what I did two years ago, and you certainly don't owe me anything, but I must ask."

Duncan regarded him knowingly, then pinched the bridge of his nose. "Bluidy hell. You want to borrow my army."

"Aye."

Duncan sat back in the chair and thought about it. "I cannot go with you," he said. "Not when I have a child on the way."

"I understand. I'll lead them myself, if they'd be willing to follow me."

Duncan sat forward and nodded. "I'll make it so."

Angus felt a strange, hesitant joy inside himself. He supposed he was afraid to feel anything that invited hope.

They clinked glasses and drank in a sober, wary silence until Angus realized that hope had very little to do with anything at the moment. He had an army to lead and a castle to invade. That was all that mattered.

He leaned forward and rested his elbows on his knees again. "I don't suppose, in addition to the men, that you have a battering ram I could borrow?"

Duncan chuckled and downed the rest of his whisky.

Chapter
Twenty-eight

Gwendolen's bedchamber felt like a cold tomb in the deepest, darkest hour of the night, as she lay in bed unable to sleep, staring tensely at the silk canopy above.

It had been four days since Angus escaped the noose and vanished like a ghost into the forest, and four days of heavy, soul-crushing agony, for she did not know if he was dead or alive. After his escape, her brother's men had returned from a fourteen-hour search that had yielded no results. There was no sign of Angus in any direction—north, south, east, or west. For all she knew, he could be dead from the poison she had given him. He might have fallen off his horse somewhere and rolled down the side of a ravine. Or he could have drowned in a river or loch, and no one would ever know what had become of him.

Morbid thoughts, all of them, but it was impossible not to imagine the worst. Her entire existence was tightly coiled around the fear that she might never see him again. And even if she did, would he believe she had not, from the beginning, set out to betray him? She had done nothing here for the last four days except play the part of a sister who had accepted her brother's rule, and had therefore earned her freedom from imprisonment.

A successful reunion with her husband, therefore, would depend on the unfolding of events over the next few days. If everything went according to plan, there would be a great deal of activity at Kinloch, and her allegiance to her husband would be revealed.

She rolled to her side and rested her cheek on her hands. Perhaps that would be proof enough to convince him that she loved him, and that Raonaid had always been wrong with her prophecies.

Perhaps there was still hope, as long as her brother didn't kill her first—which he might very well do, once he learned what she had done.

Three hours later, a faint gray light from the dawn sky spilled across the floor of Gwendolen's bedchamber. She sat up in bed, startled awake by the sound of a horn blaring in the bailey.

They're here.

She tossed the covers aside and rose quickly, hurried to her dressing room and pulled on a plain woolen skirt, stockings, and stays. With fast fingers, she tied the ribbons in front, then slipped her feet into shoes. A moment later, she was racing up the tower stairs to the rooftop, where the pink sun was just striking out from beyond the horizon.

A few MacEwen clansmen were leaning over the battlements and arguing with each other. Dissension and fistfights were breaking out in all directions. Men were shouting at each other, while the ground beneath her feet shook with the deafening crash of a ram at the gate.

It was all so familiar, and yet none of it was the same. Last time, nothing could have stopped her from picking up a weapon and joining in the fight to defend her home.

This time, the castle was divided, and she felt no such inclination. Her heart drummed wildly against her rib cage. God help her. She was responsible for this.

Her mind swarmed with dread, for a battle was about to begin. The violence was already exploding all around her. Pray God it would be over quickly and end justly with as few casualties as possible.

Boom! The ram crashed into the gate, and *crack!* The sound of wood splitting compelled her to the edge, where she looked out over the side.

What she saw made her breath catch in her throat. This was not the invasion she had expected. This was not Colonel Worthington's army!

"Who is that?" she asked the clansman who stood beside her. "Who is attacking us?"

She had expected the English army, but these were Highlanders. Was this some other clan bent on possession of Kinloch? Was this a completely different vendetta she knew nothing about?

"It's the Moncrieffe army!" the clansman shouted over the deafening sounds of gunfire. His cheeks were white with fear as he loaded his musket.

Moncrieffe?

Gwendolen rose up on her tiptoes to lean over the battlements again, just as the heavy battering ram pushed through the thick gate and shook the foundations below.

"Is the earl with them?" she asked.

"We don't know, madam! All we could make out were the Moncrieffe banners and the MacLean tartan!"

Indeed, from this high vantage point, Gwendolen could make out no one's face. But she would know Angus from any angle or distance. Was he among them? Was he invading again, just as he had done before? Had he found sanctuary with his old friend, Duncan, the Butcher of the Highlands, and enlisted his help? Many times she had wondered if that was where he had gone, but she had shared her hopes with no one, for it was information her brother would have used against him.

The clansman beside her fired his musket, and she jumped at the thunderous noise, while down below, the Moncrieffe army was pouring through the gate into the bailey. Gwendolen raced to the other side of the roof and watched the invaders enter the heart of Kinlcoh, where they met little resistance. No one seemed willing to defend the castle or fight for Murdoch. Both the MacEwens and MacDonalds were laying down their weapons or fleeing altogether. Some were fighting among themselves, arguing over conflicting loyalties.

Except for Slevyn—Murdoch's witless ox, who was cutting down one Moncrieffe warrior after another . . . shouting like some kind of giant, ugly troll.

Where was Angus? Gwendolen wondered desperately, searching the bailey for a flash of golden hair. Was he even among the invaders, or was this something else? A political struggle? The Hanoverians against the Jacobites? Or was it a battle for retribution?

Then she spotted him—her husband, the great Highland Lion—riding recklessly into the castle atop a lathered black stallion, cutting a straight line through the center of the army, which parted for him like the waters of the Red Sea.

With a ferocious battle cry, he galloped toward Slevyn with his sword high in the air, gleaming brightly in the sun. Slevyn whirled to face him, while the thundering hooves pounded over the tough earthen floor. Angus swung his sword and knocked Slevyn's shield from his hand, then dismounted in a run while the horse was still galloping.

Fear squeezed around Gwendolen's heart, as she watched the two men meet and come to blows with their heavy claymores. The clang of steel against steel rang through the early morning air, while the warriors of all three clans looked on in a motionless hush of fascination.

Her eye was caught by Murdoch at that moment. He was late to arrive, rushing out of the Great Hall, while buckling his belt around his waist and adjusting his decorative dress sword. He looked like he'd just rolled out of bed.

Her attention swung back to the fight. Slevyn was a giant of a Highlander—bald-headed, muscled, and thick as a bull—but Angus was leaner and faster. His lunges and strikes were lightning flashes of movement. It was all too quick for Slevyn, who barely had a chance to turn before the point of Angus's sword pierced him through the heart. Slevyn fell to the side like a big tumbling tree. He bounced heavily on the hard ground, then went still.

Gwendolen saw Murdoch back away and melt anonymously into the crowd.

Angus raised his sword and called out, *"Murdoch MacEwen! Show yourself!"*

No one moved or dared to speak. Gwendolen too

was transfixed by the iron force of her husband's will, while another part of her was rejoicing. Her husband was alive! And he had come here like the invincible conqueror she always knew him to be, and had triumphed over those who had wronged him.

She had never loved him more, nor had she ever felt such longing and desire.

Delirious with the need to be reunited with him, she raced down the tower stairs and burst forth into the crowded bailey, shouldering her way through the crowd. Three clans were gathered, waiting to see which leader would prevail.

She pushed her way to the center, where Angus stood with his bloody sword in his hand, turning in a slow circle, his fierce eyes scanning the rooftops.

"Murdoch MacEwen!" he shouted a second time. His deep voice echoed off the stone walls. *"Come and fight me!"*

Gwendolen pushed her way into the open circle. "He won't come," she told him. "He's afraid of you."

Their eyes met and locked. Her veins pulsed with awareness and sudden, unexpected terror. She had envisioned their reunion many times in her imagination, but it had never been anything like this. She had not expected to feel the same suffocating fear that she had felt the first day they met, when his eyes were as cold and hard as steel. But again today, his whole being was raging with bloodlust. He looked as if he might lunge forward and run her through next—for the mere audacity of daring to speak.

"Where is he then?" Angus asked.

His lips curled contemptuously. It was as if he did not know her. As if they had never met, never made love or held each other in the tender silence of the night. He was looking for his enemy. That was all that mattered to him.

She pointed toward the powder magazine. "I saw him go in there."

Angus glared intently. "Is this a trap? Do you lie to me, woman?"

"No!" Her distress mounted to the surface. Her husband loathed her. She could feel it like a bitter winter wind. He blamed her for this, and he believed she had betrayed him.

Suddenly, her courage failed her. She could see in his eyes that he wanted only to fight. He needed to face her brother, who had taken his home and thrown him from the rooftop.

Angus was going to kill him. There was no escaping that fact, nor was there any possibility that Murdoch would defeat him. Her brother was not a skilled swordsman. That was why he kept Slevyn so close—to fight his battles for him.

He was a coward in many ways, and yet, she did not want him to die. Despite everything, he was still her brother.

"Please don't kill him." The words spilled softly over her lips, even while she knew it was the worst possible thing to say. But she had to say it. She had to plead for her brother's life. She couldn't simply send her husband to the powder magazine to hack him to pieces.

Angus's pale blue eyes narrowed. A muscle clenched at his jaw, and his fist tightened around the hilt of his sword. He pointed at two Moncrieffe warriors. "Seize her. Take her to the prison in the South Tower and lock her up."

"No, Angus, please!" She struggled against their hold, while a few brave and loyal MacEwen clansman rushed to defend her. They were quickly subdued, however, by Moncrieffe men, who held knives to their throats.

"Let me explain!" she shouted, while they dragged her away. "I didn't know this was going to happen. I didn't betray you. I didn't know the wine was poisoned. It was all part of their plot, and they used me!"

Angus pointed his sword at her from across the distance. A harsh loathing darkened his voice. "I don't wish to hear it. Not now. Take her away." He started to go, but turned back. "Do not harm her! She carries my child!"

He strode off to find Murdoch, while Gwendolen was dragged in the opposite direction. She fought hard, struggling the entire way. In the end, it took four burly men to get her up the curved tower stairs and into the cell, where she finally collapsed to her knees on the floor and wept uncontrollably with frustration and despair.

Chapter Twenty-nine

Angus strode with steely purpose to the powder magazine, all his muscles flexed, his mind sharp and ready for another fight. He would not think of the agony he felt at seeing Gwendolen again. Not now. Not at this crucial moment.

He pushed the door open and stepped inside, but stopped dead at the sight of Murdoch standing over a powder keg with a burning torch in one hand, his fancy jeweled sword in the other.

"One step closer," Murdoch said, "and I'll blow this entire castle into the clouds."

Angus eyed him shrewdly for a few tense seconds, then boldly marched forward. Murdoch sucked in a breath. His eyes grew wide with fear.

Before he had a chance to even contemplate the smallest defensive move, Angus snatched the torch out of his hand.

"You bluidy fool," he growled. He returned to the door and handed the flaming torch to one of his men. "Get this out of here." He faced Murdoch again. "I ought to run you through right now. You're too stupid to live."

Murdoch lifted his sword and lunged forward.

"What the fook is that?" Angus asked. "Have you been play-fighting? Did you think you'd be ready for me?" He shook his head with disdain, strode forward again with his heavy claymore, and knocked Murdoch's decorative weapon to the floor with a light, bouncing clatter. Murdoch raised both hands in the air and stumbled backward along the wall of powder kegs.

"You won't kill me," he said in a shaky voice.

"You don't think so?"

"Nay."

"Why not?"

"Because of my sister. If you lay one hand on me, she'll curse the day you were born, and everyone knows you are obsessed with her."

"Move away from the wall," Angus warned.

Murdoch moved to the center of the chamber. "All right," he carefully said. "Let's talk then. Clearly you have the advantage in a swordfight, but I have the advantage of social connections and the right politics. Your father was a known Jacobite. Surely you'll consider joining me. We can rule here together, and when England's war with Spain begins—"

"England's war with Spain?" Angus replied irritably. "I want no part of that."

"It's a chance for Scotland to have a king again," Murdoch insisted.

Angus looked him up and down from head to foot. "Nay, it's a chance for you to wear a coronet on your head. That's right. I learned of your treachery just this morning. You're dreaming if you think you'll ever be a duke, and I won't let you use Kinloch, and the blood of my clansmen, to seek your fortune."

Angus touched the point of his sword to Murdoch's chest.

His brother-in-law frowned at him. "If you're going to do it, do it now. Then everyone will know which side of the border *your* sword falls on."

Angus clenched his jaw and felt the old familiar fires of violence and vengeance burning through his body. It was a darkness unlike any other, and he wondered suddenly how many men he had killed in his lifetime, without a single thought to repercussions. The death of one man had never mattered to him before, because he had had no regard for human life, not even his own. *Especially* not his own.

But this man was Gwendolen's brother. He was Onora's son.

Without lowering his sword or taking his eyes off Murdoch's, he stepped back and said to his men, "Lock him up. But take him to the West Tower. I don't want him anywhere near his sister."

Murdoch offered no resistance as three clansmen quickly escorted him out. He looked as if he fully expected to triumph in the end.

Angus secured the powder magazine, then returned to the bailey where dozens of clansmen—MacEwens, MacLeans, and MacDonalds alike—all stood in fearful silence, staring at him.

Were they judging him? he wondered, as he moved to the center of the crowd. Did they think him weak for sparing the life of his enemy?

He stood before all the men and said nothing for

a long time as he looked into their eyes. He turned a full circle, scrutinizing each one of them individually, challenging anyone to voice disapproval, or raise a sword against him.

No one uttered a word. They simply watched him, waiting for something to happen.

He looked up at the morning sky, then at the four corner towers of Kinloch, and thrust his sword into the dirt.

"I am Angus Bradach MacDonald," he shouted, *"and I am chief and laird here!* If anyone standing in this bailey is a Jacobite, so be it. You may fight for the Stuart King if that is your choice. But Kinloch is neutral ground. All wars will be fought on distant battlefields. Not here." He turned around. "Men of Moncrieffe! I thank you for joining me in this fight today! Remain and feast with us tonight, then you may go home to your own laird, your wives and your children, knowing that you have an ally in me, Laird of Kinloch. Everyone else—pledge loyalty to me now, or begone!"

The Moncrieffe clansmen began to back away while all those who remained got down on one knee. There were none who were willing to fight him, nor did anyone turn away.

Angus spotted Gordon MacEwen standing in the arched doorway to the Great Hall. The old steward met his gaze, nodded at him, then dropped to one knee.

Afterward, Angus pulled his sword from the ground and moved through the crowd to address Gordon. "You're that quick to desert your MacEwen chief, when I locked you up like a turncoat and accused you of treachery?"

Gordon met his gaze directly. "Murdoch MacEwen wanted to drag us all into the war between England

and Spain. Even me. He told me I had to fight, or he'd have my head."

Angus studied the man's stricken face. "Your head has better uses elsewhere, Gordon. You're a good steward. You work well with numbers. The treasury needs you, and I'll have you back in that position if you're willing."

Gordon's eyes warmed to him. "I am, sir."

Angus rested a hand on his shoulder. "Good. Now tell me something. Where is Onora?"

He needed to know the situation here at Kinloch and make certain that she would not try to free her son, or seduce other men into doing it for her.

Gordon's face paled. "I'm afraid you won't find her."

"Why not?"

"She fled the castle two days ago. She ran off to marry your cousin and Laird of War."

Angus dropped his hand to his side and regarded Gordon questioningly. "Lachlan is alive? And you say he intends to marry Onora?"

No, that was not possible. It was a trick. Angus knew Lachlan too well. He would never marry Onora, or any other woman. Marriage was not for him. Never again in this lifetime.

"Aye, it's true," Gordon insisted. "Onora freed him from the prison and wrote a long, poignant message to her son, informing him of their love for each other and begging him not to come after them. She said her happiness depended on it and promised they would not interfere with his plans. Imagine that."

Angus was exceptionally pleased to hear that his cousin and friend was alive.

As for his unlikely marriage—it was a clever ruse

and means of escape, nothing more. Angus was confident that time would soon prove him right.

"What about your wife?" Gordon carefully asked. "If you truly want peace here, sir, you cannot keep her locked up. Her clan won't take kindly to it. How long will you hold her prisoner?"

Angus opened his eyes and gazed toward the South Tower, where Gwendolen was being held. Where was her heart at this moment? he wondered with a wretched pang of dread. Had she indeed done the worst and tried to poison him so that her brother could be a duke? If she had, he would have no choice but to divorce her and take custody of their child.

Or was there some other end to all of this? Had she spoken the truth when she claimed she did not know the wine was poisoned?

All he knew was that he had to proceed with caution, for he wanted, more than anything, to believe her. But how would he ever know for sure? If he spoke to her now, he might take one look into her wounded eyes and believe anything she said, for he loved her still. There was no denying it. He knew, however, better than anyone, that love had a way of clouding one's judgment.

He regarded Gordon MacEwen with sober eyes and resheathed his sword. "I don't know yet," he said. "I believe I will need to think on it a while."

Chapter Thirty

Gwendolen wiped the tears from her cheeks, gathered her skirts in her fists, and rose to her feet. She was thankful at least that she had been taken to the South Tower prison and not the dungeon in the West Tower, which was damp and infested with rats. Here, she at least had a shuttered window and a chair to sit upon, and the floor was planked with dry wood that had been swept clean recently.

None of that helped to lift her spirits, however, for here she stood, powerless to save her brother from the steely blade of her husband's wrath. Nor could she explain herself to Angus and make him understand that she had not betrayed him. At least not intentionally. There was no one who could confirm her story. Her mother was gone from the castle, and nothing had worked out as she'd hoped.

At least not yet.

She moved to the chair and sat down, folded her hands together on her lap, and did her best not to think about the dark and bitter hatred that had burned in her husband's eyes when she faced him in the crowd just now. No matter what happened, she could not lose hope. If there was justice in the world, he would learn the truth and forgive her for all that had gone wrong. And if he could not, perhaps she would need to consider the possibility that the love they shared had never been real in the first place.

She looked down at her hands on her lap and fought hard against the sickening wave of anguish in her belly.

There was still hope, she told herself. This was not over yet.

Gwendolen rose from the chair and went to the window, and kept her eyes fixed on the horizon.

Angus sank down into the hot tub in his chamber and rinsed the grime from his aching body. It had been a grueling two days, traveling through dark glens and dense forests with the Moncrieffe army, and an even more grueling morning, breaking down the gates of his own home, not long after he had just rebuilt them.

He had faced his brother-in-law and come very close to killing him, but he'd chosen to spare him and was still reeling over that decision. Six months ago, he wouldn't have given it a second thought. He simply would have rid Kinloch of the enemy. Love for a woman would have played no part in it.

But he was not the same man, and indeed, he did love a woman—even though it was possible that she had deceived him and colluded in the attempt to have him executed.

She had told him it was a lie—that she had been used and had not known the wine was poisoned. Did he believe it?

He wanted to. There was nothing in this world he wanted more than to feel the way he had felt with her before Murdoch's arrival. In his wife's arms, he had experienced some sort of rhapsody and had begun to believe that he was not cursed or destined for hell. He had never known such joy was possible, or that he could feel such pleasure with a woman.

But not just any woman. His wife.

He leaned his head back over the rim of the tub and closed his eyes, knowing that he was going to have to see her very soon. He needed to know the truth. He needed to look into her eyes and determine what was real.

A short time later, with his hair still wet from the bath, he stood in the South Tower, outside the door to the prison, watching the guard raise the iron bar. The door creaked open and he stepped inside.

Gwendolen faced him from the opposite side of the room, her hands at her sides.

He had come here intending to remain objective, but the moment he saw her, he felt a jolt. She was the most beautiful woman he had ever seen, and he desired her— even when he knew he should be wary. All he wanted to do was drag her to his bed and prove that she belonged to him and could be conquered like everything else inside these walls.

Another, less familiar part of him, however, wanted to get down on his knees and beg her to swear that she had always been faithful, and that she loved him, despite the fact that he was her brother's enemy.

"Did you kill my brother?" she quickly asked.

The breath sailed out of his lungs, as a harsher reality came crashing down. "Nay."

"Did someone else kill him then?"

"Nay, he still lives. I placed him in the dungeon."

Was that all that mattered to her?

The intensity in her eyes relaxed slightly, and she seemed to breathe for the first time since he'd entered the prison cell.

"I am relieved," she said. "I realize, of course, that you had every right to fight him to the death after what he did to you. So if your answer had been different, I could not have blamed you. But I am pleased. Thank you for sparing him. I am . . ." She paused and her gaze dropped to the floor.

"You are what, lass?"

Say it, dammit! Say again that you were innocent in all of this! That you never stopped caring for me. And look me in the eye when you say it!

But she continued to look at the floor. "I am grateful."

"Grateful?" He moved closer to her as his blood began to simmer. "Is that all? Do you have nothing else to say? You gave me poisoned wine, and I'm lucky to be alive. I should be beating you to a pulp right now. It's what most husbands would do in my position." He hesitated a moment, then began to pace back and forth in front of her. "You said in the bailey that you didn't know it was poisoned, and that they were using you. Is that true? And if you tell me it is, how can I ever know for sure?"

At last she looked up and regarded him with eyes as wide as saucers. All the color had drained out of her face. Her lips were parted. Her chest was heaving.

"You'll just have to trust me," she plainly said.

"*Trust* you?" He was finding it difficult to think straight. His emotions were rising up like an ocean tide and he wanted to hit something. Or walk out and never come back.

"Aye." She shrugged, as if to suggest there was no other answer.

"You think it's that simple?"

"Aye. You follow your heart, Angus. I know you never believed you had one when you first came here, but I know that you do. I may not want my brother dead, but my loyalty lies with *you*. It always has. I knew nothing of this plot. It was my mother who orchestrated it, and she kept me in the dark the entire time. And Lord knows, it was easy for her to do. I was so infatuated with you, my head was in the clouds."

"As was mine," he said. "And I paid dearly for it."

They stared at each other until he couldn't take it any longer. He was filled with such rage and frustration over the confusing mix of emotions flooding through him. On one hand, he wished he'd never met this woman— for she had knocked him onto his back. He had lost the steely edge of himself that made him an effective warrior. He had been set up and caught off guard by his enemies, and lost his castle as a result.

On the other hand, he was desperate to know if he could simply trust Gwendolen, with no hard proof, just her word. He certainly wanted to, and he thought he'd be able to recognize the truth—or perhaps the deceit—in her eyes, but it was not that simple, and he was afraid to trust his heart.

All he knew was what he yearned for—which was to hold her in his arms and claim her again. To force everything to bend to his will.

That was the kind of man he was, he supposed. He took what he wanted by force. He always had. It was how he had won her in the first place, wasn't it?

Wasn't it?

Unable to think anymore, he closed the distance between them and pressed his mouth to hers in a fierce kiss that roused his body and lit a fire in his loins. He wanted to bed her now, to possess and conquer her, and yet there was still a part of him that ached and pined for what they'd had before, when politics and deception had had no part in it, when everything had been tender and joyful.

"Oh, Angus," she sighed. "Do you believe me now? Do you believe that I played no part in this?"

No, he wasn't ready to believe it. Not yet. But in this sweltering instant, all he cared about was holding her. He had been away from her too long, and he needed her now. For some reason, he needed this, and only this.

He pushed her up against the wall and cupped her breast in his hand while he kissed her hungrily. She slid a hand down over his tartan and lifted his kilt, then massaged his privates with her warm, roving hands.

"Make love to me," she whispered, as she kissed his throat and chest.

Of course, he wanted to, but he wasn't thinking with his head or his heart. He was completely, mindlessly seduced by desire, and was secretly hoping that sex would give him the answer he required.

Then all at once, his hands were cupping her shoulders and he was taking a disconcerted step back. "Nay," he said.

"Why not?" She looked stricken.

"Because I still don't know for sure, lass, and this won't help."

A rush of anger skirted across her face. Or maybe it was disappointment.

"If it's solid, irrefutable proof that you need," she said, "you may have it soon enough."

"How?"

Her passions cooled as she moved away from him. "Because *I* was the one who freed Lachlan from his prison cell. I instructed my mother to write a note about an elopement. I told her exactly what to say, then I sent them both to Fort William to inform Colonel Worthington of my brother's traitorous activities with Spain. When your cousin returns, he will attest to that. And incidentally, the English army could arrive at any moment to arrest Murdoch and restore Kinloch to you—our proper laird."

Angus regarded her with surprise in the midday light. "You betrayed your brother?"

And why had she waited until this moment to tell him?

She turned her back on him. "I prefer not to think of it that way. I want to believe that I did the right thing, because I was faithful to *you,* my husband, and the Union of Great Britain. Another rebellion against England could only end badly, I am sure of it. Besides, after what Murdoch tried to do to you . . ." She paused and steadied her voice. "But I thought you would have more faith in me, Angus. That you would return and believe me when I told you that I had nothing to do with Murdoch's plan. How could you truly believe that I would do such a thing to you? That I would poison you? My own husband?"

He stepped forward to touch her, but she held up a hand. "Please, don't. Just go, and come back when—and *if*—you find the proof that you require in order to trust me."

Perhaps he should have argued with her and convinced her that he needed no other proof, that her word was enough, but for some reason, it had not been. If she had not offered him this evidence of her devotion, he would still be as doubtful as he was when he first walked in.

He wished he felt differently, but he supposed he was too jaded to take such a leap of faith. He had been wronged and injured many times in his life. He had even betrayed his closest friend, so he knew how easy it was to deceive someone. It was not so easy, therefore, to trust that it would not happen to him again. He had certainly earned it.

He turned to leave, but she stopped him. "Wait. What will you do with my brother?"

He paused. "I haven't decided yet."

"Will you have him executed?"

Angus inclined his head and studied her expression carefully. "Perhaps I will follow your example and turn him over to the English."

She relaxed her shoulders slightly. "I know that what he did to you was wrong, but as I said before, he is my brother, and I don't want him to die. For that reason, I have written a formal plea to Colonel Worthington to be lenient with his sentencing, in exchange for my testimony against him. I've promised written evidence of Murdoch's activities in Spain."

"And you'd trust the English to let him live, once they convict him of treason?"

Her shoulders rose and fell with a heavy sigh. "Perhaps I am more willing to trust a person's word, once given. You taught me that once. Remember?"

Angus shook his head in disbelief. "Even after what

your brother—and your own mother!—did to you? How they used you, Gwendolen?"

She answered without the slightest hesitation. "Aye, because what is the alternative? To give up on trust completely? People make mistakes sometimes, but if we care about someone, and he or she is truly remorseful, then we must forgive. And occasionally, a second chance is all that's required for true redemption. You of all people should know that."

He inhaled sharply. "Does your brother not deserve a second chance? Or do you offer your forgiveness selectively?"

"He tried to kill you, Angus, and I believe if given the chance, he would do it again. So there are limits to my forgiving nature. My brother feels no remorse. That is how I know I am doing the right thing. He is not the man I once thought him to be."

They stood apart in the prison cell for a long time, saying nothing. After a while, Angus realized that the fiery rage he had experienced earlier was gone, and he felt a great admiration for his wife.

He was quite certain now that he believed her about the wine and everything else, but he wasn't sure why he had been so blessed to have claimed such a woman as a wife. He did not feel worthy of her.

Perhaps that's what was holding him back. Or was it something else? Perhaps he was simply incapable of giving his heart to another person. Perhaps it was too deeply scarred, and there was no hope of absolute, fearless love. Not ever. Perhaps this was the best he could do—to love cautiously.

He thought of his mother just then, and experienced a jarring flash memory of her face as she lay dead in the snow. He was only four years old when she was taken from him.

His eyes fell to Gwendolen's abdomen, where his own child was growing in her womb. Somehow he knew this child would be brave and strong and sensible. How could he, or she, be anything but, with this woman for a mother?

He gazed serenely at Gwendolen from across the distance of the room. "You are free to go," he said. "I'll not keep you locked up."

"Thank you, I suppose."

He turned from the room and instructed the guard not to bar the door behind him, for his wife would be returning to her own private apartments. Then he descended the stairs and headed for the treasury. He needed to speak to Gordon MacEwen and send an important dispatch.

An hour later, after the battering ram was removed from the drawbridge and the debris from the broken gate was cleared away, Angus stood on the rooftop, watching his dispatch carrier leave the castle. The young clansman trotted over the bridge and broke into a gallop on the midday field. He circled around to the east, in the direction of Fort William.

Angus walked along the stone battlements, watching the clansman grow distant, and already, he felt impatient for his return.

Chapter Thirty-one

Gwendolen pulled off her shoes and stockings and sat down at the small table in her bedchamber, which she had dragged closer to the fire. A kitchen maid had delivered supper on a tray. It was a tasty meal of rabbit stew with chunks of hearty bread for dipping, and sweet fig pastries for dessert, but her appetite was sparse, for her mind was consumed by thoughts of Angus and what had passed between them that day.

She was angry with him. There was a part of her that wanted to shout and scream at him, and call him a fool for assuming the worst about her and failing to see the love she bore him.

The other, less volatile part of her understood why he was so guarded. Her family *had* tried to poison him after all. On top of that, he had lived a violent life, and not only had he witnessed considerable cruelties, he had inflicted a great deal of cruelty upon others. He was fierce, vicious, and brutal, and openly admitted that he had done things he was not proud of. Because of all that, he was damaged—which was why she felt she must be patient and allow him some time to accept the idea that she would never intentionally cause him pain.

A knock sounded at the door, and she sat forward in

the chair, her heart beating fast. Was it too much to hope that Angus had come at last to reconcile?

She dabbed at her mouth with a napkin and struggled not to get her hopes up. Pushing her chair back, she rose and padded across the plank floor. "Who is it?"

"It's Mother."

Gwendolen sucked in a breath of surprise, then quickly opened the door. "You've returned. What happened? Did you bring the English army with you? Please tell me that you didn't change your mind about—"

Her mother entered and shut the door behind her. "Nay, I didn't change my mind, and aye, we brought the English army. Colonel Worthington is here, and they are taking Murdoch into custody now." Her eyes darkened with remorse. "But I don't know if I will be able to live with myself, Gwendolen. What have I done? He is my only son."

Gwendolen recognized the depth of her mother's sacrifice and took her into her arms. "It cannot have been easy, but you did the right thing. Murdoch would have dragged us all into a hopeless war for his own selfish gains. You have saved many lives and ensured peace for our clan. It's what Father would have wanted. He never believed in the Jacobite cause. He was a Hanoverian." Gwendolen stepped back and looked into her mother's eyes.

Onora wiped a tear from her cheek.

"Come and sit down," Gwendolen said. "Tell me everything. What news is there of Lachlan? Did he return with you?"

Onora sat before the fire. "Aye. He's with Angus and Worthington now. They are discussing everything over a bottle of whisky. As it turns out, your husband sent a dispatch to the fort, confirming what we already told Worthington about Murdoch, and we crossed the rider's path on our way here. The colonel sent his army back to the fort and pushed on with a smaller number of men to arrest Murdoch. It seemed all the hard work of breaking down the gate had already been done."

"Indeed it was." And now Angus would know that she had been telling the truth about sending Lachlan to Fort William. "Have you heard anything of Raonaid?" Gwendolen asked. "No one has seen her since Angus escaped."

"I've heard nothing, except that she promised to curse Lachlan for taking Angus away from her in the first place."

They sat in silence for a few minutes, each reflecting upon the events of the past week.

"What happened between you and Lachlan over the past few days?" Gwendolen asked. "Did he forgive you for what happened in the passageway?"

Onora looked down at her hands on her lap. "He was upset with me, to be sure. As soon as we were out of sight of the castle, I thought he was going to wring my neck. Thankfully he kept his mind fixed on escaping and helping Angus reclaim Kinloch. By the time we sneaked away and made it as far as the forest, he was grateful for my assistance at least. As for gaining his forgiveness . . . Well . . ." Onora shook her head. "He has accepted my apology. That will have to be enough."

Gwendolen poured her mother a cup of wine and gave her a moment to compose her emotions. "Is there no hope at all for something more between you? Perhaps someday in the future?"

Onora looked as if she had already given that question ample consideration and had made peace with the answer.

"None, darling," she replied. "There is absolutely none, and strangely I am not heartbroken. I have, after all, done something brave this week. I stood up to my son." She lowered her eyes to her lap. "I hope Murdoch will see the error in his ways and become a better man. It is possible, I believe, because I have just discovered that there may be something more to me than looks alone. I am beginning to understand that I do not always have to rely on my feminine charms to exert some influence in the world. I never believed it before, but I believe it now. People can change." She glanced up at Gwendolen and managed a small smile. "Perhaps I, too, will learn how to handle a claymore."

Gwendolen regarded her mother with a smile and raised her goblet into the air.

That night, the lion came to Gwendolen in her dreams—a beautiful golden spirit stalking across a lush green meadow. He sat down in the tall grass and waited for her to approach.

Gwendolen knelt down and smiled, and stroked his soft, tawny mane. The lion sniffed her ear and nuzzled her neck.

"I don't know why you are so angry with me," she said. "I didn't do anything wrong." Then he roared in her face. It was so loud, she felt it rumble in her chest and had to cover her ears and shut her eyes.

Gwendolen sat up and looked around her bedchamber. Everything was dark. Her heart was racing. "Angus? Are you here?"

But the door was shut. The room was silent. She laid her head back down on the pillow, and tried to go back to sleep.

Murdoch MacEwen was removed from Kinloch Castle the following day in a secured prison carriage. Gwendolen stood at the battlements over the East Tower, watching as her brother was taken away, escorted by Colonel Worthington, a few mounted officers, and a small company of foot soldiers.

A part of her felt unspeakably ashamed, for she had orchestrated the capture and arrest of her own brother. The more logical side of her knew, however, that it had been the right choice. Tragedy would have befallen their clan had she allowed Murdoch to continue toward his selfish ambitions of securing a dukedom for himself. She had to think of the welfare of her people, as well as her unborn child, and there was never any doubt in her mind that she was absolutely, unconditionally loyal to her husband.

She hoped that one day Angus would come to appreciate that fact and understand that she wanted the same things he did. Peace, most importantly. She had, after all, sacrificed her brother for it.

"I have it now," a voice said, behind her.

Startled, she swung around to find herself gazing at her husband, the great Scottish Lion. His hair was tied back in a neat queue. He wore a clean white shirt, and the brooch that was pinned to his tartan was polished to a fine, bright sheen.

"What is it, exactly, that you have?" she asked, determined to challenge him, for he had certainly challenged her in recent days.

"Proof. Proof of your loyalty to Kinloch. And to me." He strode closer, slowly, and a warm breeze lifted a lock of his hair that had fallen forward at his temple.

"How wonderful for you," Gwendolen coolly replied. "Now you can rest easy at night knowing your wife isn't going to poison you, or dirk you in your sleep."

She saw a spark of amusement flash across his eyes. It was not something she'd expected, nor had she seen it often in the past. He was a very menacing sort of man, most of the time.

"Unless I take up with Raonaid again, or some other woman," he added, seeming quite determined to correct her on that point. "You threatened me once about that, if I recall, and I took you seriously, lass."

She strolled closer to him. "Ah yes, I remember. It was after you raised my skirts and had me on top of a desk. It was not our finest hour, Angus. You had just accused me of lying about carrying your child, and you suspected me of plotting your death."

"But you enjoyed the lively shagging, didn't you?" he asked, ignoring all the rest. "I'm quite sure you did."

They stood before each other on the rooftop, barely a foot apart, and Gwendolen wondered if it was possible for a woman to collapse from the overwhelming effect of conflicting emotions—for despite everything, her husband was still the most beautiful, fascinating man alive, and she would have done anything at that moment just to touch him.

"Maybe I did enjoy it," she said, "but the fact remains, you thought the worst of me. You did not believe I was loyal. You later thought I knowingly gave you poisoned wine when I did no such thing. I would never have done that, and I told you so, but still—you could not trust me."

His thick, broad chest expanded with a deep intake of breath, then he drew his sword. Gwendolen stepped back, unnerved by the threatening sight of Angus the Lion, looking as if he were preparing to engage in battle. To her surprise, he dropped to one knee and rested the point of his sword on the stone floor in front of him. He gripped the hilt in both hands.

"I am Angus Bradach MacDonald," he softly said, "and I pledge my allegiance to you, Gwendolen MacEwen—my wife, mother of my child. I was wrong to doubt you."

He closed his eyes, as if he was waiting for something.

"What do you want me to do?" she asked. "Tap you on the shoulder and say that you are forgiven?"

He looked up. "Aye, that would do."

She frowned and smacked him across the side of the head. "Are you mad? I did nothing but pledge allegiance to you repeatedly and satisfy you in bed—also repeatedly. I was fertile enough to make you an expectant father after a mere month of marriage, and still, was that enough? No. I admit, my mother was a devious vixen and my brother was a self-seeking scoundrel, but *never* did I do anything to betray you. I was a good wife, who was deceived, just as you were. Yet you treated me like a woman deserving of punishment. You locked me up like a criminal and didn't believe me when I told you I was innocent. Bluidy well right, you are on your knees now! I ought to tell you to stay there for a year!"

Her husband looked up at her with surprise, then his lips widened into a smile, and he bent forward, laughing.

It was the first time she had seen her husband smile in such a way, let alone laugh. She had *never* seen him laugh. Not once.

Gwendolwn frowned. "Are you laughing at me?"

He nodded, as tears spilled from the outer corners of his clear blue eyes. "Aye, lassie! I just realized that you're madder than the witch I lived with in the Hebrides for the better part of a year. You're fookin' insane!"

Gwendolen began to laugh, too, and wondered how it was possible that she could forgive him so easily for all the pain he had caused her.

"It's not funny," she said, deeply offended, irritated, and amused—all at the same time. "I held true to my pledge, so you never had any right to be angry with me. I did nothing wrong."

He slowly rose to his feet, and his smile faded. "You're right about that, lass. I was the one who was wrong, and it had nothing to do with you. It was me." He paused. "It's just that . . . I've never loved anyone before, so I'm a bit . . . I'm a bit raw."

Her heart softened immediately at the sound of the word "love," spoken so openly from his very own lips. How she had dreamed of hearing him say it, just once. How she had wanted to feel his affections. "Aye, that you are."

"It's not that I didn't believe you about the wine," he continued. "I did. I knew you were telling the truth, and that your brother tricked you. I think I knew it all along, but I was afraid to believe it, afraid of being disappointed somehow—because I've had a hard life, lass.

I lost the only two women in the world I ever cared about."

"Your mother and sister . . ." she finished for him.

"Aye. All my life, I've lived for vengeance and nothing else. Even when I first met you and claimed you as my bride, there was a part of me that wanted to hurt you, to be cruel to you, because I saw you as the enemy. I saw *everyone* as the enemy—even those I cared about. But since being with you, lass, my desire to fight and take my revenge out on the world has waned. It's a part of me that has gone very . . ."

Gwendolen stepped forward, curious. "Very what, Angus?"

He squinted toward the horizon. "Very quiet."

Reaching out with a shaky hand, she touched his cheek. "I'm glad."

He turned his lips into her palm, held it tight, and kissed it. Then he pulled her into his arms and embraced her for a long, shuddering moment. At last, he pressed his mouth to hers. His lips were like sweet, warm honey, his tongue like an intoxicating wine that made her melt with delight. Backing her up against the stone battlements, he kissed down the side of her neck and cupped her head in his hands.

"Oh, Angus," she sighed, "I want to stay mad at you, but I cannot. You make my knees go weak when you talk like this, because it's such a revelation. The first day I saw you, I was terrified. I still am, in so many ways."

"There is no need to fear me now, lass. I'll never do you harm. I'd die to protect you from it."

She pulled him down for another kiss. It was tender and deep, and she felt as if she were drowning in endless rapture. Her hands moved slowly up the hard muscles of his arms and came to rest on the tops of his broad shoulders. She ran her palm down the length of his tartan, draped across his chest.

"I dreamed of the lion last night," she told him, recalling her fantasy encounter with the beast in the meadow. "And I don't think I am an oracle after all."

He drew his head back. "Why is that?"

"Because I dreamed that I told him he had no right to be angry with me, and he roared at me and made my insides tremble. But you are not roaring at me, Angus. You are kissing me and loving me."

He gazed down at her in the dazzling morning sunshine. "Aye, but there are many ways I can make you tremble, my darling Scottish lassie." He lifted her skirts and slowly slid his hand up her leg. "Like this, for instance."

Her whole being flooded with desire. "Ah, I believe you may be right . . ."

He gently massaged her behind. "And what about this?"

She closed her eyes and nodded, then her wild lion nuzzled her ear and kissed her neck until she was overcome by waves of sweet agony.

"Do you know what comes next?" he asked.

"I think I do."

"Then it appears you're still having premonitions."

Gwendolen smiled. "I'll believe it when you make me cry out in ecstasy from all the roaring passion that is yet to come."

He slid a finger inside her heated depths and stroked her with great finesse. "I'd better get busy then, because clearly I have something to prove."

And indeed, Gwendolen MacDonald, wife of the great Scottish warrior, Angus the Lion, trembled amorously from head to foot on the roof that day, and the trembling continued later in the laird's private chamber—on the bed, on the floor, and on top of his desk—until well into the night.

Read on for an excerpt from
Julianne MacLean's next book

PRINCESS IN LOVE

Coming in October 2012 from St. Martin's Paperbacks

June 22, 1814

"What is happening? Dear Lord, we are all going to die!"

The coach swerved ominously like a snake's tail behind the frightened team of horses. With terrifying violence, Rose was tossed out of her seat and thrown against the side door.

"We are not going to die!" she shouted to the dowager Duchess of Pembroke. It seemed a rather silly assertion, however, spoken from the floor of the coach where she was blind as a bat because her bonnet had fallen forward over her face.

She tugged it back and groped at the seat cushions to remove herself from the floor, when suddenly the coach veered sharply again in the opposite direction. She shot across the interior like a cannon ball and slammed into the window.

"Oh, my word!" the duchess cried. "Are you hurt?"

The coach was still careening left and right. Rose scrambled to her knees and reached for something—*anything*—to hold on to for she had no wish to go flying through the air a third time.

"I am well enough," she replied, though she'd landed hard on her wrist and it was throbbing painfully. "And you, Your Grace? Are you hurt?"

A cacophony of shouts and hollers began outside the coach as the team was brought under control and the coach at last drew to a halt. Everything went suddenly still and blessedly quiet.

"What happened?" the dowager asked in a daze.

Rose struggled to her feet and tasted blood on her lower lip. It was already beginning to swell.

"I am not certain," she replied, "but we at least seem to be out of harm's way."

She was just climbing onto the seat when the coach door flew open. "Everything all right in here?" the driver asked with wide eyes. The dowager's footman appeared in the open doorway beside him.

"Yes, I believe so," Rose replied, though she was aching all over and the dowager was white as a sheet.

"My apologies," he said. "We hit a slippery patch and one of the horses kicked another before they all went stark raving mad. We're lucky we didn't flip over and roll down the hillside."

"Lucky indeed," the dowager replied with notable sarcasm.

Rose leaned her head back against the seat and shut her eyes. *Thank God we are all safe.*

Quickly recovering her senses, she sat forward. "What about you, Samson? And Charles? Unscathed I hope?"

"Yes, ma'am," Samson replied. "Just a little shook up, is all. It was quite a ride. I thought we were done for."

Perhaps it was the fragile state of her nerves, or a

sudden burst of euphoria at having cheated death, but Rose found herself laughing.

"I believe we are in agreement there, Mr. Samson. If only you could have seen me! I've never been airborne before today, and I am quite certain I do not wish to repeat the experience."

Samson's shoulders relaxed and he bent forward with relief. "Indeed, madam. I saw my life pass before my eyes. It made me realize I didn't eat nearly enough cakes and pies."

She laughed uproariously, despite the fact that her lip was throbbing and she was having some trouble moving her wrist without considerable pain.

The dowager shook her head at them. "You young people are half mad! We all nearly met our maker just now, and you are laughing!" Then she, too, joined them with a smile. "But I daresay there are times one must appreciate being spared from near-fatal disaster. We are still breathing, and that is what matters."

A short while later, they were all standing outside the coach staring at the rear wheel that was up to its axle in a puddle of sticky muck, while the wind gusted across the rolling green hills and whipped at the ladies' skirts.

Samson had tried with considerable effort to motivate the horses to pull, but the coach simply would not budge.

"Whatever shall we do?" the dowager asked. "It will soon be dark. We cannot remain here all night."

"Have no fear, Your Grace," Samson replied. "We will unhitch one of the horses and send Charles to fetch help. He'll be back before we know it."

The men set to work to prepare a horse to ride, while the ladies returned to the coach. An hour later, it was pitch dark outside, and they were still waiting.

"How much longer do you think it will be?" the dowager asked as a few raindrops went *plop* on the roof.

Seconds later, a thunderous downpour began.

Rose looked up. "Oh dear. Poor Samson. He'll drown out there. I must invite him to wait inside with us."

She opened the door and poked her head out into the driving rain. "Mr. Samson! Please come inside! I insist!"

"Thank you kindly, madam, but I am fine here at my post. Must keep an eye out for help when it arrives."

"No, you most certainly are not fine out there, and you have done your duty a dozen times over. Come down here at once, or I will drag you out of that seat myself."

The wind shook the coach while raindrops, hard as pellets, pummelled the rooftop. At last, Mr. Samson surrendered and joined them inside. He was soaking wet and shivering as he took a seat across from Rose and the duchess.

"How much longer do you suspect it will be before help arrives?" the dowager asked. "I am beginning to believe we may be stranded here all night. What a shame. Don't you have tickets for the play at Covent Garden tomorrow evening?"

"Wait a moment . . ." Rose cupped a hand to her ear. "Listen. Do you hear that? A vehicle is approaching."

Samson peered out the dark window. "It is too soon for Charles to return. It must be someone else."

"Oh dear Lord, save us," the duchess said. "What misfortune will befall us next?"

"What do you mean?" Rose asked.

The duchess sighed heavily. "What sort of bad character travels anywhere on a night like this? A highwayman, no doubt. I suspect we are about to be robbed."

Rose scoffed. "I am sure that is not the case."

Though her skin was prickling. She had witnessed far too much violence in her life not to feel some unease in a situation such as this, for she was a princess from a country that was still raw from the wounds of a revolution that deposed the former king and put her own father—a military general—on the throne in his place.

Though it happened twenty years ago when she was barely old enough to toddle, she would never forget the night an assassin snuck into her father's bedchamber while she was sitting on his lap in front of the fire. The man had brandished a knife that gleamed dangerously in the firelight. Absolutely terrorized, Rose had watched her father strangle the villain to his death.

She felt that same paralyzing fear now and tried to tell herself it was not rational. This was not Petersbourg where her father's enemies still gathered secretly to plot an overthrow of the New Regime. She and her brothers were in England on a diplomatic visit.

There were no enemy Royalists here. She was quite safe, except for the wind and the rain, of course, but surely the passengers in the approaching vehicle would offer assistance and everything would be fine. In an hour or two, she and the duchess would be enjoying a hot meal while sipping tea in a cozy inn.

As the vehicle rumbled to a halt behind them and the horses shook noisily in the harness, Rose clasped her hands together on her lap to hide the fact that they were trembling.

Samson opened the door and got out. A strong gust of wind blew into the coach and the door slammed shut behind him.

Voices shouted over the roar of the storm. Good Lord, what was happening? Was Samson all right?

Rose slid across the seat to look out the window and nearly swallowed her tongue when the door flew open again and she found herself staring up at a tall man in a top hat and black overcoat, holding himself steady against the wind. It was too dark to make out his face, and the terror she experienced in that moment was more piercing than the panic she'd felt when the coach nearly flipped over and toppled down the hillside.

"Your Royal Highness!" the man shouted, and she was taken aback by the familiarity in his tone. "May I join you inside?"

Before waiting for an answer, the stranger swung his large frame into the vehicle, removed his hat, and sat down on the facing seat.

As the golden lamplight reached his face, Rose sucked in a breath of surprise.

"Lord Cavanaugh? Good heavens, what are *you* doing here?"

"I am here to rescue you of course!" he replied with a magnificent smile that melted all her fears about highwaymen, and reminded her that they had once flirted quite shamelessly in Petersbourg, but as soon as her heart had become involved, he had rejected her. Quite cruelly in fact.

Her pride was still bruised by those events, but she would die a thousand deaths before she'd let him see it.

"My word," she replied. "How is this possible? Did you somehow learn we were stranded? I was not even aware you were in England."

Removing his black leather gloves, he shook his head charmingly, and as usual her heart stumbled backwards into that old infatuation that simply would not die, no matter how many times she tried to beat it into submission.

But how could she when Leopold Hunt was the most charming and attractive man in the world?

At least, when he wanted to be.

Damn him, and damn her stubborn attraction to him. She hated that he made her feel flustered. She thought she was over that by now. It had been two years, for pity's sake, and she had done very well since then, behaving with complete indifference toward him as if none of it mattered at all.

"If I had known," he said, "I assure you I would have come much sooner, so I must confess the truth. This is an utterly odd coincidence that causes me to wonder if there are higher forces at play. Of course I knew you and your brothers were visiting London, but what in the world are you doing *here*, Rose, on this remote country road?" His stunning blue eyes turned to the duchess, as if he realized only then that they were not completely alone. "My apologies for the intrusion, madam. We have not yet been introduced."

"I do beg your pardon," Rose quickly interjected.

What was wrong with her? Oh, but she knew the answer to that question. As soon as she recognized the impossibly charming and gorgeous Lord Cavanaugh, the rest of the world had simply disappeared. She had become distracted and forgotten about the duchess entirely.

In fact, she had forgotten about everything. The fierce gales. The stinging rain.

Most importantly, her recent engagement which had not yet been announced.

"Your Grace," she said, "may I present Leopold Hunt, the Marquess of Cavanaugh and a great hero in the war against Napoleon. Lord Cavanaugh is an old friend of my brother's. They went to school together in Petersbourg." She gestured with a hand. "Lord Cavanaugh . . . the Dowager Duchess of Pembroke."

"I am delighted, Your Grace," he replied. "And what brings you both out on a night like this?"

How perfectly gregarious he behaved, as if the awkward, humiliating end to their affair had never occurred.

The coach shuddered in the wind, and another blast of rain struck the windowpanes.

Rose gave the duchess a sidelong glance. "We attended a charitable event in Bath, but were late leaving town. We didn't expect to encounter such treacherous roads."

"Welcome to springtime in England," the duchess said with a chuckle.

Lord Cavanaugh smiled. "Indeed. Well then. I have already spoken to your driver, and I insist that you both join me in my coach. I, too, am on my way to London, but I've made arrangements to stay at the Crimson Flower Inn for the night. I can deliver you both there safely, and your good man Samson is transferring your bags to my vehicle as we speak. He promises to meet you in the morning to continue on your way, providing there is no damage to your vehicle of course, in which case you may ride the rest of the way with me."

Rose's pride reared up, and she wished she could reject Lord Cavanaugh's assistance, but the fact remained—they were stranded and in desperate need of help.

"We most gratefully accept," the duchess replied. "How fortunate for us that you came along when you did, Lord Cavanaugh. You are the hero of the day!"

He turned his arresting blue eyes to Rose. "Shall we?"

She managed a polite smile.

The next thing she knew, he was handing her up into his own well-appointed vehicle with warm bricks on the floor, lush velvet seats, and luxurious cushions with gold tassels thrown freely about. The light from a small carriage lamp filled the space with a warm glow, and it smelled cozy and inviting—like apples and cinnamon.

Cavanaugh climbed in and sat down across from her. Though he wore a heavy greatcoat, she could still make out the lean muscular contours of his body beneath it. Or perhaps she simply remembered all too well those particular details of his appearance—along with the rich, chestnut color of his hair and the unruly manner in which it fell forward around his temples.

It was difficult not to stare at those long black lashes which framed teasing, pale blue eyes—a rare and striking feature on a man. And that mouth . . . so full of mischief and temptation.

He was a devastatingly handsome gentleman by all accounts and she wondered if he had any notion of the sexual power he possessed. Did he know that he could make a woman swoon and ruin her for life with a mere glance in her direction?

Oh, probably.

As Rose sat back in the seat and settled in, she wondered if his chance arrival and open chivalry was an event too good to be true, or if it was the worst possible thing that could ever happen—for he was dangerously beguiling. She certainly did not wish to be tempted away from her fiancé. Not only was Joseph Hapsburg heir to the throne of Austria, he was, by all accounts, utterly besotted with her and would never in a thousand years break her heart.

If only she could be more indifferent toward Lord Cavanaugh.

She feared this was going to be a bumpy ride.

Chapter Two

As the coach prepared to depart, Leopold sat across from Princess Rose and wondered irritably if this was some sort of test of his Royalist allegiances, for what the devil were the odds of running into a Sebastian on a deserted country road on a night like this, when he was on his way back to London to meet a Tremaine?

Rose of all people. *Rose*.

Discreetly he watched her while she arranged her skirts and unbuttoned the top of her cloak to reveal her lavish bosom beneath. She should have looked ragged and weary after what she'd been through this evening, but somehow this rather remarkable princess always managed to appear delicious and fetching in pretty silks and ribbons and lace. One more gust of wind a few minutes ago, and he might have ended up in the ditch lamenting his damned inconvenient carnal desires.

For he had no business desiring a Sebastian.

The coach lurched forward unexpectedly, and Rose reached out to grab at something, as if she half expected to be tossed to the floor.

A rather unfortunate metaphor for her future, he supposed, which did not help his mood in the least.

Nevertheless, Leopold frowned as he watched her wrap a hand around her wrist and wince in pain.

"Are you hurt?" he asked.

"Not at all," she replied, which prompted the duchess to speak on her behalf.

"Princess Rose is very brave, Lord Cavanaugh, and too proud to describe how she was thrown about with such violence, it is a wonder she still lives."

His eyebrows drew together with concern. "Is that true, Rose? Do you require a doctor?"

"Of course not," she casually replied. "It is a mild sprain, nothing more. I am perfectly well."

He sat back, not entirely convinced she was telling the truth. "We will send for a doctor nevertheless, as soon as we reach the inn. Best not to take chances."

"Quite right," the duchess said, while the coach picked up speed.

Rose lifted her compelling blue eyes to meet his just then, and despite their polite discourse when he entered her coach a few minutes ago, she was now regarding him with an unmistakable note of disdain.

He couldn't pretend not to understand why, for he remembered all too well that bright sunny day two years ago when they went riding together during a shooting party on his father's estate. The Sebastian Royals of the New Regime were the guests of honor, which had been a ruse to prove Leopold's loyalty and secure greater power for him in the Sebastian Court.

Rose had just turned twenty, and he hadn't been able to take his eyes off her, for she was an exquisite beauty with unparalleled intelligence and a boatload of charm to go along with it.

During the hunt, her brothers—the princes Randolph

and Nicholas—had raced ahead with the hounds barking at their heels. Leopold and Rose chose to follow at a more leisurely pace and flirted up a storm while discussing books and theater and the latest gossip at court.

Rose was coquettish that day, and he knew if he'd wanted her, he could have had her at the altar before the year was out, for there was an obvious spark of attraction between them that exploded like cannon-fire each time they met. She aroused him to a wicked degree, and he knew the feeling was mutual. They were wildly attracted to each other, and despite the look she'd given him just now, he suspected not much had changed.

As he turned his gaze to the window, however, he fought to remind himself that nothing could ever come of it, for she was a Sebastian and he a secret Royalist. One day he would help knock her usurping family off the throne of Petersbourg, and from that moment on, Rose would count him among the very worst of her enemies. And she had more than a few.

He sighed with regret and glanced back at her across the dimly lit space, while cursing this damnable weather for thrusting them together again.

It had not been part of the plan.

"Do tell us, Lord Cavanaugh," the duchess said. "What brings you to England? Are you part of the shipbuilding campaign to strengthen our allied navies?"

Rose tried not to stare too closely at Leopold as he lounged back casually in the seat like a gorgeous lion.

"Not at this time, Your Grace, but I understand Prince Randolph is making excellent progress in that regard."

It was not lost on Rose that he hadn't answered the question, and though she wished she could care less about his comings and goings, she rephrased it.

"Are you visiting acquaintances, my lord?"

His seductive blue eyes turned to her while the rain beat hard upon the roof.

"I've been traveling with my father for the past month," he replied. "He is journeying to Scotland tomorrow, but I shall return home to Petersbourg in the next day or so."

"Sailing out of London?" the duchess asked.

"Yes, that's correct." He then steered the conversation to the celebrations in France since Napoleon's capture. Thank heavens there was much to discuss on that front.

Later, as the coach rocked and swayed on its stormy path to the inn, the dowager's head began to nod and her eyes fluttered closed. Soon she was snoring softly.

Uncomfortably aware of the fact that she had just lost the company of her chaperone, Rose glanced across at Lord Cavanaugh, who was resting a finger on his temple and watching her with those sly, devilish eyes.

"Don't look at me like that," she said, "as if we are alone here and I am something you find amusing."

"Amusing?" He shook his head as if baffled by her remark. "That is not the word I would choose." He casually began to unbutton his overcoat. "Do you not find it strange that we've bumped into each other like this? Honestly, what are the odds?"

"Very slim indeed," she replied. "I am beginning to

wonder if it is some sort of punishment. Though I am not quite sure what I did to deserve it."

"Punishment." He sighed heavily. "Ah, Rose, I thought we were beyond that. It's been two years."

She shifted her body on the seat and rubbed at her aching wrist, which had begun to swell. "Has it truly been that long? I hadn't thought about it. I am happy to hear *you* are keeping track, though."

The dowager snorted and jumped, as if startled out of a bad dream. Then her eyes fell closed again.

Lord Cavanaugh leaned forward, weaved his fingers together, and rested his elbows on his knees. He regarded Rose carefully with narrowed eyes, as if he were studying her mood, trying to decipher her like a riddle.

As usual, she felt very exposed. He was too close, and she didn't want to smell the appealing fragrance of his cologne, or look at those strong, manly hands, for they reminded her of the past.

"Can we not be friends?" he asked.

Her breaths were coming faster now, and she swallowed hard over the urge to tell him what she *really* wanted him to do with his friendship.

"Does it even matter to you, Leopold? Because I don't believe it does. I think you want my approval only because we are stuck here together and there is no escaping the awkwardness of it. You want to have the upper hand again. As soon as I tell you that you are forgiven and I adore you, you will sit back in that seat, quite satisfied with yourself, and you will stop working so hard to be charming."

In the very next instant, he sat back. "You never fail to astonish me."

"How so?"

He frowned. "I've never met a woman who speaks as candidly as you. You don't mince words. You say what you think."

She scoffed. "No, I assure you, Leopold, I do not. If I said what I really thought, you would be a great deal more than astonished."

His eyes smiled with admiration, and he leaned forward again. "I am sure you are quite right about that, but let us travel back a bit. I certainly don't think you adore me. Quite to the contrary, I believe you are very unhappy with me, and I cannot blame you. What happened between us two years ago was . . . it was . . ."

He paused, and she clenched her teeth in anger. For the love of God, she couldn't stomach any more of this unnecessary degradation.

Raising a hand and shaking her head, she said, "Please, Leopold. There is no need for us to discuss it. It was a long time ago and I'm completely over it. I am very happy now. I no longer wish that you would become the man I once wished you to be."

He regarded her with shrewd eyes. "Now *there* is an artful insult if I ever heard one."

"Not at all," she helpfully replied. "You are who you are, and two years ago, I was simply mistaken in my impression of you." She waved a dismissing hand through the air. "I was very young."

He chuckled. "You were twenty. And what *was* your impression of me, exactly?"

He appeared quite genuinely curious.

Rose paused. If she were being honest, she would tell him she believed him to be the most handsome, fascinating, and intelligent man she'd ever imagined could exist, and that they were destined to be together, and that she wanted him to father her children—at least a half-dozen of them.

But that romantic first impression had died a swift death when she showed her true feelings and he blatantly rejected her. For that reason, he did not deserve to hear such praise.

"I thought you were very charming," she simply said.

"There's that word again." He shook his head and waved a finger, as if he knew she was holding back and would have none of it.

She let out a frustrated breath. "What do you want me to say? That I fancied myself in love with you? That I thought you might feel the same way, and I was heartbroken when I realized it meant nothing to you? Or that I still dream of a proposal from you?"

His lips parted, and he was about to answer the question when the dowager snorted and startled awake.

"Oh, I do beg your pardon," she said, sitting up. "Was I sleeping? Are we almost there?"

Leopold inclined his head at Rose, as if to say, *We are not done here.*

Look for the magnificent Highlander series by
bestselling author

JULIANNE MACLEAN

CAPTURED BY THE HIGHLANDER
CLAIMED BY THE HIGHLANDER
SEDUCED BY THE HIGHLANDER

…and don't miss

BE MY PRINCE
First in a new series!

From St. Martin's Paperbacks